TESTIMONIALS

There sure are a lot of stories in this collection.

—A. READER

Maybe now that the stories are in a published book, I won't keep hearing about these characters at every holiday meal.

—SOMEONE WHO MIGHT BE RELATED TO THE AUTHOR

I'll be honest, I was hoping for something more than just pages with words on them. I could've gotten a sandwich and fries for the price of this thing.

—BAR GAINHUNTER.

BOOKS BY K. M. HERKES

RELICS FROM A TRAVELING SHOW

K. M. HERKES

DAWNRIGGER
Publishing

For Paul.
He knows why.

For Taia.
This book wouldn't have happened without her.

CONTENTS

RELICS FROM A TRAVELING SHOW

UP ON THE ROOF

This one comes first because it marked a lot of "firsts" for me. First story published in a paying venue, first story to win a prize, and the first story written by using idea prompt cards (banana, library, gargoyle). Still one of my favorites, so perhaps someday I shall write more adventures for Grawlix and her friend.

———

EVERY FRIDAY, the girl on the roof planted snowmen. I watched her in silence every time she crept out the fire door and did her little ritual, and every Friday it bugged me more. Patrons aren't allowed on the roof. The hulking HVAC units, the crunchy gravel, the slanted, begrimed skylights, and above all the wide parapets that made such perfect roosts—all those things belong to me and my sister and brothers.

That's the Agreement. The Librarians guard the contents of the building, both the mundane and the secret, and we guard the outside. Four times a year the Administrators do their dances and chants to refresh our wards, and twice a year the Pages scrub us and the skylights, spread a new layer of tar on the gravel and change air filters. We watch over them all, and they go away when they're done.

The roof was ours. Patrons stayed in the Down-below. Except this one.

Every Friday this winter, this little girl showed up with her puffy red coat zipped up to her tiny nose and a cup full of ice cubes clutched in both hands. She would spend an hour sticking ice cubes into every snowdrift and whispering to them, and then she would creep away. She never once looked at us, the watching guardians. It was insulting, that's what it was.

The kid was so *sure* those ice cubes would grow into snowmen, too. She told each chunk of frozen water what she wanted it to do until it dripped through her fingers, but of course the trick never worked. She didn't have the power to make the magic work. She said 'please,' and 'you can do it,' and 'I believe in you,' as if the words would make a difference, but power has nothing to do with faith or courtesy.

Like all the other Patrons, she was nothing but blind ignorance wrapped up in wet flesh.

The ignorance didn't bother me. The way she kept ignoring all of us did. We're huge, all of us. We're designed to look terrifying, but she just didn't care. It *irked* me.

This Friday she crept out the fire door onto the icy gravel just like always, and after a look around, she headed straight for the snow piled in the lee of the north parapet. That put her right under my great big nose, just like the previous week and the one before that, and she still didn't even look up.

It was enough to make any gargoyle feel insecure. Why couldn't I impress a kid whose whole head would fit in one nostril? What was wrong with me?

I should've kept my mouth shut. *Be silent* is one of the big Rules, right up there with *never let them see you move*. We have a lot of rules. No one can follow all of them all the time, and there's only so much rudeness a person can take.

Besides, the kid broke the rules first. Patrons didn't belong on the roof. She must've sneaked past two locked doors to get to the roof stairs, and children weren't allowed to wander unsupervised. That made three rules she'd broken right there. Who knew what else she'd done?

So I opened my big mouth, figuratively speaking. <What'cha doin,' kid?>

She shrieked, which was satisfying, and she ran all the way to the fire door. I laughed so hard. Her stubby, little legs almost blurred, she was moving so fast.

Then she stopped and turned around slowly, with her little brown hands all tight-fisted and her lumpy brown face scrunched up in an expression any gargoyle would be proud to display.

"Rawr," she said, and marched right back to me. "Rawwrr."

Right. In. My. Face.

She waved her hands over her head and did it again. "RAWWRRR!"

I admit, I was taken aback. I have big ears. The yelling was actively painful.

She was missing three teeth on her lower jaw, and the remaining teeth didn't look useful. I'd never noticed how pointless Patron teeth were. Not that I use mine for biting, but they're nice and sharp. The Pages see to that, filing off mineral buildup from rainwater and polishing them smooth.

Maybe she was defective. That would let me off the hook for talking to her. I decided to risk satisfying my curiosity. <Is that supposed to frighten me, or are you incapable of forming words?>

She lowered her arms and closed her mouth, only to open it again immediately. "Ha! I knew it. You did talk. Your mouth doesn't move, but you speak. You're alive."

I'm not, actually. I'm a construct. That's an important technicality when it comes to things like souls and immortality and blah-blah-blah secrets of the universe stuff. Precision is important. I turned my thoughts to condensing those ideas into idiot-Patron vocabulary without revealing any secrets.

Something wonderful distracted me.

There was a smell, a scent so penetrating and rich that it stopped all thoughts except one: want. This scent was delight distilled; it was sweet and pungent, so thick with creamy tones and smooth notes that my nose went into spasms trying to catch them all.

I did mention the nose, didn't I? It's big. There's a reason. I'm not simply a grotesque, not a mere stony ornament. I'm a gargoyle, and gargoyles are designed to channel things in through their bodies and out through their noses and mouths.

Traditional gargoyles channel water off roofs. That's why they face outward. Library gargoyles? We channel magic. We're designed to capture the universal forces drawn to stored knowledge. We catch it and safely direct it all down into the building where it can be tapped, stored, or eliminated as the Librarians choose.

The work is done by huge wings, broad backs, and colossal bellies, yawning cavernous mouths, and big, bulbous noses—and our noses are sensitive, too. How else could we sniff out evil trying to thread its way into the guarded places? Forget sampling parts per million. I can detect the odor of one fallen demon among the infinite crowd of angels in an air molecule. We're all about the sniffers.

I had never smelled anything like this in my life.

<What is that?> I demanded. <What is that smell?>

The kid jumped back, tripped, and bounced her butt on the gravel. That defective mouth of hers gaped open again, and her eyes filled up with water. I braced myself to be deafened. The screams from Patron families dragging kids out the front door Down-below always hurt my ears, and this little creature was a lot closer.

She sat and made sniffly noises. No screams. I tried again.

<You smell delicious. What smells so delicious?>

"I don't know. Are you going to eat me?"

The idiocy of Patrons never ceases to amaze me. The

Library histories are full of their incredible feats of intellect, but most of them are as thick as bricks. <Don't be absurd. I'm made of stone. How could I eat anything? Please come back so I can smell you better. You smell wonderful, and I want more.>

The kid got up and came closer. The smell came with her. When she wrapped both her hands around my upper tusks where they curved over my lip, the heady, powerful scent grew so thick that I thought I might pass out from it.

<So sweet. So tangy. So perfect. Can you stay there forever?>

She climbed higher, onto my front paws, and tugged my ear. "I don't think so. Uncle Hector would miss me. Mom and Dad, too. What does absurd mean? Is it worse than stupid? Uncle Hector's assistant calls me stupid all the time."

Most of that went in one ear and out the other. Despite the vast knowledge the Library gives me, my area of expertise is pretty limited. I've never left the same rooftop where I was brought to life seventeen years ago. I know Patrons have complicated hierarchies and relationships inside and outside the Library, of course, but assigning meaning to facts is diffi-cult without a frame of reference.

The name Hector had meaning. <You know the Head Librarian?>

"Is he head of something? He has the tiniest office. Mom has to work late on Fridays in her new job, and I can't walk home alone because it's too dangerous, so I come here until Uncle Hector can take me home. He brings groceries and stays for supper."

That explained how the kid got here. If she was under the Head Librarian's protection, no door in the building would be locked to her, and his office was above the wards that made Patrons ignore the floors filled with curiosities and books in dead languages. His office would look like an archivist's cubby. All the Librarians have mundane job titles as well as supernatural duties. Patrons don't do well with magic past a certain age, not even family members.

This kid obviously hadn't reached that age. She was climbing all over me now, poking at my decorations and brushing snow off my eyebrows, perfectly comfortable with a talking statue. It felt delightful. Spring equinox cleaning was a long way off, and grimy city air always gets into crevices. I decided to add to my Patron experience base while my neck fringe was being scratched. Relationships were hard things to work out.

<Do you love your uncle?>

"Of course I do. Don't you love your family? Aren't those your family?"

A little hand waved in my peripheral vision. I decided that if I was going to ask questions, it was only fair to answer some. <Those are my brothers and sisters, but gargoyles don't do love and families. We have audacities.>

"That's a funny word." She hopped down to duck in front of me. "Do you have names? Do the others talk too? Why are you here?"

<I'm Grawlix. My sister Nittle is facing us, and my brothers Agitron and Briffit are on the left and right walls. They sleep more than me.>

They sleep almost all the time, honestly. Our cornerstone was only laid twenty years ago, and it takes a lot of time for a construct to build up enough residual magic to awaken without a Librarian's help.

<We collect magic from moonbeams and starlight at night and pour it into the Library.>

We also guard against the demons who lurk in darkness and storms, and we assist the Librarians in repelling attacks against the minor works of Power stored here. I didn't mention that. Kids don't need to know everything. I'd been awake ever since this one started puttering around on the roof, but she didn't need to know that I'd initially thought she was a threat.

"Gathering starlight sounds pretty," she said. "I'm Krissy Pollux. Nice-to-meet-you-Grawlix."

I couldn't see her now with my nose in the way, but something bumped heavily against my tongue, and then I had the strangest sensation. <Are you inside me? I thought you were afraid I'd eat you.>

Krissy's voice echoed. "You said you wouldn't. How odd you are! Hollow like a cave, and warm. May I eat my snack in here? It's nicer than the corner of the top floor where I usually go to hide from Barton."

The kid was sitting in my belly with her feet on my lips. It had to look undignified, but oh, heavens, who could care while that happy smell permeated my body? <I like you there. Why do you hide from Hector's assistant? Patrons aren't usually allowed on the roof, you know, and children are supposed to stay with adults.>

"I'm not a child. I'm almost six. And Barton is a snotty snotball."

Wet smacking noises punctuated her words, and the glorious scent intensified a million times. Its sweetness gained deeper, richer tones, some earthy, some astringent, and I belatedly realized something. The smell was the kid's snack, not her.

<What are you eating? Where did you get it?>

"It's a banana. Oh, I'm so sorry." She squirmed a bit, which tickled. "Are you hungry? I should've split it in half."

Banana. Associations fell into place. Chemistry. Botany. Horticulture. Shapes and sizes, nutritional profiles, growing conditions, shelf life and pricing—I tore my attention away from the data flow. Nothing in it hinted at the incredible wonder of the smell, not even descriptions of aromatic molecules like crystalline spindles. Nothing could substitute for the experience.

<I never know anything could smell that good.>

"I've eaten most of it," Krissy said, "but you should have the rest. You said you wouldn't eat me, so I—I'm sorry. Being hungry is awful."

If gargoyles had hearts, mine would've melted right then and there. <Don't be sorry. I don't eat anything. Not little girls, not bananas. If I did eat food, I think I would only eat bananas forever. Where did you get it?>

"Uncle Hector. He gave it to me. I didn't steal it."

Of course the kid hadn't stolen it. Hector was the Library Administrator. A thief couldn't take dust from this building without his knowledge. Where she'd gotten it wasn't important. I was more interested in why no one ever brought us one before now, and most of all, how soon I could get more.

Those weren't questions Krissy could answer, but she could keep helping me understand Patrons better. <Why don't you stay in your uncle's office?>

"He's always busy, and Barton is mean whenever he isn't looking. He says I'm a stupid little ape, and every time he loses things, he says I stole them. I like the stacks better, and the pictures in the books. And it's pretty out here on the roof, only I get cold and lonely."

<Is that why you want to make your snowmen dance? To keep you company?>

"No, I'm doing it because Uncle Hector wouldn't do it for me this winter. He says I'm too old now and should start forgetting about them soon. I don't want to forget. I want to make my own dancing snowmen and prove that Barton's wrong and I'm not stupid."

The last few words came out so loud they made my ears ache. A limp, yellowish-brown thing landed with a splat on the roof nearby. Sweet rapture trailed along behind it, which meant it was the remains of the banana. I forgave the littering, just that once.

"You never told me what absurd means," Krissy said more quietly. Her gritty boots pressed against my teeth.

<Your banana distracted me. Absurd means deserving of derision or mockery. See also ridiculous, silly or frivolous.>

"So it is like stupid." She kicked my left lower tusk. "I guess I'm all those things. I'm stupid, and silly, or ridiculous."

Kick, kick, kick, kick. Every syllable.

<Ow. If you keep doing that, I will call someone to take you away.>

Silence. Snuffling. "Go ahead. I don't like it here anymore. I hate being too stupid to do magic."

<Who told you magic was about brains? That's absurd too. Magic is about spirit. You can't do magic because you're a Patron, that's all. It's how life works.>

Krissy kicked my other tusk, gently this time. "I don't want to be a Patron if it means forgetting magic. I don't want that. I want to make dancing snowmen, and learn to read books, and grow up and work in the library so I can come at night to watch you collect starlight."

Her breath hitched, and her voice got very small at the end.

I'm a gargoyle, not a monster. I may be made of stone, but let me tell you, there's no force on heaven or earth as powerful as the cry of a heartbroken child. It could move mountains.

It moved me, that's for sure. She'd shared banana with me. How could I send her away in tears? Short answer: I couldn't.

She might only be a Patron, but when I thought about it, there were no Rules against Patrons doing magic. If one could do magic, one became a Page and then a Librarian. Patrons couldn't, and that was that.

One did not become the other. That didn't mean it was impossible. Only one thing in the universe was Unchanging, and it surely wasn't a mortal's state of being.

No matter what happened next, my siblings and I were going to get a good few decades of debate over the existence of this epistemological loophole. Meanwhile, I had an unhappy kid to console.

<Stop sniveling. Please remove yourself and stand where I can see you.>

Hiccupping and scuffling led to crunching across gravel. Krissy picked up the banana carcass along the way and put it in her pocket, and my heart got all mushy inside, seeing that. A Patron who picked up after herself. Miracles did happen.

She wiped at her eyes and frowned up at me. "I didn't mean to upset you, Grawlix. I'll come to visit until I forget, I promise. And I'll bring you your own banana, next time."

<I'm not upset. I might be able to help. Even if I can't, you can visit any time, with or without bananas.> Although she wouldn't. Patrons stopped playing when they reached a certain age, or so the research on file indicated. <Today, if you're willing to listen hard and do exactly what I tell you, we might be able to make snowmen dance together.>

That would make a nice beginning, I thought, and Krissy showed all her defective little teeth at me in a big grin. "Really truly?"

<Really truly. Is that a yes? You'll do exactly what I tell you?>

"If it means I get magic, yes! You can give that to me? Will it hurt?"

<I don't know. I need to make a call first.>

Gargoyles channel power. We don't control it, and we don't direct it. Librarians do, and Administrators of course. What I wanted to do, though—this was out of their league, too. None of us on the lower planes handle States of Being. This kind of philosophical paradigm shift would take the work of a Higher Power.

So, I called on the Powers. It's another thing gargoyles can do.

All the records indicated there would be a wait to get an issue like this into the queue for resolution. I was prepared for multiple delays, involving explanations, consultations, passing to other Powers for discussion, and then lots and lots of specific instructions about prayers, drawings, and rituals.

Sometimes there was singing. I expected to receive a lecture and a liturgy and maybe a hymnal. At least.

I was wrong.

Someone Up There must've already had an eye or six hundred on little Krissy, because no sooner did I pass along my request than an answer came back. A shaft of white light lanced down from the sky and struck the kid like a bolt of lightning.

If I'd known she was going to scream, I never would've made my offer to her, because the kid had a set of lungs on her fit to call down Judgment Day. At least she only had time to scream once. One long shriek, and it was done.

She sat down on the gravel and sat there blinking. The sky felt dark without the light of Heaven coming down. My ears rang with the sound of more than Krissy's screams. Then the music of the spheres went silent again, and I strained to catch the last echoes.

Krissy jumped up and squeaked and started dancing around like a tiny little dervish. "I'm full of ants!" she yelled. "Ants, and rainbows, and baby camels, and a narwhal, and so many other nice things are filling me up, and oh—" She stopped dead and said in the tiniest voice ever, "Oh, but some of this doesn't feel good at all."

<Having magic won't only be about playing with the pretty parts of the universe, or the nice ones. It's about the dark and the painful and the dying, too.>

I felt sorry for her, in that moment, I did. But not too sorry. <Do you want to make dancing snowmen now?>

"Yes!" She walked over to her line of ice cubes and poked at them. "I have all these bubbles inside now, but I still don't understand what I did wrong. I said all the words Uncle Hector did."

<You did everything wrong, and nothing. You couldn't tap into the energy of Creation until now. Say the same words you were whispering earlier. You'll see the difference.>

She picked up an ice cube and told it that she would love it to become a snowman please, and then she laughed like a ringing bell when snow spun up in a cloud that condensed into a lumpy, bumpy white mannequin around the symbol of her heart's desire.

I might've added a little power boost. A tiny, tiny bit. Just to be sure it worked, her first time. The snowman bumbled over to her and hugged her finger.

Krissy laughed like sunshine and birdsong and rainbows. "Go and play, now," she told her snowman. "I'll make you some friends."

By the time Hector arrived, barely a minute later, Krissy had a whole parade marching around the roof, up and over my paws and down again, and the commotion in the aether was beginning to wake my siblings.

The Administrator watched from the fire door. He wore a Patron suit, not his official robes, and he had on one of those expressions that might make more sense to me when I have more experience. His mouth was open, which could be surprise or fear or anger, and his eyebrows were moving up and down too, which made the rest hard to interpret.

He has extremely bushy white eyebrows.

I had no doubt he'd heard the noise of Krissy's baptism in power, but he didn't approach her. After a long interval of silence broken only by Krissy's laughter and ridiculous instructions for the snowmen, he looked right at me and frowned.

There was no fooling a Librarian. <Hello, Administrator.>

Now he definitely looked surprised. He came over and peered closely into my right eye while snowmen danced a jig over his feet and Krissy said, "Hi, Uncle Hector. I'm sorry I yelled. I know I'm s'posed to be quiet in the library, but I'm outside, so I don't think it should count, and look! I made my own snowmen this time!"

"I see that, honey," Hector said. "And I'm not angry about the scream. I was only worried for you, and I see you're safe and sound. Those are excellent snowmen. Why don't you let them have a snowball fight?"

She squealed, painfully high-pitched, and started lining up sides for an epic battle. Once she was distracted, the Administrator put a hand on my nose and leaned in close to me.

"Hello, Grawlix," he said. "No one expected you four to be so alert for another few decades. I would've kept a closer eye on Krissy if I'd known. I apologize for the disturbance."

<I'm not disturbed, and it's no surprise we're coming into sentience on the early side. This is a powerful Library, and you manage its collections with great skill.>

"Not surprising? I might dispute that, but it's never wise to argue with a gargoyle." Hector regarded his niece for several moments before sighing. "Those damned snowmen. I knew it was a mistake, but she has such a happy laugh. Do stop powering them, Grawlix. I'm sure you mean it for a kindness, but it's only dragging things out. It's hard on us, watching our Patron relatives grow up and forget magic, but we have to let them go."

<About that…you're going to have to put her in Page training now.>

"What?"

I explained.

He looked at Krissy, then at me, then at her again. "Well, now. This should be interesting."

That was a singularly uninformative statement. <Could you clarify, please?>

He laughed, and it was Krissy's laugh, only softer and deeper. "I could try, but I won't. You'll understand eventually."

I wanted to understand now. <Is this one of those knowledge-to-experience gaps?>

"In part. You've done something amazing today, so amazing I can't begin to predict all the repercussions. Frankly, I don't care about any of them. Thank you, Grawlix. You've given me a precious gift, and I don't know how to express my gratitude."

That was the opening I needed. <I know the perfect way. Please tell me more about bananas.>

KNEE HIGH TO A GRASSHOPPER

This bit of silliness was my first original contribution to a lovely webzine titled Far Horizons. *The publication was a labor of love produced by a talented all-volunteer staff of writers, artists, and editors from 2014 through 2018, and I was a regular contributor during my peak Facebook years, 2014-2016.*

———

OFFICIAL RECORDS
FUTURE MAGICIANS TECHNICAL INSTITUTE
FORMAL EXPULSION HEARINGS: TRANSCRIPTS
TESTIMONY OF PETRIA COOPER, REGARDING THE EVENTS OF
FLOWERS 17, YEAR 3219 OF THE NEW CALENDAR

I DIDN'T START the fire. I'd like to make that clear right now. It was my fault, yes, but the bugs started the fire. I'm just the one who accidentally enchanted the bugs. My mistake.

If you have to blame someone for the fire, blame Master Grandin. What kind of teacher attacks one of his own apprentices? A bad one, that's what kind. Also, I thought I was about to die, or I never would've attempted the spell that enchanted the bugs. It was self-defense. Sort of.

Let me go back to the beginning. Yesterday morning was bright, remember, and warm, the first fine day in forever. Of course I was staring out the open window of the Spell Tower. How could anyone concentrate with all the birds outside chirping louder than anything? The cool breeze smelled like flowers, and the sunlight was making Tony's red hair sparkle.

Tony is the handsomest boy in our whole class.

Master Grandin is the one who put my seat behind Tony. If he'd made Tony sit in the back of the room, everything would've been fine. But no. Tony was in front of me, and the lecture was more boring than usual, so I was playing instead of listening. That isn't a crime.

Rope-Dance is such an easy spell I could draw it on my desk and mouth the words without making noise. I was using it to make Tony's hair move, because it looked like flames in the sunshine, but it was also good practice for both verbal and physical spell components. Everyone is always telling us we're supposed to practice.

So I was concentrating when Master Grandin called on me to recite the verbal components for a Buff-and-Polish. He wanted to startle me, and it worked. I was so surprised and flustered I said the first thing that came to mind, which was the spell I was already doing.

The rest of it was a mistake, I swear. Yes, I always keep a few joke spells cued up and ready to go, but this wasn't one of them. How was I supposed to know the gestures for Egg-On-Your Face were that close to the ones for Rope-Dance? I'm only an apprentice, and Spell Associations is a journeyman-level class. And the finger-roll component that multiplied the spell a hundredfold? That was a total accident, too.

Anyway, Master Grandin startled me, so it's his own fault he ended up with egg all over his face. And his robes. And his desk, and the wall. I was only doing my best to answer when called on like a good student. He's the one who lost his temper and started yelling.

He called me an annoying little pest, which I expected, but then he said a lot of syllables really fast and loud and spat on the floor. That was disgusting. Who knew you could use bodily fluids as a physical component instead of gestures? When were we supposed to learn that—officially? Third year? Fourth?

At the time, I had no idea what he was doing. One second I was waiting for him to give me a week of detention, the next, the classroom was gone and a huge, dark hunk of something was looming overhead, blocking out the light.

Now I know he was casting a Size-Me-Up-Size-Me-Down spell, but yesterday all I knew was that the world had stopped making sense.

The slab was only the underside of my desk, but I didn't know that. When a big hunk of rock appears out of nowhere, who thinks, "I bet my teacher just hit me with a master-level transformation spell and shrank me into an insect-sized version of myself!"

Not me. I thought I was about to be squashed. I panicked and used one of my stored spells to get out from under that rock as fast as I could.

Fun fact: casting Feather-Float on yourself is a great for running up stairs and hopping high enough to see what's on tall shelves. That's why most of us short apprentices keep it stored.

The problem yesterday was that I didn't know how small I was.

The spell built to make Big-Me lighter sent Tiny-Me flying. Zoom, out over the floor I went, up, up and away. Not what I wanted at all. But hey—I did successfully call up a stored spell under pressure. That's a silver lining, right?

Huge, blurry shapes were whirling all around me, and air currents threw me from side to side. Thinking back, I guess those were the hands of people trying to catch me. At the time, they were another terrifying mystery, and they were worse than no help at all. Everything was total chaos for a while.

Did I mention the window was open? Yeah.

I went flying right out of the classroom into the school courtyard. Hilarious, right? Well, here's another problem with Feather-Float. It isn't one of the spells that stick to their target and maintain themselves, like, oh, the one Master Grandin cast on me.

Feather-Float requires constant maintenance and concentration, like Rope Dance, and it's super-hard to concentrate while you're dizzy, and confused, and nearly heaving your guts up.

I lost the spell and dropped like a rock from two stories up.

I thought I was going to die. The school is lucky that physical forces work differently on objects as small as I was. Gravity is the same, but air resistance and other factors come into play. So I didn't die. The landing only knocked me out cold.

The headache woke me up. That's when I finally realized how tiny I was.

The world looks weird from half an inch off the ground. The grass was a forest of huge, green, swaying stalks. Every pebble was a boulder. The air was warm and eerily still, even though I could hear wind blowing through the grass. All sounds were amplified. The ground vibrated. Light came at me from crazy new angles. Oh, and everything stinks, at that size. I could actually smell dead plants and spit and mouse poops rotting.

Picture waking up surrounded by swaying green blades thirty feet high, smelling poop and worms and wondering if you're deaf. It was a little like that, only scarier. I might've screamed a little. I'm sure no one heard my tiny little voice.

A troop of ants came marching by. They were little ones, the ones that show up to picnics, but their pincers were as big as my hands, and those eyes of theirs—well. They were as beautiful as gemstones, but let me tell you, they sent shivers of fear through me.

I will never forget the sounds they made. Their chitin squeaked, their mouthparts clicked, and their quivering antennae *hummed*. I sat there, mesmerized, until one of them snatched at me with those pincers and claws.

Then I ran away screaming. I went the wrong way, as it turns out. If I'd run past the ants, I would've hit the gravel path in a few minutes and been visible to all the masters and apprentices who were pouring out of the building to search for me.

That small stretch of lawn was effectively a mile wide for me in my condition, and I couldn't see the path. So I did the logical thing and ran away from the ants, further into the yard, right into the flowerbeds.

It was probably for the best, honestly. With my luck, one of the searchers would've squashed me flat before seeing me.

All afternoon, people ran back and forth on the lawn, darkening the sky and making the earth tremble. The heavens shook with the roar of their voices. I spent most of that time scared out of my wits, if that isn't clear yet. I was working on survival instinct. That's why I made the choices I did. Not making excuses, just explaining.

Where was I? Ants. Searchers. Not getting stepped on. Being scared out of my wits. Right.

It wasn't all terror. I recall stealing cracker flakes from a mouse's bed of dried leaves when I got hungry, and sipping sweet dewdrops from cool hollows at the base of grass stalks. There was beauty in that world of tiny things, too. Specks of sand were a rainbow dazzle of sharp-edged gems. Flowers petals bobbed overhead like giant umbrellas made of bright velvet and lace.

Around nightfall, the air cooled, the searching noises stopped, and I began to worry that I might be stuck out there in the yard at the size of a thumbnail for a year and a day. Or until some ant ate me, whichever came first.

If I'd known all the Size-Me variants were from the Time Limited spell class, I wouldn't have quite been so anxious. I would've been looking for somewhere to hide until sunrise.

But I didn't even know the spell had a name, remember? What I *knew* was that Master Grandin looked really angry when he was casting.

So I wondered, what if he'd been angry enough to forget about adding a time limit to his enchantment? What if he wasn't even looking for me?

I'd been out there for hours by then with no one to talk sense to me.

That's when I got the idea of designing my own counter-spell. If Master Grandin could make me small, I figured, surely I could work out a way to reverse it. The way I saw it, I had nothing to lose.

Yes, it was a bad idea, but in my defense, my brain was the size of a pinhead.

The moon rose and turned everything to silver and shadows while I sketched out ideas and pondered outcomes. In retrospect I should've thought through the possible side effects of an improvised spell more carefully. I should've drawn a protective circle and done a lot more preparation to contain stray energy. Shoulda, coulda, woulda.

Maybe if my brain had been bigger than an eyelash, I would've thought of those things. Maybe not. I can be a little impatient and goal-oriented. Also, did I mention the noise?

I was surrounded by chirping crickets the whole time I was working, and it wasn't nearly as peaceful as it might've been if I was bigger. The noise was mind-numbing.

Crickets bury themselves in the dirt during the day. Did you know that?

Right after sunset a half-dozen of them came up out of the soil near me like zombies from fresh-turned graves.

Immensely creepy. They also ignored me, which was a relief, since I barely came up to their leg joints, but every time they dragged one wing across the other, the scraping noise was loud enough to make my teeth hurt.

Despite all the distraction, I almost had the spell perfectly framed in my mind when a huge monster frog popped up from beneath a leaf.

Maybe it was a toad, but seriously, who cares? It was huge, it had glistening eyes the size of me, and it was *fast*. Zip-slurp. One noisy cricket gone. *ZIP*. There went the second. The others sprang away over the tops of the grass.

The frog looked at me. Excuse me if I panicked all over again.

I recited the words of the spell as fast as I could and made all the proper gestures while dodging between grass blades and leaping over pebble-boulders.

Think about that. I cast a complicated master-level spell while running for my life. Tell me that isn't impressive! That spell was something special, really. Most apprentices never would've pulled it off.

I did. Between two steps I grew back to my proper size, and I'm sorry if my screams woke everyone in the dorms, but at least they were awake when the fire started, right?

Plus I stopped yelling as soon as I realized I was back to normal size.

All the rest of the screaming, that came from other people who looked out into the moonlit yard and saw the giant crickets flailing around in a panic, scraping out their alarm songs and casting sparks off their giant wings. *Huge* sparks.

I hadn't thought about the spell's area of effect. Among other things.

Me, I didn't stop running until I was safe inside a dorm with the thick oaken door shut tight behind me. I ran right up to my room and slammed that door behind me too.

By the time I looked out my own window over the shoulders of my roommates, the whole yard was in flames and some masters were out there casting amazing water fountain spells. They disposed of my giant garden companions as soon as they got the fire under control.

I am sorry about the fire. I keep thinking about all the poor little mice and insects that must've been caught up in the destruction, and I feel guilty.

In the end, though, it's not like I caused permanent damage to the school. If the gardener wants help restoring the beds, I'll be happy to volunteer. I don't want to leave. I like learning magic here.

Really, it was all Master Grandin's fault. He started it.

RECORDED JUDGEMENTS:
Based on this and the testimony of other witnesses, the case review board makes the following recommendations:
1. Award Master Grandin Landry two weeks paid compassionate leave.
2. Move Petria Cooper into the journeyman's fast-track program.
3. Assign Journeyman Cooper a tutor in Ethics of Magic.
4. Add two notations to Journeyman Cooper's profile:

    (a) Provide student with daily challenges to prevent boredom.
    (b) Under no circumstances allow student to work unsupervised.

HOUSEWARMING

I live in an area overrun by homeowner's associations, so I've heard a lot of horror stories about the bigotry and the spitefulness of small-minded people drunk on petty power. I decided to write a little revenge fantasy. Here it is.

———

BECK PLACED the phoenix on its damp, reeking nest of combustibles, gave its shimmering feathers a last affectionate stroke, and backed carefully away. "Bye-bye, birdie. Good luck."

Its peeping countdown sent them hurrying up the basement stairs. They retreated to the loaded dragon waiting at the curb and called Cassidy on their magic mirror. "Hello, Cassidy, my sweet hearth witch. How's the unpacking going?"

"All done!" Beck's wife beamed at them, then angled the mirror to show off a cozy room with full bookcases and overstuffed chairs. "Everything marched out of the boxes into their new places without a single complaint, and the resident ghosts are excited about the cookies I'm baking. We're going to like this house. How's our farewell gift to your Homeowner's Association shaping up?"

"All wrapped up. I'm just waiting for the big finale."

"You're the best, love. Thanks for arranging it for me."

"It was easy, like packing and unpacking are easy for you." Fire was totally overused as a symbol for renewal, but Cassidy loved grand gestures, and Beck loved Cassidy. They smiled at their beloved. "It's like you always say. You handle the hearth spells, I manage the bestiary..."

"...and we make a great team!" Cassidy blew them a kiss. "See you soon!"

Down in the basement of the old house, the phoenix exploded into flame.

The force of its rising blew out the basement windows. The openings gaped like furnace mouths, filled with a red-orange brilliance.

Ticky-tacky houses up and down the tree-lined street vomited up occupants to stare at the spectacle. No one noticed Beck on the parkway.

No one in the nosy neighborhood association had ever noticed Beck until Cassidy moved in. Beck had made themself small, tried to fit in, tried to survive by being too boring to bother. The strategy hadn't ever worked well, but it stopped working entirely once they'd met Cassie and invited her to move in.

Cass was a tiny woman, but her big hair, big voice, big emotions, and big ideas made her impossible to overlook. Her enthusiasm for all things home-related was even bigger than that.

She read all the bylaws and all the homeowner's association records. She went to every meeting. She made good suggestions. She asked reasonable questions. The HOA board eyed her and Beck with disdain, muttered about the wrong kind of people, and stonewalled Cass every chance they got. They also made it their mission to pull every petty intimidation trick in the book against the 'troublemakers.'

Everyone underestimated hearth witches. Cass enjoyed the challenge. She had Beck's golden-egg laying goose to pay for supplies, and she cheerfully countered every complaint with approved improvements no one could fault.

The board eventually ran out of violations to file claims over, and peace reigned until the following spring, when Cass learned she needed an exemption for some new shrubs she'd picked out.

She went through the proper channels. She put out flyers, canvassed the whole subdivision, collected signatures, and organized her support. The attendance at that HOA meeting spilled out of the clubhouse into the street.

The board still denied the exemption.

Cass got all her paperwork in line again and filed an appeal. The board denied the appeal, too. In a closed meeting, that time.

That was the last straw.

Cass had found them a new house in less than a week. Beck sold a few golden goose eggs to pay for the new place and sold the old house for a single copper coin to a certain old acquaintance with a very particular set of needs.

Now Beck's dragon hummed impatiently, watching smoke and flame rise into the sky. Beck patted its blue-green scales. "Not quite yet. We'll leave once the phoenix rises safely."

A minute later, the building was a raging inferno. Billows of thick, stinking smoke obscured the bright flames seeking— and finding—new targets. The firebird was aloft, and the guidance spells were holding. The wards would prevent any living things from being harmed, but the flames wouldn't stop burning until they consumed everything marked for destruction.

Beck would've marked a lot more buildings, but Cassidy had been firm about that. "Just the ones who voted against us every time, sweetie," she'd insisted.

Sirens wailed closer. People screamed and ran. Beck swung into the saddle and nudged the dragon into flight.

The HOA board really should've let Cassidy plant her lilacs.

THOSE WHO CAN

Here you find one of my earliest writing efforts, set in a world I developed for a high fantasy roleplaying game. The game campaign ended before the players met one of my favorite non-player characters, so I wrote her a story. It first appeared in print in the webzine Far Horizons.

———

THE BOY CROUCHED low over his small brazier and made an intricate gesture across the fire within the bowl. Weak tongues of flame rose and licked the edges, melting a tiny pool of light from the darkness. The boy grasped the rising smoke with one sooty hand, molding the tendrils with a careful flick of one finger. A blue crackle of energy burst upwards, embroidering the ceiling with fire.

A lean, gray-haired woman robed in silver and black stepped from the shadows and sharply clapped her hands. The flames subsided until only the brazier's flickering remained. "Igniting my storeroom is not the intended result, Guthrie," the woman said. "Does that happen when you cast the spell in class at the schola?"

"It happens every time, Master Linnea." The boy rubbed

his eyes, smearing ashes down one cheek. "Master Gerrold says he'll feed me to the Well-Thing if I don't start practicing, but I do practice. I practice until my hands cramp, but the spell always slips at the end."

Linnea patted Guthrie's shoulder and walked off through an archway, muttering a trigger phrase to light a trio of lanterns. Under the bright glow, bolts of rich cloth, chains of polished stones, carved pieces and other wares sparkled below glass and glimmered high against white walls. Guthrie scurried after her.

When Linnea plucked a wooden ball from a box beneath a tray of gemstones, the boy groaned. "Ball exercises? But I—"

"But you will listen to me when I say you must do them." Linnea raised a long finger and balanced the wood ball on the tip. "Both hands. Every finger. Every day. I promise you, you'll mold perfect smoke ghosts if you practice with the ball. I'm certain Master Gerrold is teaching you magic requires three elements—" She paused expectantly.

"First, the talent to use one's own essence to harness external forces at will, second and third, the words and gestures required to manipulate those forces," Guthrie recited. "But it's a twin-moon night, so the world's essence is almost as strong as it'll ever get, but it still doesn't work, and Master Gerrold says I slur and he's never satisfied and—and—and he scares me, Linny."

"Your inflections are perfect," Linnea assured him. "Forget Gerrold. Forget waxing and waning essence. Trust me. Your off-hand needs more strength to support your dexterity, that's all." She handed over the ball and coached the boy through a set of the proper finger exercises.

Guthrie soon departed, clutching his hopes and the ball tight to his chest. Linnea watched from her front door until the boy had safely entered the gate to the nearby schola. She was polishing her brass door-gargoyle's nose with her sleeve when the scent of sliced oranges drifted to her from inside the shop.

She closed the door with a smile and faced the shadows. "Why do you journeymen waste good essence on teleports to visit my worthless trinket shop? You could walk here in five minutes."

"And risk meeting an apprentice on the street after curfew?" A figure moved between the shadowy displays and spoke in a husky, familiar alto voice. "Gods forfend. We would both would die from embarrassment."

The voice's owner stepped into a patch of moonlight, revealing a narrow face and a silvered black robe draped over feminine curves. "Besides, I have two moon's worth of energy to spend."

"Shandra!" Linnea embraced the young woman, then held her at arm's length. "Back so soon from Geferell? And wearing master's black already, as well. Congratulations!"

"Thank you. Barely a handful of us passed this season, of a triple score of candidates."

"Geferell has the profession's reputation to consider," Linnea said. "Not everyone has the discipline to be trusted with master's prerogatives." She stopped herself. Praise was in order, not a lecture. "Your strength and your discipline are to be commended. What are your plans now?"

"For now I'll take over some of Forten's classes. The staff has been shorthanded ever since Varice took off without giving notice."

"That's two masters gone this summer," Linnea said, surprised none of the apprentices had mentioned the desertions. "A few of the journeymen left without notice too. That's a lot of attrition, even for a small provincial schola like Haresford."

"And yet the labs are still overcrowded," Shanda said drily. "I love the old place, but it is tiny, Linny. I'm not surprised the journeymen flew the coop. There's barely space for the new apprentices and their antics as it is. I think I'll enjoy teaching the little rats manners." She hesitated, then said in a rush, "I took your name, by the way. Forten agreed that it was proper."

It was custom for a new master to take a mentor's name for their new surname, as a gesture of respect. "But I was never one of your official masters," Linnea protested. "I'm not a master at any schola. I'm only—"

"Only what? 'A road-weary old caravaneer seeking a warm place to rest her old bones?' Bah. That story doesn't fool the youngest babes. Your robe is real, and so is that magnificent aura. Call yourself whatever you like, but everyone here has known for years you're a master mage."

"I chose a trader's life," Linnea said firmly. "Everyday magic is enough for me."

"Yes, but think of the things you could do with a lab. Even if you stayed itinerant, you could enchant far more of your wares. You might have to set up the lab in a broom closet, but you could do so much more."

"Why should I?" She let annoyance creep into her voice, wanting to bring the interrogation to an end. "I left such drudgery behind years ago, and I've prospered ever since. If not for some certain unruly apprentices, I never would've thought about practicing higher craft again in my life."

"Well, you did think about it, and you've done well by every one of your unofficial students." Shandra smiled, and her fond pride shone like the moonlight itself. "Which is why I took your name. You can't talk me out of it, either. I'm not a client to be bargained with or bullied, merchant. I'm a master mage, thanks to your tutoring, and I'll have the world know it."

Linnea bowed in surrender. "You honor my small efforts too much. Your work and your talent won that robe."

Shandra waved off the compliment and changed the subject. "What was wrong with Guthrie?"

"Other than his weak left hand? Gerrold's rolled out some monster story to make the apprentices work, and the child is terrified. What is a Well-Thing?"

"It's a gruesome old schola legend." Shandra shuddered delicately. "They say a demon lives in the water essence cisterns and comes out at night to eat lazy apprentices. New students usually learn it from older children, but masters are known to invoke it now and then."

"That's a good story." Any schola's source of water essence would make a good monster's lair. Linnea recalled the schola where she had spent her childhood. The echoing chambers and bottomless wells had seemed to hide the world's mysteries in their dark depths. "Still, fear is a bully's motivator."

"That's Gerrold for you. Not the schola's best teacher. Speaking of which, why have you never applied to Haresford to teach officially? The quorum would give you a post in an eye-blink, especially if you didn't want a lab for yourself."

"I don't want to teach a class. That would be worse than doing dull lab work. I don't want any official position."

"Why not? Think of how much more good you could do as—"

"Enough, Shandra. I don't want it. Leave it alone. Haresford is a fine schola, but it's your heart's nest, not mine. You are making me feel old and tired. Fly away home. I've had a long day."

"And I'm no longer a child," Shandra said fiercely. "Don't brush me off. I deserve an answer."

Linnea snuffed the lamp wicks between her fingers, glad Shandra could not see her expression. "I like playing the mysterious stranger, and some children respond best to lessons that come with a touch of the exotic. I'm honored by your gesture. Now, leave me to my rest, and go baptize your new robes in spilled wine with your friends. It's far past my bedtime. Good night, Shandra."

"Good night, teacher." Shandra's disgruntled tone warned

she wouldn't leave the subject alone for long. With the sound of a popping bubble and a faint scent of cinnamon, she was gone.

Linnea shivered. Her robe weighed on her shoulders like a cloak of ice, numbing her skin through the padded shirt beneath it. She untied the sash. The spell-encrusted cloth slid to the floor, rippling as it fell to avoid direct contact with her feet. She herded the robe into a corner of her bedroom in the rear of the store. Then she sat down and buried her face in her hands.

Sometimes she could forget that she utterly lacked the talent she nurtured in others. Sometimes, though, she was brutally reminded that she was a fraud. She might have a master's hands and mind—and a god's essence trapped in her aura—but she could no more cast a spell than she could touch the moons in the night sky.

Shandra's questions mocked her through a sleepless night. Linnea had never sought friendship with adult mages, knowing a trained eye would see through her simple tricks, but she hadn't shunned her students once they grew beyond her instruction, either. It had never been necessary. No journeyman had returned to Haresford after reaching mastery until now.

Now she saw the danger in her sentimentality. Shandra would not be deterred forever by vague refusals. She would keep pushing Linnea to teach.

If only she had kept to herself more, if only she had insisted on cutting ties with the older students. Better yet, if only she had never meddled, never agreed to help any of them. She bought respect with lies, and now the bill was coming due.

Guilt and shame gnawed at her through a sleepless night.

When bright sunlight gilded the windows, she rose stiffly to face the day. By noon she was tending customers by rote habit while she concentrated on her abacus. The stones clicked and slid on their wires, showing her the path she must take to escape the snare of her shop. Unless she accepted huge losses, liquidating her holdings would take more time than she wanted to spend.

"Counting your blessings?" someone asked.

Linnea bumped the abacus frame, erasing the calculations. She drew on all her negotiating skills to hide her shock behind a smile. "My apologies, Master Maclin. I didn't hear you arrive."

"I was quiet," said the bearded old man at the door. His hands stroked the embroidery of his robe. "I hope you didn't lose your calculations."

"I'm glad for the interruption. What tempts your fancy today, oh favorite of customers?"

"Nothing." Maclin stood silent after that unlikely declaration. Linnea waited. The master finally said, "This is not easy to say, but I've come to beg advice for myself. Please don't protest. We both know what you do."

Linnea swallowed the polite evasions she normally used. Her time in Haresford was short. She might as well do some good with it. "Then we should have privacy."

Maclin took his time examining the walls, floor, and ceiling of the storeroom. Linnea both feared and envied his sight, which saw, as clear as firelight, the intricate net of enchantments protecting the room. The net was there, Linnea knew, but she was as blind to its beauty as she was unable to create it.

"Nicely done," the old mage said at last. "The work must've been exhausting."

"Worth the effort." Linnea said. Her nervousness eased. The creation of those wards — costly, not tiring — had been accomplished secretly by itinerant journeymen. She had always expected any experienced mage to spot the room's patchwork origins. Perhaps she had been over-cautious.

"Master Maclin, I'm honored by the visit, and compliments, but we are both too old to waste time. What help can I offer that your own quorum cannot?"

"I don't know. I think my essence has turned on me." Maclin sat on the stool in the center of the room, which triggered the engraved wardings. The enchantments indicated their ready state with a visible flash for Linnea's benefit.

Master Maclin blinked at the unusual embellishment. Then his shoulders slumped. "I've lost spells in hand. Twice, now."

"Every practitioner casts foul, now and again."

"I've not miscast in ten years." Maclin's angry tone flattened to a despairing sigh. "Until now. If I confess it, the quorum will blame age and give my labs to another. I want an objective opinion before I submit to that humiliation. Haresford is an old, proud school, for all its small size. I will not disgrace it by clinging to my position out of vanity, but I find that I'm not ready to step down."

Linnea found his attitude admirable, if a little extreme. Then again, attaining master's rank demanded a touch of fanaticism, as she well knew. Privately, she suspected age was at fault too. Old hands lost their dexterity. Old voices wavered.

She asked for a demonstration. While the mage chanted, Linnea concentrated on voice and gesture. Her specialty, of necessity, had always been magical theory and the practices of the craft. Few working mages were willing to admit that their success was even more dependent on the precise physical patterns than on their innate talent for controlling essence.

On that plane, at least, the casting was perfect. Maclin's words swelled firm, his hands wove a cradle of motion, and at its center, dust and air swirled. A delicate flower shimmered into existence. The mage looked relieved.

Linnea, who had expected nothing less, discussed the results with him and had him try again. Maclin cast progressively more complex spells, each successful, until a half-completed summoning dispersed in a burst of smoke.

Maclin sighed. "Could you feel it?"

"What?" Linnea had felt absolutely nothing, as usual. Dread coiled thickly around her guts.

"The difference," Maclin said. "At the end, in the essence. That what happened the last two times I cast higher spells in my lab. The more power I fed in, the odder it felt. As if—" he paused. "It's as if the essence is being leeched away. As if something was pulling it out of my hands. It didn't start as quickly here, and it built up more slowly, so I was able to feel it more easily."

Linnea opened her mouth and then closed it. She had never heard of such an effect. "Perhaps you distracted yourself?"

"Bah. I was interrupted, not distracted." Maclin's words were firm, but a shadow of doubt fell across his face.

Linnea felt a twinge of sadness as she spread her hands wide. "That, I cannot judge," she said, "but I saw no flaws in your casting until the end, and I saw no outside cause for your failure. I'm sorry, Maclin. I can say nothing more helpful."

Maclin's face fell, and he looked years older in an instant. "Ah, well. Perhaps it is time to step down after all."

The copper bells on the shop door chimed mournfully in the wake of his exit. Failure sat cold and heavy in the air. Linnea returned to her counter and set up her abacus again.

She had been a fool to think she could help someone whose talents she could not even sense. Something might be wrong at the schola, but solving the problems of the schola was not her job. Its mysteries were not her business. They never had been.

The sooner she left Haresford, the sooner people would stop looking for miracles she could not provide. Everything would be better once she was gone.

She told herself that, over and over, but regret and worry made her fingers tremble on the abacus beads.

————

THE NEXT FEW days brought departure no closer. With apologies and regrets, Linnea began to call in the debts owed to her, but her customers could only pay what they could afford, a few pennies at a time. A week passed before she collected enough to begin closing accounts with her own suppliers.

That raised eyebrows, as did the bargain prices she charged for her remaining merchandise. As blank spaces grew like white mold on her shelves, as her trunks and barrels emptied, the curiosity of her customers increased. Linnea let the questions slide off a shell of frosty politeness. Rumors twined back to her along the gossip grapevine; she had come into a fortune in foreign lands, she missed the excitement of caravan life, she had heard news that some crime was about to catch up to her. The last rumor amused her least, since it was uncomfortably near the truth.

Cutting financial and social ties was painfully difficult, but she had anticipated those challenges. She had not foreseen how troublesome her apprentices would be. She tried to wean the circle of casual students by refusing to open her doors after dark, so they started visiting during business hours when she had to admit them.

They would not be put off, and Linnea found herself noting how fearful and tired they were looking. She started to feel guilty about abandoning them. They sounded more desperate than ever in the past.

The twinges of shame were easily smothered by the weight of a single truth: no one was indispensable. She was grasping at reasons to stay, but it was vanity. Shandra was notably absent from all the comings and goings, as were the older journeymen. Linnea saw that as proof enough that no one would miss her for long.

A little of the guilty remorse remained. When five apprentices invited her to an unofficial farewell party on the day she officially closed down her shop, she appeased them with an acceptance. They assured her that no one would object. All the masters and most of the journeymen were working late, eagerly awaiting the power flux from a true lunar conjunction.

Getting into the schola didn't require much sneaking. Linnea walked right in. A chill passed over her as she passed through the moon-shadow of the schola gates. The sensation became a bone-deep ache that would last until she quit the grounds. It was a familiar pain, reminding her of the reasons she had rejected magic once already in her life.

Eleven years had passed since she last stepped within the heavily warded confines of a schola. Eleven years since she had slunk away in disgrace from Geferell's respected walls, taking her bruised ego and her master's cloak to the tent of a caravan leader who needed an investment partner.

Eleven profitable, satisfying years, full of travel and discovery. She had made a good life for herself.

So why, Linnea wondered, did entering Haresford make her feel as dull and clumsy as an apprentice again? The rebellion of her body against magic-harnessed essence was familiar, but she deeply resented the emotional numbness that grew with every step she took.

She hadn't felt this apathetic and defeated since the night after her master's investiture, but she'd never forgotten how close she'd come to entirely giving up on life. Unfair, that visiting this schola in the present should so easily open past wounds.

She sternly reminded herself that a merchant lived by her word. Attending the party was an obligation, even if she was in no mood to celebrate. Her shadows walked before her across the school courtyard, already overlapping as the moons neared their meeting.

The door to the main hall opened at her approach, sensing her aura. A waiting pair of apprentices proudly marched her through their domain.

All scholas were built on the same basic plans, a necessity created by the magical demands of warding the stone. Once built, they could be made no bigger.

Haresford had clearly reached its capacity. The empty classrooms looked cramped, the library had outgrown its shelves, and the halls felt oppressive, filled by their own darkness. Even the gaping stairwell to the basement kitchens and laundries seemed smaller than it should be.

Shadows within the entrance lapped at the stone walls, sucking at the edges of the apprentices' magelights. Linnea glanced quickly away, recalling with resentment all the long hours she had spent scrubbing clothes by hand when others had spelled theirs clean in minutes.

She stuffed the anger away, reminding herself how far she had come, to be here now. She was no longer a homeless apprentice accepted at the world's largest schola, her presence tolerated as a novelty joke, nor even the master she had become, jeered by her students and denigrated by her peers.

Here, tonight in little Haresford, she was an honored guest. However little she might deserve the generosity, it would be as rude to meet it with surliness as it would be to refuse it.

Her escort led her up narrow stairs to the student dormitories, beneath the master's quarters and private labs. Their steps slowed until they shuffled along as if they were going to a funeral rather than a party, and their eyes flashed sidelong at Linnea as they walked.

She wondered if her dreary mood was affecting them, but surely not. If her face were so easily read, she would have starved her first year working as a merchant trader.

The door to the dormitory hall opened, and Linnea forgot her puzzlement as a small mob of students—both apprentices and journeymen—cheered and clapped at her arrival. The size of the crowd stunned her. They seated her on a bed festooned with streamers and paid court with giggles and jokes.

Bright lights banished the darkness to the corners, and the silence was filled by laughter. The warmth of hugs and shy farewell kisses replaced Linnea's memories of empty loneliness. Small gifts were pressed on her until simple amulets and herbal sachets and tiny carvings pooled in her lap like a stack of snowballs.

Memory provided Linnea with names for only half the faces present, but they were easy with each other, and their happy faces shone with confidence. Then Shandra appeared, a dark spot of dignity in the jostling flock, creating a stir of uncertainty among the apprentices.

Linnea braced herself for questions from her old student, but that worry proved unfounded. Shandra barely had time to hand Linnea a small book engraved with runes before someone pulled her away to help with an uncooperative keg.

Food had been smuggled from the kitchens; small cakes and cheese and bowls of hot, popped corn, washed down with cider and watered ale that even the youngest apprentices were allowed.

Some of the youngest became a bit noisy and tipsy, and as the evening wore on, the party broke into smaller clumps, as parties often did. Linnea set aside her icy, uncomfortable presents and presided over the festivities from the sideline. Gossip and spirited argument flowed around her unheeded, and weariness caught up with her. She ought to depart, but she didn't want to cause a fuss by leaving such a happy atmosphere.

She closed her eyes to rest them a moment, full of good food and good feelings. Sleep brought discomforting, restless dreams, and she opened her eyes to the sight of a clump of people at the door. It looked like every student in the school was crowding into the apprentice hall now, and all of them were talking at the same time.

The loudest voice rose from the center of the crowd in a near-hysterical cry. "I said he's gone. We both saw it. We were sneaking trays back to the pantry, and he disappeared!"

"Into a shadow?" The question came from multiple throats.

"Yes!" That was Guthrie's high reedy voice. "Close the door! Can't you see it out there?"

The darkness in the hall shimmered over the children's heads. Someone slammed the doors shut. Complete silence fell, then shattered into fragments of excited commentary.

"...like Reyja last month. I told you...what if it's...didn't care when it only took dogs, but..."

Linnea cut through the babble with a voice trained to shout over desert winds. "What in the name of Beral's ninth hell is going on?"

The crowd split apart, then reformed around her. In front were Guthrie and a curly-haired girl who wore a shiny new journeyman's badge. The pair looked frazzled and yet oddly calm. Their hair was wild, and their clothes disarranged, but their faces were empty of emotion. The hysterics had already passed, leaving behind numbness. No one quite touched them, as if sensing a taint that might spread.

"Well?" Linnea asked. Everyone answered at once, the flotsam of information floating in a sea of confusion. Linnea waited for the tide to ebb, then sifted through the detritus. Her head started to ache. "You're telling me that a master, five journeymen and dozens of pets have been eaten by a monster over the last few months, and now it's eaten an apprentice right in front of someone?"

Heads bobbed energetically.

"It was the Well-Thing," said the curly-haired girl. "It sucked Falis into a hole."

"It ate him, Marena." Guthrie's correction sounded

hollow. "Just like it ate Master Forten. What should we do, Linny? We were never sure before, and whenever we told the masters, they made excuses and looked indulgent and didn't believe us. What if they still won't believe? Please. You have to help us."

A parade of sensible explanations marched through Linnea's mind.

Journeymen often bolted after their promotions, chickens fell to raccoons, cats hid, dogs ran away. She wanted to make those rational arguments, but she also felt the heaviness in the air, saw the darkness pooling in the corners of the room. Her imagination could not explain those things, and her imagination had certainly not made a boy disappear.

It was easy to believe that something was deeply, dangerously wrong with this schola—almost too easy.

The ring of expectant faces awaited her judgment. She summoned up her most authoritative tone of voice. "If this a prank on your old teacher, I will make you regret it."

Their protests were too varied and too desperate to be passed off as acting.

Linnea sighed. "All right then, you believe in this Well-Thing, and you believe it's eating people. What else can you tell me about it?"

"I told you weeks ago, Linny." Shandra moved forward through the throng as she spoke, until she was gazing somberly down at Linnea. "It's a demon that creeps from the schola's well at night and tracks down lazy students by the excess essence in their auras. Some say it also drains blood or life force from its rightful prey. If it is real, if it is stalking its prey here tonight, we need to stop it. Protecting the schola is the responsibility of its masters."

"Then by all means," Linnea said dryly, "be responsible. I have no authority here. If you find the evidence persuasive, raise the alarm, roust your peers from their beds, and go hunting."

Haresford's newest, youngest, and lowest-ranked master tried out her best glare. Linnea glared placidly back.

Shandra's glare wavered, and she looked away first. "First, no one is in their beds. Everyone with lab space is working the moon essence, which means that second, my interruption wouldn't be appreciated. Third, I doubt they'd believe me— and that's if I survived the halls to reach anyone. I need your help, Linny."

Part of Linnea's mind still urged her to refuse. *You're leaving town in the morning. Don't get entangled. Let those with real power kill their own magical pest. Escape while you can.*

Another part — not her conscience, but her common sense — doubted that she could leave safely. When she had arrived, the hallway shadows had seemed to be lapping at her feet. She had no desire to tempt them to show their teeth. The smart choice was to help, if she could.

"Where would Master Maclin be tonight?" she asked. "Can we get to his lab?"

Some of the apprentices tittered. Shandra sighed. "He resigned his position a week ago and split up his classes. He's been sulking in his rooms ever since. The quorum will probably revoke his privileges at the next meeting. Why?"

"I think we should visit him, you and I." Linnea rose, brushing cake crumbs from her shirt. "I have an apology to make, and I have reason to think he'll help."

Shandra looked warily at the door. "Do we dare risk the halls?"

"I wouldn't," Linnea said. There were other ways to travel. "Can you jump us there? You know the destination."

Apprentices and journeymen alike began to protest being deserted to their own fates. Linnea raised a hand to quiet them. "Those of you who know the spells, ward this room as heavily as you can. Layer them like you're building an onion, weakest to strongest, and don't set foot outside it until we return with help, as you value your souls."

Once she was certain that the order would be taken seriously, she nodded to Shandra. "When you're ready."

The young mage raised her hands into the spell's first position. "Behind me, please. Hands on my shoulders."

A knot of foreboding tightened under Linnea's ribs as she complied.

The spell would work. She was not worried about that. She knew from experience that she could be passively wrapped in a jump spell, as long as it did not center on her. Interaction with magic was not impossible for her, it was simply difficult and personally unpleasant. The magical route of a transport always battered Linnea's senses with stinks, flashing lights, and deafening noise.

She braced herself for the usual nauseating trip through icy pain and disorientation. This time, though, a new kind of chaos snatched at her in the instant after the dormitory disappeared. Tentacles of smoke and frigid darkness yanked her sideways into limbo.

———

THE ATTACK WAS TOO UNEXPECTED, too overwhelming to resist —and it was over too quickly to scream. One instant, oblivion was sucking at Linnea, draining the life from her, and the next, a chill pool of magelight surrounded her where she crouched, shuddering, on a flagstone floor.

A hand brushed her shoulder, and Master Maclin's voice filled her ears. The mage's fingers clutched at the air, and his chant took on an imperious note. Maclin was wearing only a nightshirt, and his bony feet stuck out beneath the hem.

An odorous cloud appeared before them and split with a wet, ripping sound. Shandra staggered from it into clear air and then, white-faced, abruptly sat down. Oily black vapors spilled from her robes and soaked into the stones at her feet, staining them dark.

Maclin sank to his knees with a muttered curse, then pointed an accusing finger at Shandra. "You! You don't deserve that robe, you hooligan. First, you wake me by bursting past my personal wards, then you require rescuing from your own miscast spell, and *then* you nearly drag a demon in here with you?"

Shandra whimpered, then lifted a hand to her forehead.

Maclin scowled. "A backlash headache is no more than you deserve, fighting like that when I pulled you in. I nearly lost you both to limbo."

"I wasn't—fighting." Shandra's voice fell to a whisper. She seemed not just weak, but drained of vitality, her expression a blank mask of exhaustion. "Didn't miscast."

A shudder ran through Linnea as she realized how close she and Shandra had come to dying. Magical transport had clearly been no safer than mundane means after all.

"She's telling the truth," Linnea said. "Your spells are being disrupted."

"You found the cause?" Maclin glanced at her, then pulled the covers from his bed and wrapped Shandra in them, fussing over her like a nanny. "Tell me everything."

While Linnea explained what she had learned about the Well-Thing and her suspicions that it had escaped and was feeding freely, the master mage dug his robe out of a packed traveling bag and dressed himself.

At the end, Maclin shook his head. "If I hadn't seen the shadow creature that came in with you two, I would think this a story devised to ease my humiliation. You're certain I was not losing the essence of my spells? That creature was feeding on it? That's why it felt different in your shop?"

"Yes, I think so. When you came off the schola grounds to me, it took longer for the creature to find you. I'm sorry I couldn't sense it. It must be affecting everyone, but you were the only one perceptive enough to identify the interference."

Maclin snorted. "Flatterer. It's a relief to learn that my talents were not turning fickle, I'll admit."

"It's sucked me dry," Shandra said numbly. "I couldn't cast a candle flame right now. How could that monster be living here without anyone knowing?"

Linnea said, "Everyone always says Haresford schola is old. How old, exactly? Do either of you know?"

"Far older than the town," Maclin said with a shrug. "As are most scholas this close to the desert. It's been settled and abandoned tens of times over the generations. When the sands come, the wells fail, and the people leave. Stone endures. When the desert retreats, settlers return. Every time, the schola has been here."

The current incarnation of Haresford town was over a century old: a prosperous, bustling, trade nexus. "And how long have these tales about your 'Well-Thing' been around?"

"Forever," said Shandra. "There are old records that the children use for copy practice which mention–oh! If some earlier quorum bound an essence-eater inside the schola wards and we lost the warnings, it might have squeezed out a little at a time over the years."

"Getting stronger every time," Linnea agreed. "The schola is overcrowded, and there have been so many moon passes this season—all the activity could have helped it break through old, failing bindings. It makes sense."

"It doesn't help us destroy it, though." Shandra sighed.

"Might there be clues about its weaknesses in any of the legends?" Linnea asked.

"None that I've heard. They're simple morality tales."

"We need to think of something, and fast." Maclin tugged at his robes. "The truth is, most purely magical creatures can't be destroyed. They can only be trapped or—"

He stiffened, eyes wide, then rose to his feet and approached his door, staring at it as intently if he could see *through* it. Shandra was staring the same direction. The little color remaining in her face drained away. Her lips shaped a prayer or a curse.

Linnea wondered what her blindness was hiding from her.

Maclin clutched the door handle with a shudder, then pulled it wide open. The portal was filled from floor to ceiling with a knotty, whirling darkness. It was too solid to be shadow and moved too intentionally to be smoke. A veil of blue and silver shimmered in front of it; the room's wards were becoming visible to Linnea as their power drained away.

The frail membrane bulged inward, then flattened again. Maclin stepped back without taking his eyes from the creature his magic was holding at bay. "Well," he said with false cheer, "at least we know it isn't terrorizing the children right now."

Tendrils tapped and swirled, testing at the wards. The motion was mesmerizing. Maclin gestured, and the silver brightened a little.

"I can't hold it long alone," he said. "Linnea, cast a second warding. Quickly, please."

Linnea's heart jumped in her chest. Cold sweat trickled down her spine.

"I can't," she admitted in an agonized whisper. "I'm sorry. I can't."

"Linny, please." Shandra huddled in her blanket, as if to make herself a smaller target. "I don't care if you hate magic. I've nothing left to pour into a spell. There's no one else. You have to do something."

A single hysterical laugh escaped Linnea's control. "What do you want me to do? Dance? Tell it jokes? Don't you understand, Shandra? I couldn't light a candle on my best day. I never could."

Maclin glanced at her. "What? But you're a master."

"Mastery is awarded for knowledge," Linnea said bitterly. "I know the craft inside out, well enough to impress even the hidebound quorum in Geferell. I'm adept in every aspect of the art except one. I can no more channel essence than a rock or a twig can. No, a rock has me at a disadvantage. A rock could be enchanted. Any spell cast directly at me rebounds on the caster, sometimes violently. The results for me are equally disagreeable."

"Of course they would be." Shandra sat up straight. "Natural resistance combined with that strong an aura would cause a phenomenal level of physical interference."

"But how—?" Maclin retreated from the door as his wards began to sizzle and spark. The bubble of light retreated with him, drawing inward from walls and ceiling. In the center of the smaller glowing bubble, surrounded now by living darkness, Maclin turned on Linnea. "How can you be essence-resistant with that magnificent aura?"

"It's a complete mystery," Linnea agreed. "Everyone told me so, from the moment I passed Geferell's gates on Testing Day, to the night I left with my master's cloak in my backpack."

The fragile wards overhead sizzled and quivered under the pressure of the shapeless monster outside. They all looked up.

The darkness swirled. Linnea found she could not take her eyes off the Well-Thing. It was beautiful, in its way. Mesmerizing.

Intellectually, she knew it must be one of the creature's weapons, but apathy was subtle to enough to slip past the physical resistance turning her bones to ice. She knew she was in mortal danger, but she no longer cared enough to panic.

Maclin sank to the floor beside her. He did not bother to dispel the wards, but without his active attention, they inexorably shrank, the energy absorbed by the shadows.

Static crackled as the creature's tendrils pierced multiple weak points. Linnea closed her eyes.

Maclin asked drowsily, "For faith's sake, Linnea, why study magery if you can't practice?"

"I love the patterns," she answered, watching the mosaic

of darkness and light against the backs of her eyelids. "Magic is all about patterns and precision and beauty."

The pattern shifted. She opened her eyes to see it in better detail. Tendrils were merging midair, spreading around Maclin's head like a hood of midnight clouds.

Shandra grabbed the master's arm and dragged him out of the path of destruction. Blackness splashed to the floor beside Linnea. It rose into a wobbling, quivering mass, its motions excruciatingly slow, its growth still constrained by the eroding wards.

"Get up, you old fools," Shandra shouted. "If I can resist its psychic attack, surely you can. Don't just sit there and wait for it to swallow you. Stop it."

"Stop it how?" Linnea asked. "Shall I teach it manners? Hit it on the nose with a stick?" She swatted idly at the swelling mass. "Bad monster. Bad. Go home to your well and stay where you belong, warded and bound beneath flowing water."

Her arm sank into the shadow and went dead to the shoulder. That loss of sensation finally penetrated the mental numbness that had been smothering her fear.

She leaped away, staggering into Shandra and Maclin. To her surprise, the shadow mirrored her retreat, shrinking into itself and withdrawing beyond the shredded remains of Maclin's wards.

The respite was a short one. The blackness crept forward again, squeezing slowly but surely through the fractures in the wards. Linnea examined her hand, which was stark white and chill to the touch.

"It spat me out," she observed.

"Maybe you taste bad," Shandra said.

Linnea clenched her numb fingers into a weak fist. The thing had not been able to absorb her. Her arm was useless with cold, the inevitable aftermath of a close brush with magic, but it had *not* been eaten up.

What would happen if she gave the monster a larger bite? She could hope that it would be enough of a shock to drive it farther back. With a lot of luck, it might be so repulsed that it would leave a gap to the door, so that Shandra or Maclin could get past it and run to the laboratories and warn the rest of the master's quorum.

Maybe, if enough mages provided opposition, the creature could be bound again or destroyed. If she was wrong, if her hope was a vain one, then she would never know. She would be dead before she knew it.

Shandra and Maclin crowded against her sides as the monster encroached on their shrinking refuge.

Its lower edge bubbled, oozing its emanations of apathy again. Linnea found time to marvel at how difficult the decision was, even when she had so little choice. With a prayer to gods she knew seldom listened, she stepped into the groping shadows.

Paralyzing cold sank through skin and muscle as soon as the creature touched her. Essence froze her lungs solid and turned her bones to ice. She barely had time to regret her actions before her thoughts ceased to move.

———

LINNEA WOKE IN A WARM BED, with a warm feather pillow cushioning her head. Sunlight caressed her face, and the scents of dust and flowers tickled her nose. Her bones still felt as if they were made of ice: brittle, fragile, and cold. Magic, muted but strong, surrounded her.

She sat up, slowly. Her bed was in a room that appeared to double as a storage closet. Shelves lined all the walls, even above the single small window.

Master Maclin was sitting on the window ledge, chatting with a sparrow. When Linnea moved, the old mage sent the bird away and grinned at her. "None the worse for your adventure, I see," he said. "And what an adventure it was."

Linnea could think of nothing polite to say. A peek under her blankets confirmed that her body was whole and dressed in a light robe. Everything that should move did, although her muscles all complained of stiffness in a chorus of aches.

Maclin continued talking at her, unperturbed by the lack of reply. "That creature — whatever it was — shrank down around you like a shroud and proceeded to go through the most amazing contortions you could imagine. It couldn't absorb you, but it also apparently couldn't stop trying. Quite an impasse."

"Mmm."

The old mage shot her a piercing look. "You couldn't have known that would happen, of course."

The rest of Linnea's clothes were draped over a nearby chair. She used dressing as an excuse to ignore the comment.

Maclin cleared his throat. "Shandra ran as soon as the door was clear, and she brought the whole quorum. The sight of you was quite sufficient to move them to action. We did bind the thing below running water, if you're interested. This time the wardings are carved into the walls, so that no one will forget to renew them when they weaken with time."

He caught her gaze before adding, "Your actions saved the whole schola last night."

That remark relieved Linnea's biggest worry—that she had lost days or weeks to unconsciousness. She still had time to catch the caravan before it departed. "I did what I could," she said as she pulled on her boots. "It was little enough."

"But it was enough," the old mage replied. "Imagine how you'd feel now if you'd hung back in fear and let it eat Shandra and me first."

Linnea imagined it. She swallowed a lump of painful emotions. Maclin left his perch to sit on the bed. Linnea braced herself for the question she knew was coming.

It came.

"Linnea, why did you keep your nature a secret? Shandra told me how upset you were when she took your name as her mastermark. Is that why you're pulling up stakes and moving on? You're afraid of exposure?"

It would have been too much to expect that detail to be forgotten in the excitement. "Yes," she said, pointedly ignoring the first question. No one reached master rank without understanding the power of pride. "And now, with thanks for the night's lodging, I'll be on my way. I have an expedition to manage."

The old mage spread his hands wide. "Why not stay? There's no secret to protect now. You've no reason to be ashamed. No one would think your resistance a handicap, not after last night. Take a posting here, Linnea."

"Did Shandra put you up to this?"

"No. The quorum had time to discuss it, while they—we —worked out the binding spells. It was a unanimous vote. We could use a master with your skills, discipline, and courage."

Linnea saw gratitude in the old mage's eyes, and she saw respect as well. That was something she had never truly expected to receive from another mage, and the gift warmed her. "And besides, I wouldn't need much lab space?"

Maclin laughed. "Truth. You'll stay, then?"

"No," Linnea said. "I'm grateful for the offer, but no."

The old mage's smile disappeared. "If you're afraid the children would lose respect once they knew —"

"No," she interrupted. "I'm not afraid."

"No?" Maclin's voice betrayed his confusion.

"I never liked structured classes. I learned to love being a merchant. I'm not running away. I'm choosing what I want. I want to ride the trade routes again." She waited until a full measure of disappointment settled over Maclin's face before she added, "At least once more. My money's already invested, Maclin. You can't expect me to throw it all away."

The other mage's smile returned with a sly edge. "And after that? If you chose to settle in a backwater town on the edge of the desert, and if you happened to open a shop with evening hours ..."

"Then I might not object to a student or two coming my way," Linnea finished cheerfully. "If they needed a little help."

They sealed the deal with a handshake.

Linnea left for the caravan grounds, glancing back over her shoulder at her future every so often, and smiling the whole way.

SOLSTICE DANCE: A MIDWINTER TALE

I wrote this one for a themed charity anthology titled Winter Wishes, *put together by some members of an inclusive, supportive, science-fiction-oriented, writer-friendly Facebook group—back in the days before Facebook groups became completely unwieldy and overrun with spammers. Many of the stories were Christmas-related. I went out of my way to write one about a different kind of celebration.*

———

Long ago in a little town far beyond the farthest sea…

Wren's brother elbowed her in the bruised spot under her ribs. "I dare you," he whispered in her ear. "Don't be a scared little baby. I did it last year."

She shoved him with her shoulder. "Shut up, Danyl. Just stop it."

He dropped a dusty cup painted with holiday patterns into her dishpan instead of carefully handing it to her. Water splashed high enough to soak her apron and drip onto the sideboard where they were working, and she tensed, knowing what was coming next.

"Be more careful, Wren," their mother said calmly from

behind them. "If you break any of that china, your father will be very upset."

"I know, Mama." Wren's heart thumped faster, and she widened her eyes at Danyl, pleading with him. *Don't get me in trouble.*

He smirked at her and mopped up the spill. "We are being careful, Mama."

Then he mouthed, "You have to do it."

Wren shook her head: *no.*

She did not want to spend the bitter cold Midwinter night waiting in the snow for creatures that didn't exist. She was twelve now. She was too old to believe that magical spirits gathered in the deep forest to dance for the returning sun. That was a story to tell babies in the church attic while the grownups shuffled through rituals down below. So what if she was the oldest child in the village this year? She couldn't dance, and she wasn't going to sneak out of the attic for a stupid old tradition.

After Midwinter Night would come Midwinter Day's feasting and partying, and Papa always hosted a dance on behalf of the Royals, whose tithes he collected. If Wren spent the night in the woods, she would be too tired to enjoy any of it. She had been working twice as hard as usual to be ready for that party, and she was not giving up the payoff.

"I am not going to the stupid woods," she said under her breath, so Mother wouldn't hear.

Now their mother sat at the head of the formal dining table with her head bowed over the crystal glasses she was cleaning. Wren dried down the plate she had rinsed and picked up the cup. Danyl grabbed a stack of her clean dishes and added them to his stack.

He looked down his nose at Wren, and his eyes twinkled. They weren't brown like Papa's, they were green like hers and Mama's, and he had fine, thin bones like them too. That was why he'd often gotten the side of Papa's hand when he was younger.

"No son of mine will be soft," Papa would roar when he shoved Danyl out to hunt rats in the barn or worked him in the fields like the older, bigger boys. Now Danyl was older and bigger and technically a man after spending his thirteenth Midsummer in the Youth's Cabin.

Sometimes Danyl tried to be as mean as Papa, and he was always sneakier. Now he raised his eyebrows over those green mischievous eyes, and then he quite deliberately chipped a bowl against a plate in Wren's stack.

Their mother looked up at the noise, and when she saw Wren's horrified expression, her frown was the stormy one that always made Wren feel slow and useless. "What did you do now, Wren? Can't I trust you with anything fragile?"

A pained whimper escaped Wren's throat. She knew better than to rat on Danyl. She'd learned that lesson years ago. Mother loved him best and didn't even pretend otherwise. She backed away as Mother approached to inspect the damage, and of course she tripped on the knotted rag rug. Her fall made the dishes rattle and added bruises on top of bruises.

"I'm sorry," she said from the floor. "I'm so sorry."

"Oh, honestly, Wren." Mother set aside the cup and put her hands on her hips. "How can one child be clumsy enough for two? Danyl, pull the ornament box down from the attic for her to unpack. She can't break those."

Wren burned with resentment, but she only bared her teeth at Danyl when he gave her a hand up and led her away. He was not Papa or Mother, and she did not have to obey him. Not even if he tormented her straight through until Midwinter was done.

"Midwinter is stupid," she said, following Danyl upstairs and then up the ladder into the attic crawl space. "None of it is real. It's all an excuse for dancing and drinking. No one believes the stupid old stories."

"You will," said Danyl. "Once you go."

He set the dark box on the carpet in front of the parlor couch where Mother and Papa sat and read on cold evenings next to the fireplace. He even loosened the tightly knotted string for Wren and went to fetch a polishing cloth from the dining room.

The box lid squeaked when Wren lifted it, revealing a patchwork rainbow of fabric pieces. The ornaments smelled of dust and sweet oils, and tears welled up in her eyes. Every year, she forgot how much she loved this part of the holiday—the memories of laughter and fun, the moments of peace, the tingle of anticipation before the Day—she always forgot all that, until it was almost time.

After every Midwinter's giddy whirl came the months of cold and fear and counting every last grain of wheat. Midwinter was a promise that the world would survive the season's icy grip. The sun would come back, spring would follow, and times of plenty would come again. All the stories, all the songs, all the traditions came down to one thing: hope. It was easy to forget about hope most of the year.

Danyl knelt beside her and offered her the cloth and a smile. This smile was softer, even a little sad around the edges. "Please, Wren. I know you don't believe, nobody does, these days, but it's important, it truly is."

She pulled out a figurine at random and began gently unwinding it from its wrappings. The brass points of a sun emerged. "You said it was cold and boring. You said you didn't do anything last year."

Danyl rose to his feet, and for a weird instant he didn't look like her stupid brother, standing there with that odd smile on his face and his hands dangling loose at the ends of his too-short sleeves. He looked like a sad stranger.

"I lied," he said. "I'm begging, Wren. Swear to me."

Wren shook off a chilly touch of apprehension. He looked

so *serious*. The promise burst out of her in a surly growl. "All right, fine. I swear. I'll go."

Danyl nodded firmly, just like Papa did sometimes on those rare occasions Wren pleased him. After he left, the fire crackled in the fireplace, and in the other room, Mother began to hum a hymn to Rayani: a jig tune for the Midwinter Day celebration, not one of the mournful pleas for the night services.

Wren wiped away the tears and went to work. One by one, she polished the carved gods and goddesses until every inset glass chip and line of silver gleamed bright.

Arranged on the mantelpiece with evergreen boughs around their feet, they made a pretty display. Rayani stood off on one edge with wooden hands outstretched, holding the brass sun. The lesser gods of field and forest stood on the other edge in a clump with their backs to her, discussing how to tempt her back to the world and keep humanity from drifting into never-ending cold and darkness. Wren stroked a finger down the backs of her favorites: Chiala the Fox, lover of fools, Brack the Frog, lord of change and clean water, swift Heffel of the long mane and tail, protector of pasture and paddock. In the center stood Rayani's children Stella and Steil; earth and sea both abandoned when Rayani went wandering away.

Tomorrow night, the other gods would join them, and Papa would light candles that made their shadows dance. In the church, everyone in the village would perform the songs and dances of the faithful. And Wren would dance in the deep woods. Oldest child of the village this year, on the dividing line between immaturity and adulthood, on the night that divided the season in half, she would beg Rayani to come back to the world for one more year.

Alone of course, because it was all just stories and rituals.

At least no one would see her stumble and trip. Clumsy child, all thumbs and elbows. "No child of mine will be this stupid and slow," that was Papa's roar for her, and she didn't even have Mama to defend her. *Honestly, Wren,* was Mother's favorite phrase. *I'm not angry, I'm disappointed.*

Mother called out, "Honestly, Wren, how long does it take to set up some statues? Are you done yet? The pies are baking, and we need more wood for the oven."

Wren touched the sharp points of the brass sun, gleaming now from her hard work. Rayani's joyful smile, carved into the wood grain, taunted her. "If I had a choice like you get every year," Wren whispered, "I would go where no one laughed at me and never, ever come back."

———

SNOW FELL on Midwinter's Eve. Fat, fluffy snowflakes came down in veils of white, piling high and heavy on the roofs, and drifting in the village streets. By the time the family trooped from the house to the church, Wren was wading knee deep in it and wishing she had never given her promise to Danyl.

At least she had on her thickest socks. Her felted boots were waxed and waterproof, and her woolen cloak was lined in fur. She wore her warmest winter clothes beneath her holiday finery, and her gloves had not a single hole. Tonight would be dreary and cold, lonely and pointless, but she wouldn't freeze to death.

Once inside the attic, she didn't even have time to take off her coat before she was being pushed towards the window, hugged and jollied along the way. Everyone had a gift for her to take along. She had to stand there and accept them all.

The strap for a flask of hot cider went over her head, paper packets of cookies ended up in her pockets, and handmade trinkets were pressed into her hands. One of the younglings still in diapers presented her with a lumpy, wet clay horse daubed with ink. His older sister hushed him when he ran giggling back to her.

Wren's arms were full in no time, and she started to drop things, of course. Her best friend Gerri tidied everything into an embroidered knapsack—the bag was her gift— and helped Wren open the attic window.

After the gifts came more hugs. Gerri hugged her last. "Make up a good story for tomorrow, won't you? Danyl was so dull, last year. I'm teeny bit jealous, too. If Mama had popped me out one day sooner, it'd be me getting all the treats tonight. Goddess bless, and oh, be *careful*, Wren. You know how you are."

Wren *was* careful, sliding down the icy cedar shingles. She only slipped once, bruising her elbow on the copper gutter and catching splinters under her nails. Then she was standing in the dark, snowy street, sucking on her torn fingernail and feeling a tingle of excitement. She hadn't expected the gifts. It was tradition like all the rest, but she really hadn't thought anyone would care, not with it being *her* this year. Tears stung her eyes, an upwelling of happiness so sharp it hurt coming out.

The congregation's singing voices pushed her toward the sheep pasture and the trees beyond. She hummed the same tune and mouthed the words, and the rhythm carried her feet forward. "Return to us, Rayani bright and kind, return your blessings to the world this night. To us give light and warmth again, embrace your sad and lonely children."

The falling snow muffled all other sounds, wrapping her song in a veil of silence, and her breath fogged before her face. The moon rose beyond the clouds, teasing a faint glow from bare birch limbs and the white-draped evergreens. Wonder overwhelmed her, a chill that was somehow also warm and exciting. Magic might be a story for babies, but this night was beautiful and wild, and it was all hers.

She still had one verse to sing when she reached the Midsummer fire circle, deep within the forest. She spread wide her arms and shouted it to the sky, grinning to herself. Maybe this wouldn't be a bad night after all.

She reached for the cider and was taking the first, sweet swallow when someone spoke, behind her. "You have a donkey's voice, but I like your enthusiasm. We'll have a fine dance this year."

She dropped the flask and fell on her butt trying to spin around. Laughter filled the air— one voice at first, then a hundred, a thousand. *Thousands.*

Wren gaped up at an audience she *knew* had not been there a moment earlier. She had walked past row after row of empty log seats, lumps under drifted white snow. Now the whole clearing was packed with bodies.

Gods and goddesses surrounded her in a crowd so closely packed she could hardly pick out one form from another. She glimpsed thick leaves and narrow reeds, ears and antlers, beaks and black noses. Scales and fins flashed, here and there.

Every power in the universe was represented in that throng, and they were all laughing at her. Humiliation soured her happiness, and a lifetime of being a disappointment poured out of her in outraged tears.

She got to her hands and knees, then stood with hands fisted in rage. "I can't help being clumsy! Don't laugh at me. Stop it! Shut up and be nice!"

Silence fell as if all noise had been emptied out of the world. The crowd of gods stood waiting with wide eyes, laid-back ears, and flattened crests. A stand of grass rippled uneasily.

One form separated from the rest, treading forward on delicate paws until it stood nose to nose with Wren. The fox's eyes were like glowing emeralds, green and bright. The red fur on her back was as bright as the snowy white of its belly, and the black around her muzzle and feet was as dark as the midnight sky between stars.

The vixen looked like Wren's favorite statuette come to life.

Wren's heart clenched in her chest. *Is this real? Can that be Chiala? The goddess of fools and mischief is real?*

The fox licked her cheek. Her tongue felt real, warm and wet, and it left behind a chill track of slobber. Wren sat back on her rump and scrubbed her face against her coat sleeve. "Hey! Behave yourself."

Chiala sat in the snow, tucking her fluffy tail around her feet, and her tongue lolled out of her open mouth in a fox smile. Then she tilted back one triangular ear, as if to say, *Well? What now?*

Wren stared back. "I don't know. Why don't you tell me?"

The goddess's laugh was as soaring and joyful as bells ringing, as fresh as the first cool breeze of autumn blowing away summer's humidity. The other gods murmured and stirred, looking worried, especially when Chiala trotted proudly around the ring with her tail flagged up high, yipping the whole way.

"Tell me what's so funny," Wren said when the fox sat down in front of her again.

"You, child. Humanity. Chaos. Look at them." Chiala indicated the crowd with her muzzle. "You silenced us, and now you've asked me what to do. *Me.* I'm the family trouble-maker, yes? What if I say, 'dismiss us all, and let the world freeze'? What if you listen? Oh, yes. You've put a proper scare into them. Well done, child. Well *done.*"

Wren looked at the sea of faces large and small, and they did look fearful, but why? *How could I silence gods?*

Then she remembered. They danced for Rayani this night, and only a child could lead them. They were hers to command, for this one night, for these few hours.

For a moment, one horrible, unworthy moment, she wanted to say, "Let Rayani run free forever if that's what she wants." There would be no more disappointing her mother and enraging her father. No more mockery and embarrass-ment. Let it all freeze.

Paper crinkled in her pockets, and in her mind, she heard Gerri's voice. "Bring home a good story."

She bit her lip, remembering little Ben giggling as he handed her a stupid ugly horse statue. She would not wish to see that joy die starving in the cold and dark.

"It's tempting," she told Chiala, "But I promised to do this right. If you ask me, it's a really stupid idea letting a twelve-year-old decide the fate of the world."

"It was my idea, can't you tell?" Chiala's mouth dropped open in a smile, and her green eyes twinkled. "Now pick your three partners, and we will square off to dance the sun back!"

"I would rather sit and watch the rest of you," Wren said. "I'll only trip and fall."

A rumble of disapproval ran through the gods, and Wren shrank back.

"I can't," she whispered. "I'm afraid. You'll all laugh at me again, and it hurts, when people laugh at me."

Chiala came close and licked at her hand. "Mirth is no small gift to give the gods," she said. "I've made it my specialty. Not all laughter is cruel. Watch me now, and I will show you what I mean."

The fox made a sound like bells and breezes, and then she leaped into the air, giving her body a twist. She landed on her back in a drift of snow, so deep only her black legs showed, sticking up out of the whiteness.

The rest of the gods roared with laughter, and this time Wren could hear the happy note in their voices. It *was* funny when it wasn't her.

Chiala stuck her head up, and her mouth dropped open into a toothy smile. "Grace is not the gift we need tonight, child," she said. "Pick me for your first partner, and we shall be joyful fools together."

As soon as Wren nodded, the other gods flowed around her, a sea of furry backs and leafy branches, until she could not help but laugh while they all murmured and buzzed and bragged about their dancing skills. They made her stumble among them, but she shoved and tickled and laughed her way to where Heffel stood waiting, one rear leg cocked patiently, tail swishing.

"I choose you," she said, stroking his muzzle.

He swung his head to look her over with one liquid dark eye, and then he neighed happily. "I'm honored."

Wren had a feeling he wasn't often chosen. His heavy feathered feet were not made for sprightly jigs. With him beside her, the crowd was easier to manage, and she soon found her last partner lounging beside the reeds.

"There you are, Brack," she said, lifting the frog to Heffel's back.

Brack sat as tall as his tiny legs allowed and puffed out his throat pouch. "Me? Me? Me! She picked me!"

Wren explained her choices as she led them to the center of the ring where Chiala waited. "I'm not as clumsy when my feet are off the ground, you see. In the water, on horseback—there, I feel graceful. If I have to dance, however badly, then I want to do it with you two."

Chiala yipped, and Heffel snorted, but it was Brack who said in his burbling voice, "You cannot be bad at this dance. It's the doing that matters, not the how. Rayani forgets we care, and we remind her. Now, child, come and make your bows to the sun's other children before we shall begin."

A tall pale man and a taller broader woman now sat on the log behind Chiala. Wren gaped at them. Steil and Stella had arrived—or had they been there all along?

Steil waved a greeting, and his green hair floated and waved as well. He cradled a guitar in his arms, smiling as he placed his hands on the neck and belly of the instrument. His sister Stella tucked a dance drum under one strong, thick arm.

The ground shivered underfoot as her fingers brushed the drumhead.

The goddess gazed at Wren, and somehow Wren understood she was being asked a very important question. *Ready?* Stella's sad eyes asked.

No, Wren wanted to say. *No, I can't.* Fear and shame smothered her voice.

Then Chiala shoved a cold wet nose against the palm of her hand, and the fear lifted—not far, but enough. A goddess believed in her.

Wren inhaled deeply, then nodded. "Yes, I'm ready."

Brack closed his eyes, Heffel bent a foreleg, Chiala arranged her ears and tail just so, and then the drum spoke.

The rhythm pounded through Wren's bones, and when Steil plucked the first note from the guitar, the tune rippled in her blood.

There were proper steps to the Solstice dances, but Wren didn't know them well. She went the wrong way so often that her companions quickly abandoned their attempts to school her.

When Wren tripped over her toes and fell to her knees, Chiala used her as a vault to leap onto Heffel's back. He bucked, startled, and kicked a tree trunk. Snow fell from the branches and cascaded over Brack's head, burying him completely.

The frog hopped out, croaking and shaking his long back legs—and Stella laughed aloud. Wren stood stunned, knees shaking at the glory of that voice, and for an instant, the universe stood still.

Then Chiala leaped off Heffel's back and dodged between the horse's legs, Brack tripped the fox with a flick of his long sticky tongue—and Wren pelted them all with snowballs.

The other gods danced too, in a swishing, growling, lively whirl, but the center of the ring belonged to Wren and her unorthodox partners.

She laughed and ran and jumped and forgot to be careful, and when the drum stopped and the guitar fell silent, she was clinging to Heffel's mane with a frog on her shoulders and a fox hugged to her chest, while the horse god trotted in circles with his neck arched and tail held high.

That was when Wren finally noticed she had a shadow. The woods were still dressed in night's black and gray, but the sky above glowed with the rosy gold of sunrise.

Heffel stopped in his tracks, then turned, bowing so low Wren slid right down his neck, over his head, tumbling into the snow.

Brack burped nervously in her ear.

The goddess Rayani stood before them, her head bowed and her hands tucked into the sleeves of her robes.

The statue makers got one thing wrong, Wren noticed. Rayani didn't carry the sun. It followed her like a brilliant hummingbird, hovering at her shoulder.

The weight of the sun bowed the goddess's shoulders, and the power of it thickened the air. When Rayani lifted a hand, the circle was suddenly empty of all but her. Even Stella and Steil vanished, leaving only Wren and her dance partners.

Power washed over the churned snow and dirt of the night's dancing, smoothing and brightening it until no sign of foot or hoof, paw or claw remained. Wren marveled at the glistening, pristine blanket of white.

Then Rayani raised her head.

Her smile burned a mark on Wren's soul.

Every smile that ever existed had been born in *that* smile, every loving glance took its glimmer from the light in *those* eyes. All that was love, joy and the cozy contentment of belonging sprang from this goddess's essence.

"Um," Wren said. She hugged Chiala a little tighter, for courage. "Hello? Have you come to dance with us?"

Rayani's eyebrows went up, quirking at the center, and then she clapped her hands. "Oh, if only I could. I do believe that was the most entertaining dance I have seen in centuries. No, child, I must hurry along, if I'm to make my Midwinter deadline. I almost missed it, as usual. Thank you for pulling me back to face the right way with your joy. You have the gratitude of us all."

Chiala nudged Wren's ear with her cold, wet nose. "She means you get to ask her for a gift. Anything within the abilities of the gods can be yours. Make me proud, little fool. Be creative. Ask for something expensive or impossible."

Wren thought about it. She had a lot of wishes stored up. No one had ever told her about this part, and she knew, somehow, that she would leave it out of any story she told. Some secrets simply should not be shared.

"What did Danyl want?" she asked. "My brother. Last year. May I ask? What partner did he pick? What did he ask for?"

"Oh, him." Rayani rolled her eyes, which only made Wren love her all the more. "Like every boy ever, he picked dryads and naiads to dance with, and much joy he got from it, but it's so predictable, I sometimes despair of my creation. Then he asked to know who his father was, as if that mattered in the least. I hate to tell you this, but your brother is a *very* shallow person."

Heffel snorted. "He is a colt. It comes with the territory. He'll grow out of it." Brack croaked an agreement, and Wren giggled.

Chiala licked Wren on the ear. "Remember to be clever."

The fox goddess sprang away, vanishing into a shadow between tree trunks. Heffel nodded heavily and followed, tail swishing behind him as he vanished into the forest. Brack said, "Brrrack,"in a pleased tone and disappeared without bothering to move.

Their departure caught Wren by surprise and left her feeling bereft and empty.

Rayani said gently, "You must choose a gift now, child of

earth and ocean, and return to your world. Don't take Chiala too seriously. None of us do. It needn't be something showy or impossible. Ask what's in your heart."

"I want—" She wanted tonight again. She wanted this forever. "I want to bring joy and laughter to others," she said to herself, thinking it through. "I want to dance like a fool and sing like a frog and feel the earth pass under my feet as fast as if I could fly. Every day. Forever."

Silence met her words, and she looked up with a sudden lurch of fear. "Is that a bad thing to ask for? Is it something you can't give?"

"Oh, sweet one, I can give you anything except the forever." The goddess bent close, and dizziness washed over Wren. Rayani's breath smelled like flowers and cut hay and was as warm as the fire on a cold evening. Her lips brushed Wren's forehead. "I will give you a gift for yourself too, as a reward for your generosity. Chiala will be more than proud when I tell her."

Wren's dizziness turned to a light and weightless exhaustion. As her eyes fluttered shut, she heard the sun goddess mutter, "And knowing that mangy mutt, she's eavesdropping now."

A fox's squalling laughter was the last sound Wren heard as sleep claimed her.

———

SHE WOKE in the gray light before dawn, cold and alone in the fire ring. The only footprints in the snow were her own, and her stiff muscles were the only proof that she had danced away the night alone or in company—those, and the crushed cookies in her pockets.

She grinned, remembering how they'd been crunched to crumbs after landing a dive over Chiala's back.

Her stomach growled, and she shivered. If she hurried,

she could be home in time to come downstairs for Midwinter breakfast like nothing had happened at all. If she *really* hurried, she might have time to sneak in a snack first.

It was worth a try, and the exertion would keep her warm, at least until she planted her face in a snowdrift.

Wren took off running for town, working on her story for the other children all the way down the trail. Only when she got to the pasture did she realize that she hadn't tripped once.

She scared a few goats, whooping with surprise and joy, but no one else heard. She danced every step home from there.

It was the best Midwinter Day ever.

GRIEF'S REWARD

And now for something completely different: three dark fantasy flash fiction pieces originally published on my blog at dawnrigger.com. This first one was an experiment in flow and description, based on a painting of the Irish coastline at night. It went off the deep end from there.

I HEARD HER CALL, in the chill night after an autumn storm, and I went to her. How could I not? She sobbed as she sang, and her lonely pain plucked at chords within my empty heart. She sang my pain, and it touched me as no one else ever had.

The surf was cold, roaring high, and the stones tore my bare feet to shreds. I bled into the salt foam between land and water before she rose to embrace me. There was beauty in her coils of iridescent scales, and she sang of joy and warmth beneath the waves. She tied me to her body with strands of kelp, and she tied me to her soul with song, and her sharp fins cut my flesh as she took me under the sea.

She brought me deep, where lay the bones of those gone before, but I did not care. They had fallen prey to her frustration and rage. This time, a happy accident brought her a widowed fishwife, not the tall fishermen her lure had ensnared in the past. She had sought always the biggest, strongest mates, not understanding how my kind differed from the creatures of the sea, and she laughed when I explained. We shared that joy and more until dawn came, when she brought me safe ashore.

She left me, but I am no longer alone. I watch the sea in springtime now, under warm hazy skies, and life grows inside me. I watch the surf, and I hope for storms.

THRESHOLDS

This flash fiction piece originally published on my website is proof that the more restrictive the story structure gets, the further into creepy places my imagination goes.

———

ONCE UPON A TIME, when I used to hike the woods at night, I saw magic on every trail. My imagination and gleaming moonlight painted the world with unearthly power. Every gap between curving beech trees marked a portal into another world. Bent arches of fallen wood became entrances to strange places filled with ancient, forgotten treasures. I walked every path with hope in my heart and listened to night creatures rustle in the darkened bushes, praying this time I would find a real gate to worlds beyond.

When I was young and innocent, when I still walked outside after sundown, I saw passages to worlds wondrous and strange everywhere I looked. I dreamed aloud, there in the night solitude, and I made oh so many wishes.

I miss those nights when I walked along lanes of pale beeches glowing white by moonlight, when each firefly in the darkness was a sparkling promise of something better.

You see, there are doorways between worlds. *There are.* I was right about that, I did find them in the end, but I was so very wrong about the rest.

Those other worlds are filled with horrors. For years, they heard me calling, there in their dark lairs. When the gates opened, they came after me.

They came with eyes glistening and the skins of their victims buckled around their slimy throats, and they creep into the shadows outside my door every day when the sun sets.

I hear them rustling in the bushes.

GOOD DOG

Flash fiction lends itself well to experimentation. I wrote this one trying to combine horror and humor in one brief tale. You can decide how well it worked.

———

DOG WAS adorable when he was a baby. When Jim looked over the litter of nine–born who knew where, abandoned at the animal shelter–the pup was a palm's worth of black fluff, with shiny button eyes and a tiny pink tongue that got stuck between his teeth when he barked. Jim tucked him into a coat sleeve for the bus ride home.

The shelter said he would probably grow to fifty pounds. Perfect, Jim thought. Fifty pounds was the perfect size for a country boy who was willing to admit that he wanted protection on the mean city streets. No mugger would ever beat him again, not with a dog like that. He named the puppy Dog, because nothing else fit. Dog grew. He read training books. Dog grew. They attended obedience classes. And Dog grew.

"Devil dog," the landlady called him, and made evil-eye signs at them in the hall.

"He's a good boy," Jim would say, and she would spit on the floor.

By six months, Dog had left fifty pounds far behind. He was big enough to pull Jim off his feet and run loose to chase rats in the alleys. When Jim would catch up to him, Dog would look up from his prey and let his teeth show. His eyes would glow red, above his red-stained muzzle. He looked evil when he wagged his tail.

Evil? No. Not my dog, Jim would tell himself as he picked up Dog's leash. He can't be evil. He's a good boy.

"Who's a good boy?" he would say, and Dog's long, pink tongue would loll out between his bloody teeth. He never left a scrap behind.

When he was a year old, he killed his first mugger. "Who's a good boy?" Jim said, and he smiled when the landlady opened her door.

MIRRORS: A SLIGHTLY WARPED FAIRY TALE

I have a thing for fairy tale themes. Long ago, I was trying to explain something about self-esteem to someone, kept grounding out, and finally gave up on dull declarative nonfiction and went straight for Once upon a time. Not sure the message is accurate from a mental-health perspective, but it seemed to help its original audience of one, so it's here as a successful experiment as well as a fun story.

IN A COUNTRY far off in the lands of adventure, there once lived a prince who was cursed by a witch on his christening day.

It was not his fault, of course. Being a baby at the time, he was simply unable to escape the hazards of his exalted position or act in his own defense. He was blameless.

His parents, a King and Queen, had done their best to protect him. They did not omit the witch under discussion from their christening guest list, nor were they so gauche as to place her at some seat unsuited to her station. They did, however, once accidentally humiliate her in public.

The slight was unintentional, of course. During the christening service, each witch, wizard, fairy godmother, and guardian angel of the kingdom stepped forth to bestow a trifling blessing or tidbit of advice. The witch who eventually did the cursing was a woman of delicate balance, and she did not wish to brave the steep steps that led to the well-warded and charmed presentation cradle. She requested instead that the child be placed in her arms for blessing.

The royal couple was torn between their sincere wish to placate their guest and even greater fear for their youngest child's safety. Such reasonable requests were historically used by creatures who inevitably chortled in maniacal laughter, shed their clever illusionary disguises, and disappeared with the poor babe the instant they got a grip on the swaddling clothes.

Rather than face their twilight years in philosophical discussion over whether their only son was being raised by Djinn of the Ninth Circle or Air Demons of the Cloud Reaches, the couple politely declined the witch's demands.

This witch's dignity was, alas, as delicate as her balance, which made refusal into insult and left the poor witch with no choice but to curse the babe.

She drew herself to her full height, ignored the nervous murmurs from the other magical guests, and performed her duty with remarkable poise and precision.

Scholars later remarked that it was quite a skillful accomplishment, especially considering that it was an off-the-cuff spell. She had a talent for improvisation under pressure.

With a complicated wave of her hands, she delivered the child's doom, and then—on the verge of tears herself—disappeared from the palace in a puff of smoke. Several in the audience applauded the display until hushed by more understanding neighbors.

It was not so bad, the guests and relatives said at the time. After all, the prince had not been trapped in the body of a toad or doomed to become a statue if touched by the light of the moon, nor had he been spirited away to a distant land to be raised in squalor by abusive strangers. The conniving old biddy had merely said that Prince John would never be able to see himself clearly.

As the child grew, his curse was first seen as a mere nuisance. All the mirrors in the rocky hilltop castle were destroyed as a matter of course, on the very day after the christening, since the experts said that knowledge of the curse might badly affect the prince's development. The blessings of the other dignitaries made their appearances one by one, and the prince's assets seemed more than enough to offset such a puny disadvantage as an inability to see oneself.

Prince John was a gentle boy, sweet of disposition, and his body grew lean and tall as the years passed, all the usual awkwardness of childhood and adolescence neatly bypassed by his various magical protections. He quickly learned all the academic and athletic skills every good prince needed to know. This surprised no one, since he had the requisite nimble feet and fingers, keen eyes, and calculating mind.

Atop all his other graces and abilities, he had been blessed with a smile that could charm gold from a miser, skin as clear as a bright June morning, eyes the color of a midwinter sky, and hair as bright as a fresh-minted gold coin.

He did not learn of his affliction for many years. He had valets and servants to dress and groom him, and he had no idea that the rest of the world commonly viewed themselves in polished metal or silvered glass to see a representation of their physical appearance. He knew nothing of an experience that would be forever denied him, and with the innocence of a child, he believed everyone when they told him he looked gorgeous and performed every task with skill.

One day in a blessedly weak show of adolescent rebellion, John escaped the confines of the tilting yard and the disciplines of his weapons master and took himself into the fields to enjoy the beauty of a spring afternoon.

John did not know it, anniversaries of christenings not

being followed with as much good-natured avarice as birth-days, but it was sixteen years to the day from the fateful after-noon when he had been cursed. In the way of such things, the ugly creature, metaphorically speaking, chose that time to make its first true appearance.

The day was a lovely one. Afternoon sunshine warmed the sweet new grass and bright flowers on the hillside meadows around the castle. John wandered the beautiful countryside with an unaccustomed and slightly disturbing sense of freedom.

When he saw a goose girl harrying her flock in his direc-tion, he immediately moved to intercept. He was, of course, as blessed in the skills of flirtatious conduct as he was in all else — those skills were among the best-exercised of his blessings. One never knew: the milkmaid to whom one spoke might be a princess in disguise, and such opportunities would only knock once. So, John gave the goose girl a brilliant smile and offered to carry her basket and stick.

She graciously allowed the favor, and John noted with increasing interest the unusual allure of her movements, the fine curved beauty of her form, and the shining black length of her hair. He then pleasantly engaged the Just-Possibly-a-Princess-in-Disguise in conversation.

Her name, she volunteered, was Selene. She and her elderly godmother had only recently arrived in the land, and she was grateful for her new employment at the castle. She chattered on and on about her geese, and John let himself be carried along on the melody of her voice.

Once the birds were peacefully grazing by a pond, the couple sat together on the hill and shared bread and cheese from Selene's basket. Afterwards, the girl took from beneath the cloth a fine tortoiseshell comb and a small shining piece of metal.

By the light of what John first believed to be a magical item, she coaxed her tousled black hair from attractive windblown disarray into a cascading glory of midnight silk — all without the help of a single maid or dresser. John watched in amazement and then asked how the trick was done.

After the device's function was explained—that it bestowed upon the bearer an opportunity to view their appearance—John sat stunned and doubting for long minutes.

Surely his family and subjects must have had a good reason for hiding such a simple device from him for so many years. Perhaps, he decided with a chill of horror, *perhaps* he was really hideously ugly; maybe even cursed to be malformed. Such tragedies had befallen other princes, as he well knew. After bracing himself to view a horrific visage, he gazed at the mirror and saw nothing. The metal faithfully showed him the grass or a cloud and the goose girl's worried pretty eyes, but of himself he found no sign.

With a cry of despair, he threw the terrible thing from him and fled to the safety of his room. He was a prince, and princes did not cry, but he did snivel a little once he reached the safety of his room.

Clearly, he could trust no one to tell him the truth. Everyone he knew had lied to him for years about mirrors. They might have lied about many other things. He was a prince. No one would ever have told him he was bad or ungainly or stupid. Princes never were, unless they were evil.

That new thought was a greater fear than all the rest: he might be evil and not even know it. He could not even examine himself for such obvious signs as a twisted leer or a beetled brow. He could not see himself.

He moped for days, inconsolable. His mother finally visited his chambers and demanded an explanation in the kind of voice only a mother can use. The prince confessed all his fears. The queen comforted him to the best of her ability, but John still doubted himself and everyone around him. He fell into a depression, refusing food and hiding himself from friends and family, and he developed the habit of sighing heavily while wandering the halls.

People avoided his dreary presence, which only reinforced his worst fears. He had never been handsome, kind, or witty. Everyone had lied to him. He was pathetic. No rational argument could satisfy him of his worth.

Only if he could truly see himself, he proclaimed with a blessed flair for melodrama, would he ever be happy.

Thus began months of proclamations and offers of rewards sent to the ends of the kingdom and beyond. The King resigned himself to holding daily receptions for charlatans and minor wizards, each proclaiming to hold the solution to his son's curse. Unfortunately, not one of the sparkler-lit spells or powdered herbal treatments removed the curse, and no mirror, however intricately carved or humbly polished, revealed the prince's true nature.

The family's first grain of hope came from an old man wearing rags and tatters. This petitioner brought no mirror, no magical potion to cure the curse, and made no demands. A man's true nature, he said in a consumptive wheeze, would be reflected in the eyes of his true love. The gnarled figure disappeared in a cloud of smoke, showing that he had been a true magician, not a simple charlatan.

The Queen thought the advice grand. She had been presenting potential mates for years, and now she redoubled her efforts with royal enthusiasm. Despite the prince's protestation of disinterest, eligible princesses and daughters of assorted worthies joined the daily ranks of hopeful spellcasters. Each day Prince John would be prodded forth to review a long line of possible matches. He felt like a judge of cattle at a village fair and began closing his eyes against the unreflecting and slightly desperate gazes of all the well-bred but boringly similar girls.

Then one day, as soon as he entered the throne room, a

girl standing quietly at the end of the line caught his attention. Surely, he thought, surely she would not be so bold.

Yet there stood his Selene, the goose girl who had so innocently exposed the lies, ignorance, and emptiness of his short life. Dressed now in the sparkling frothy finery of a princess, she curtsied with courtly grace when John stopped before her. Noting the prince's interest, the steward eagerly presented her.

John had no interest in the man's speech. His attention was locked on the vision before him. The how and why of Selene's blossoming from obscurity were unimportant to him. She was simply a princess, and a single tear glistened on one cheek. Without thinking, he raised a hand to brush it from rosy, perfect skin, and as if in a dream, he gazed into her eyes. Brilliant gray they were, like a mirror reflecting clouds. She whispered that she could not claim to hold the answer to his soul's ache, only that John had held her heart trembling in his hand from the very second they had met.

John saw not himself, only Selene's own soul within the depths of her eyes, but her love, honest and fresh as sunrise, was more than he could refuse.

The wedding took place as quickly as his parents could arrange the details. Now, everyone thought, the boy might forget his petty unhappiness and settle into his proper role as heir to the throne.

It was not to be. John spent the first few weeks of marriage in delirious happiness, but soon the couple began to quarrel, as couples do. After one such spat, the prince decided that his last chance for happiness had been thwarted by his awful curse. Within a few weeks he was so miserable again that even Selene, who did truly love him, could barely endure his presence.

A particularly fierce argument over whether the salt cellar should be placed to the right or the left of the pepper grinder sent the princess flouncing off in tears, and she did what many young newlyweds did when confronted by irreconcilable differences: she left her husband and sought the solace and advice of her mother.

John, left alone in an empty suite of rooms, soon found he missed the sound of his princess' voice. He sent word after Selene, begging forgiveness, only to learn that she had never reached her parents' castle. She had disappeared.

Nothing would please John then except to quest after her. His parents and friends, being heartily tired of dreary self-pity and egotistical tantrums, encouraged his taste for adventure.

John searched the length and width of the land, looking very fine on the back of his proud white charger, and also as gloomy as any prince possibly could look. His search proved fruitless. Either his Selene had been stolen by a wraith, or she did not wish to be found. John naturally suspected the latter, knowing in his heart of hearts that he must be as boring as sand and ugly as a brick.

Weeks of sleeping on hard ground and gnawing on hard bread took their toll on John's determination. He tired of failure and miserably turned for home, full of the bitter knowledge that he should have known he would fail. He was cursed, after all.

At a village within a day's journey of his own castle, he was forced to stop at the cottage of an old woman to beg water for his horse and food for himself. He saw no man's belongings in the little thatched cottage into which he was invited. Only herbs and hanging vegetables of a simple peasant woman decorated the place. From these details, John deduced that his hostess was a widow and recalculated the amount he planned to pay for a meal. Princes were supposed to be charitable.

The old woman said her name was Bertha, expressed great shock over the prince's road-weary condition, and proceeded to fuss over him. She refused the payment, of course. Widows always did, being too proud to accept charity.

John surreptitiously dropped the sack of coins to the floor beneath the table, as was proper.

He allowed himself to enjoy a shave using the warm water Bertha brought, and he eagerly wolfed down the hearty stew and fine white bread she set before him. After the old woman left on some errand, the prince tipped back a third glass of warm brown ale and began to wonder where his hostess had obtained such amenities if she was wasting away in the poverty of widowhood.

It belatedly occurred to him that the woman must be a witch. Hard on the heels of that realization came fear—but also a tiny hint of satisfaction. He'd made a common princely mistake, but at least he'd behaved like a good prince, not an evil one.

Now he would be asked to perform some gargantuan task to pay for his meal or else be transformed into stone or salt or worse. Contemplating his impending doom drew him into a gloomy reverie, and he jumped to his feet in surprise when the rickety door opened again.

The witch—her status now revealed by an elaborately embroidered robe, not to mention her sharp eyes and the wart on her sizable nose—made her way to the table and sat across from him. The sweet scents of fresh fruits rose from the basket she laid atop the planks.

"You wouldn't be *the* Prince John of Rambling Rocky Castle, would you?" she asked. "You only said your name was John, so I didn't place you at first."

John confirmed his identity and closed his eyes, awaiting whatever fate lay in store for him.

"Silly booby. You must've slept through your 'Identification of Hazardous Magicians' lecture. I'm a good witch. Honestly, what self-respecting evil magician would be named Bertha?"

John felt depression settle on him again. He was not even

worthy of being transformed or given an impossible quest. "Nothing I do ever goes right," he cried. "I'm cursed!"

"You are ridiculous," Bertha replied. She paced across the room a few times, waving her hands freely as she walked. "Yes, I had to curse you—rules, you know—but I came up with the most harmless little curse I could. Clearly I underestimated the blessed princely ego. Notoriously sensitive, and so easily bruised at this age."

She stopped and shot John a very significant look. Totally lost, he smiled, hoping for further explanation or perhaps a transformation.

"Now here you are," the witch said in an exasperated voice. "Totally mopey and pathetically dreary, all because you can't see your pretty face in a mirror. I ask you, is that any way for a grown prince to act?"

"I say," said the prince. "That's unfair. Everyone lied about mirrors. How can I trust their opinions on anything else? I'm cursed to never know truth, to never truly know myself."

"Oh, look who's the expert on curses," the witch said. "It's my curse, isn't it? Mirrors, boy. That's it. The rest you're making up yourself."

After opening and shutting his mouth several times, John asked, "You laid this curse on me?"

"Are you even listening? Didn't I just say that?" Bertha sighed. "Rules and all, as I said. I was insulted, I *had* to lay a curse. I snuck in a blessing while no one was watching, too. I hope you didn't mind."

"No, no. That's quite all right." John wondered if he looked as baffled as he felt.

"I'm afraid I did a rather good job," the witch said with shamefaced pride. "It's not going to come off. Quite permanent, that curse. You can stop wasting your time and crushing the hopes of all those silly razzle-dazzle wizards."

She waved a finger in John's face. "I want this nonsense to

stop. You're driving your poor parents into an early grave and making your poor, sweet wife cry. I won't have another minute of it, do you hear?"

"Uh," he said, wondering if he had a choice and doubting it. "Bertha, what am I to do, then? If the curse won't come off, how will I ever know who I am? I'm doomed to never truly know myself."

"Oh, bosh. Poppycock. Horsefeathers." Bertha reached over the table and grabbed the prince by his hand, hauling him to the door. "If you must see your silly face, have a portrait done. Or have two done, and then start practicing."

"Practicing?" he echoed as they emerged into late after-noon sunlight.

"Making comparisons," the witch said impatiently. "You learn to know yourself the way everyone else does. You look inside yourself first, where, I might add," and she did, acidly, "you don't need a mirror. I was very specific about mirrors, you know. I'm sure you were told."

"I didn't listen." He felt silly for acting as badly as he had for so long. But then, he reflected, princes were often silly. It was almost expected, certainly no cause for shame.

"Start with that, then." Bertha nodded firmly. "Listen to other people's opinions of you, balance what you feel inside with all the things you hear, and adjust yourself accordingly. That's all there is to it. It's easy to say, quite hard to master. Now shoo, before I charge you for the sage advice."

She had to push John forward, because he was frozen in shock.

Selene, wearing a peasant girl's smock and petticoats and looking as lovely as ever, was holding his proud charger's bridle. She smiled without apology for hiding so long. She thought he needed the time alone, she explained, and she had needed advice from her godmother. John made his first wise decision in a long time and said nothing.

He heard Bertha say smugly, "No one says witches can't be

fairy godmothers too. My blessings for you both, you see? Go on, silly boy. Ride off into the sunset with her before it gets dark."

John leaped into the saddle behind his princess, and after a dignified kiss and a not-so-dignified hug, they both rode home to the castle.

They did not live happily ever after. Few people, even royal fairy-tale couples, manage that. They did share a great deal of joy and love in their long and exciting lives, and that was all any prince or princess could ask.

DOG DRABBLES

Drabbles are stories that must be no more and no less than 100 words long. I love the challenge of playing inside those tight lines. These five mostly lighthearted pieces first appeared in a canine-themed charity anthology titled Ludlow Charlington's Doghouse. *All the tales in Ludlow were inspired by paintings in which a classical portrait subject had been replaced by a rescue dog.*

WHAT'S IN A NAME?

Of all the many things in the world that vexed Lone Pine Septimus Poochie Pie—mail carriers, the garbage disposal, that one shadowy corner of the vet's waiting room—his name irked him most. It had no dignity; no style.

He thought himself the most handicapped hound in creation until he was introduced to Happy Farms Who's My Boogie-Woogie Pretty Boy.

"Call me Boo," that unfortunate fellow begged with an embarrassed tail-wag. "May I call you Tim?"

"Brilliant!" Tim replied happily. "Why didn't I think of that?"

He grinned at his new best friend, and they went for a romp.

Admiral's Big Surprise

Once upon a time, the Forbidden Room had been the boring old Empty Room. Now Admiral's people spent all their time inside, and amazing smells and strange noises came out of it day and night.

They said, "Admiral, no," when he followed, and "Admiral, hush," when he barked. That meant they were doing important things. Something special was inside!

He brought them his toys to show them he understood. When they opened the door, he was ready, tail wagging.

"Admiral, this is the new baby," they said, and, "Be gentle." And he was, because he was a good boy.

Heavy Lies The Head

No one asked her if she wanted the headache of a crown. No one asked if she wanted to be weighed down with jewels or imprisoned in fine fabrics made stiff by heavy, lumpy gold-thread embroidery. It was her destiny, they told her. They washed and dressed her and put her on display, and they told her she was powerful and beloved.

She'd never known love, and she'd never had power. She didn't believe them. Not at first. They gave her a crown she never wanted. She gave them her heart and became the queen they needed her to be.

I'm No Empty-Headed Fribble

Don't be fooled by my fashionable turnout or my affable countenance. I am no empty-headed fribble whose regard can be bought cheap. You see before you a serious gentleman of discerning manners. Do not think to win my heart with treats or gain my goodwill with praise. I am proud, and I have high standards. It will take more than food or flattery alone to earn my loyal admiration.

It is a truth universally acknowledged that a good boy, in possession of a single squeaky toy, must be in want of more toys and a lively game of fetch.

Ruler Of All She Surveys

It isn't much, this worn braided rug in a sunny patch of hall between kitchen and dining room, but it is hers. It's her castle, and she defends it from all comers, evicting puppies, toddlers, toys, and other nuisances with courteous firmness.

The rug once lived at the garage door—under dirty, wet shoes, imagine!—but she knew a treasure when she sniffed it. Her claim is constantly challenged, but the thieves who return it to its old home whenever she relaxes her vigilance are no match for her perseverance.

Victory goes to those who fight for what they love.

FOR WANT OF A NAIL

I wrote this goofy tale long ago for the sole purpose of making a friend smile. We both liked fantasy tales about long journeys, impossible tasks, and magical companions, and we'd been complaining to each other about the unquestioned assumptions behind the whole concept of "Happily Ever After." So I twisted a few tropes for fun.

THE CITY WAS DEAD. A pall of yellow dust covered each empty, silent street, and ruined buildings lay bleaching like bare skeletons beneath a glaring hot sky. The quiet air stank, an invisible curtain of rot that no living breeze touched.

A solitary horse and rider moved slowly through the desolation. The horse, an undistinguished dirty gray creature, picked a careful path through the maze of half-burned timbers and brick rubble while its rider dozed, swaying gently in the saddle.

When the horse stumbled over a loose cobblestone, the rider jerked upright and looked around in bewilderment at the bleak surroundings. He peered sleepily at his surroundings, then turned and plunged one hand into a saddlebag. After a few seconds of tightlipped searching, he hauled a grass-green lizard into the sunlight.

The lizard swung by its tail, stubby legs churning help-lessly, and its wide mouth snapped open and shut in impotent anger. The man brought the creature to eye-level.

"A wondrous gem of a metropolis," he said in a sour voice. "Center of commerce, seat of political and economic power. Look at this, you miserable lying excuse for boot leather!"

He swung the lizard back and forth, providing a compre-hensive, if upside-down, view of the destruction around them. The lizard's beady eyes blinked nearsightedly, and it opened its mouth again. "Things change, my prince. Immovane was a very nice place when I was young."

"That was a few hundred years ago, Alice."

"It's not my fault I was frozen in crystal all that time, Tireus. You can't expect an enchanted princess to keep up on all the little details. If you don't like my advice, then don't listen to me."

"Princes who don't take advice from their enchanted companions never succeed." Prince Tireus heaved a great sigh and lowered Alice onto the pommel of his saddle. "Why couldn't I get a talking fox, or a bird, or a cat? What did I do to deserve an iguana?"

"You got lucky. Keep looking, my prince. There must be someone left. Maybe there's a war on."

The prince was visibly cheered by the thought of warfare. "Princes are supposed to be valiant in battle." Tireus toyed with the iguana's tail. "I can't believe any king would live in a dump like this, Alice. Are you sure the royal family didn't move somewhere else?"

"Don't lose hope so easily, my prince. Ride on and let me bask in the sun."

So encouraged, the prince urged his tired horse forward again. Alice perched happily on the saddle horn and soaked up the hot sunshine while Tireus slowly wilted under its beating force.

They emerged from the maze of rubble onto a plaza in the very shadow of a scorched and battered castle. The market was a squalid little pesthole, with beggars and uniformed guards outnumbering honest merchants and townsmen. Tireus bought a mouse-nibbled loaf of bread from a vendor who happily dispensed knowledge for an outrageous fee.

The information was of better quality than the food. The explanation for all the poverty and destruction was simple: Immovane had been overrun during a recent war with an assortment of ravening barbarian hordes. According to the indignant merchant, the plundering barbarians had left the city to rot, not even providing an occupation force to replace the customers they had killed.

The royal family still lived in their castle, and the merchant assured Tireus that the King was accepting visitors. His Royal Majesty, a few stalwart courtiers, and a gaggle of generals held a pathetic court each day.

At that good news, Tireus packed Alice safely out of sight and presented himself to the guards at the castle gate. When questioned, he admitted that he was a foreign prince and said that he had a favor to ask of the King. Before he could finish his explanation, he found himself arrested on charges of spying, stripped of his weapons, and thrown into a rocky dungeon.

Tireus had expected something of that sort: false imprisonment was a traditional hazard of questing. He settled in the damp straw and caught up on his sleep. He awakened just in time to see the sunset fade to black night in the cell's tiny window. Time crept onward. As the city clock tolled midnight, he heard claws scratching along the stone wall.

"Took you long enough," he said to the darkness.

The darkness hissed angrily.

"I was nearly crushed inside that silly pack," Alice said. "You made knots in the strings. It took me hours to work my way out. I don't have teeth or sharp claws, you know."

"A fox would've been here hours ago. Or a cat. Why couldn't you be a cat, Alice?"

"I am what I am." The iguana sounded hurt.

"I'm sorry. I was only teasing." Tireus felt in the straw until he touched the lizard's soft leathery skin. He patted Alice's head, and she climbed up his arm, curled around his throat like a necklace. The prince absently scratched her spiny back. "You're my best friend, Alice. It's only—no matter how gorgeous a princess you become once you're disenchanted, I'll always think of you as an iguana. That bothers me sometimes."

"How much does it bother you? Enough to leave me a lizard for all eternity?"

Tireus patted her head again. "Don't be silly, Alice. I won't let you down. Once you help me finish my quest, I'll bring you home, your curse will be lifted, and you'll be a princess again."

"Yes," the iguana hissed. "Of course." She puffed a little. "I could've been a toad, you know."

Tireus shuddered. "Don't remind me."

"Try to look on the bright side for once. You're almost finished. This should be the last stop. We'll be on our way home in a month."

"A homecoming. It's strange to think about coming home when I was never meant to leave. I was entirely the wrong son to go questing."

Alice made noncommittal noises.

"Jodrie was the eldest, so of course he had to stay home and think for Father after that evil warlock Kojan stole the Cloak of Judgment from us, but Barius should've gone on the quest to retrieve it. He was the youngest. It wasn't fair for Mama to make me go in his place. Middle sons go to mage school or become military advisors."

"You're special," Alice assured him. "There are exceptions to every tradition."

"Yes but Barius got all the quest lessons, not me. I went galloping off without the first idea of what I was doing. I got lost in frozen wastes and treacherous jungles and one truly horrific magical forest before I finally reached the city where Kojan lived." He paused in reverent memory. "Now *that* city was lovely. The streets gleamed with gold, and everyone smiled at me."

"Even Kojan?" Alice asked drily.

"Well, no. The old geezer wanted to skin me alive when he caught me sneaking out his window with the Cloak. I had to turn on all the princely charm to keep him from pulling out the knives." He sighed yet again. "When Kojan agreed to give me the Cloak of Judgment if I brought him the Heart of Ice, I figured I'd made a sweet deal. Even if I didn't know what the thing was, it had to be better than being skinned. So I tracked down an old soothsayer to tell me about the Heart of Ice."

His voice took on a querulous note as he quoted. "'The Heart of Ice is a wondrous crystal that gives off light without heat. It belongs to an old witch who lives east of the sunrise. Now get your silly feet moving, young man, and straighten up your spine.' I'll remember that advice until I die. I thought I was on the brink of success until I found out it would take a year and a day just to reach the sunrise."

Alice said, "Yes, but you found me there."

"No, I spent months with that awful witch first. And as soon as I stole the Heart, the shriveled old biddy caught me red-handed. I thought I'd die. Then she tells me I can have the stupid crystal if I'll only do her a small favor and kill the mule that pulls some competing wizard's magical plow. She sent me off with a beating, and *that's* when I found you."

"Oh, yes." Alice nodded, scratching Tireus' chest with her scaly chin. "You were sitting under a gnarled old oak tree at the edge of the world, crying your heart out."

"I wasn't crying. I had a cold."

"You did not. You were sniveling about being a failure and other nonsense, as I recall. The tears shattered my magical crystal prison. I was so afraid you would kill yourself in despair before I had a chance to help. You were so miserable."

"No one ever told me that getting caught was part of the plan. How was I to know that quests were traditionally divided into threes? How was I to know that every move I made was part of some greater pattern? Who made all these rules?"

"It's simply the way of the world. Good thing, too. Otherwise there'd be a chronic overpopulation of royalty and a horrible shortage of fairy tales."

"Phooey on fairy tales."

"Oh, Tireus. It hasn't been so bad, has it? The Great Birac caught us in the act—of course—but he agreed to kill his mule if you brought him the Golden Blackbird, which I happened to know had been domesticated by someone in the Immovanian royal family. I navigated you past the Kraken Swamp and the Fall of Heroes and the Caves of Doom, and to fulfill the quest now, we just need the bird."

Tireus ticked off the last few steps. "So now the King will give me a task. I'll succeed—although only with your help—and I'll get the stinking blackbird as payment. It'll probably peck me half to death, with my luck. I give the bird to Birac, he kills the old mule, and I take a trophy to that wretched witch. She gives me the Heart of Ice, I give that to Kojan, and I get the cloak back at last."

"Then you go home to receive thanks and praise and riches from your family," Alice said in a distant voice. "And there, in front of witnesses, you can propose to me. That act of gratitude will dispel my enchantment, and I'll become a princess again." The iguana finished with a hissing sigh. "We get married and live with the royal family in your castle."

"Happily ever after," Tireus agreed numbly.

Every time he thought about Alice as a princess, he felt

nauseated. Still, if he did not accept Alice's hand in marriage, she would remain an iguana forever, and that wouldn't be fair to *her*. He couldn't let that happen. Alice was his only real friend in the whole world.

Sometimes, though, sometimes he wished he could escape the trap of tradition. Sometimes he wished he could ride off into the sunset, ignore his obligations, and keep traveling forever.

"Tireus," Alice said.

"Hmm?"

"You said gold lined the streets in the citadel where Kojan lived?"

"Uh-huh. Big gold buildings too, with a bunch of castles in the center."

Alice's tail slapped lightly against his face. "You great ninny. You really were lost at first, weren't you? That was Immovane. Didn't you recognize it today?"

"I thought the towers looked familiar. Gosh, I hope I don't run into Kojan!"

"Don't worry, dear. Kojan probably snags three or four questing princes a year. I'm sure he wouldn't recognize you on sight. You're not that memorable."

"You're full of flattery, Alice."

"It's only because I love you. Go to sleep, my prince."

Dawn came at last, heralded by birdsong outside and less melodic grumblings in the hall outside the cell. Soon the door opened with a squeal of rusty hinges, admitting two unsavory-looking guards who chained Tireus and escorted him from the dungeon to the main hall of the castle.

The royal reception room was both gloomy and impressive. Despite the summer heat, a fire roared in the huge hearth at one end of the hall. Even through the obscuring smoke, Tireus could tell that the high, proud walls were bare. The invaders had looted even the palace.

A paltry group of grubby-looking courtiers made mandatory titters of derision at Tireus' appearance. Irritated, he drew himself to his full height as he approached the throne.

The king stopped the snickers with a gesture of royal authority. His hands shook with palsy and his head bobbed up and down as he peered at the meager crowd, but it was still a fine gesture.

The prince bowed. Fifty pounds of iron clanked.

The king displayed a toothless grin. "You are a prince, you say?" he said in a wheezing voice. "Yes, I see that. Definitely a royal appearance. Mmm-hmm."

The weight of the shackles stooped Tireus' shoulders, and his travel-worn clothing dripped bits of straw. "Your majesty is perceptive."

"Thank you. I'm terribly sorry about the arrest. The men are jumpy, you know. Military defeat and all. Disheartening. I only heard about you this morning. Had you released immediately, of course."

"Of course, Your Majesty."

Imprisonment and mistreatment followed by kindness and promises: these were the steps in a familiar circle dance. Kings hoped the process would leave travelers willing to accept any alternative, no matter how outrageous. Seasoned travelers knew that and endured in hopes of getting the best possible offer. Everyone knew the steps, and only beginners stumbled.

Tireus was an excellent dancer. He bowed low again. "I'm at your Majesty's service."

"No more of that 'Majesty' stuffiness," the king said airily. "Formal rank bores me. Call me Sal. I hear you've come to ask a boon. You're in luck. We could use a brave adventuring type such as yourself. Should you do a small service for the crown, anything in the kingdom would be yours for the asking."

A trill of music swept through the hall as if to underscore the king's words. The glorious liquid sound managed to brighten the gloom with a glamour of richness. Clearly, the Golden Blackbird was still in Immovanian hands.

The prince made another clanking bow to hide his disappointment. "I would consider it an honor to place myself at your service, Your Majesty."

"Sal, my boy, Sal," said King Sal. "That's excellent. We'll outfit you, of course. Wouldn't be neighborly to send you off with just the shirt on your back, would it? Servants will attend you, we'll have a little feast, and then off you go. Hmm?"

He waved, and servants ushered Tireus from the room. The prince soon learned that Immovane still had much to offer a visitor. First, valets dressed him in finery according to his proclaimed rank, then palace armorers provided him with a fine sword, polished shield, and bright chain mail. Their fussing reminded Tireus of the whirlwind preparations that had preceded the very beginning of his quest.

He wished he had Alice's sharp-tongued company to relieve the tedium of being allowed to do nothing for himself. Unfortunately, Alice had slipped off into the woodwork to do a little enchanted-companion-type spying so she could plan strategy.

Tireus let himself be primped and pressed and flattered — and ground his teeth in frustration. The lavishly embroidered doublets and hose, while attractive, would not last a week on the road, and courtly swords made better ornaments than weapons. He found himself wishing for the return of his sturdy boots and trousers, his rough knife and staff. He would have to trade the fancy dress for more practical outfittings at the first village he reached.

The grand luncheon he shared with the full court, although sumptuous, left him craving plain bread and a glass of tavern ale. The conversation, full of intrigues and murmured confidences, bored him to tears. Royal life was so very dull.

At last, the whole court proceeded to the front steps of the castle for the formal going-away blessing. Grooms brought the prince's horse. The animal's coat gleamed white now, washed and brushed to perfection. New polish scented the saddle and harness with a spicy perfume. Tireus took the reins and patted his steed's soft pink nose. The horse sneezed.

King Sal began mumbling some speech about bravery in battle and the blessings of royal duties, so Tireus tuned out the noise and thought about his future.

Soon, he would be going home to his senile father, his manipulative stepmother, and his annoying brothers. He would also be going home to marry someone who was kind, sweet, and wise…and who had once been scaly. He would be returning to endless feasts and jousts and presentations.

He wanted to leap to the back of his charger and run for the hills; without Alice, without accepting King Sal's commission, without facing that too-predictable future. The daydream evaporated in the light of reason. Alice would never forgive him.

Soon enough, the iguana arrived on the scene, skittering up the prince's leg to his shoulder where she could hiss in his ear. "The king didn't tell anyone what he planned. It doesn't matter, I suppose. It has to be something we can do together. And then we'll on our way home."

She nuzzled his neck and sighed. To the prince's practiced ear, the sigh sounded disappointed. "What's wrong, Alice?"

"I'm not looking forward to disenchantment."

Tireus whispered in astonishment, "I thought you wanted to be a princess!"

"Oh, no! I like being a lizard. But Fate made me your magical companion, and being disenchanted is part of the deal. I can't let you down simply because I don't like the way the story ends."

Tireus' heart rose. Dreams flitted through his mind again: dreams of a future free of tradition. "Alice, let's forget this stupid quest. I don't want to go home any more than you want to be a princess. We can have adventures together, and you can be an iguana forever if you like."

"Don't you tempt me," Alice hissed. "It's not *done*. You must complete the quest. If we tried to cheat, I'm sure lightning would strike us down or something horrible like that. Besides, you already gave your word to King Sal and to your father too. No one who breaks their word ever lives happily ever after!"

The prince sighed mightily and let the dreams crumble to dust. "You're right."

"I'm sorry, Tireus. It would've been nice."

The prince tuned his ear to the king's unwelcome words again. The old man was winding up to his point at last: the dreadful awful danger that only a prince could face, the awesome task that could be performed only by a quest-driven hero.

The task, like everything else about Tireus' quest, was a bit of a disappointment. Apparently, a court adviser had proved to be less than faithful during the recent war. The villain had left with the victorious barbarian hordes with much of the treasury in his greedy hands. Only a hero could pass the multitude of enemy soldiers and retrieve Immovania's honor and wealth.

"Get specifics," Alice warned him. "You're not a collection agency, for pity's sake."

"Uh, Your Majesty?"

"Hmm?" The king blinked owlishly.

"If you would tell me what single object or device most embodies the honor of your country, I will do my best to return it to you. Only this can I promise."

King Sal beamed at him. "Of, course, my dear boy. Of course. In fact, I'll give you a royal order to that end, sealed and signed by my hand. Whenever you're ready."

"I depart at your word!" Tireus vaulted onto the horse's

back in a fine princely fashion, and the king handed him a folded slip of parchment.

"Say nothing of your goal," Sal whispered. "My so-called advisers don't want me to have this. Surrender it to no one but me."

"My word on it." Tireus tucked the paper into his collar so Alice could read it at her leisure. "I'll be on my way then, to return only when I have completed this task."

His horse pranced away from the castle steps before the king could complete his royal farewell. After a night's rest in a royal stall, eating royal oats, the animal was eager for action. Tireus waved farewell and concentrated on guiding the spirited charger through the ruins of the city.

As he neared the eastern edge, he realized Alice was mumbling. He pulled the horse to a halt and held it quiet by force. "Alice, what is it? Has something else gone wrong?"

"I don't know," she said. "I can't find a flaw, but it can't be right, either."

"What do you mean?" The prince reached up and patted Alice's head. She puffed with agitation and wrapped her tail around his ear. The parchment fell to Tireus' lap.

"Look at that," Alice said.

The prince fought with the horse and tried to read the king's crabbed handwriting at the same time. The name Kojan leaped out at him, after the title of Magical Adviser. Among the semi-legible instructions were the scrawled words "Cloak of Judgment."

"This can't be right," he exclaimed. "I'm to steal the Cloak?"

Alice huffed. "To fulfill the quest rules, this has to be a task we can perform, and it is, technically. I mean, it's the task we're already performing. But it doesn't work. You can't beat Kojan. If you could, you'd've been finished questing long ago. But you *can* bargain with him, so he'll send us after something else…but if he does that, it means we'll be starting a new trio of quests."

Tireus pondered the problem. "You mean we'll have to keep adventuring?"

"Yes, and I don't know how long it'll go on," the iguana answered in frustration. "We've fallen into some kind of loop. If the quest keeps coming back to the Cloak, then we'll never wind up the chain of tasks."

Their lifetimes might be spent in various adventures, performing heroic deeds of one sort or another. Tireus grinned a very un-princely grin and let his warhorse leap into a full gallop at last.

"Alice, my dear, I think we've managed to pull off a happy ending after all."

NUMBERS GAME

This story grew from my many attempts to wrap my brain around what, exactly, my spouse's job title meant. His patient explanations of what, exactly, a financial analyst did made actuaries sound like wizards who used math magic to make sure insurance policies didn't lose the company money.

So I wondered, what if the profit-watchers had access to actual magic, too? They'd misuse it in the heartless pursuit of profit, wouldn't they? Then my question became, "Who would stop them?" Here's one answer. First published in Far Horizons.

———

THERE'S a clarity to insurance that's missing from most modern financial arrangements. Take credit cards. Those multi-page agreements are worse than deals with Satan for catch clauses and loopholes that benefit the card issuer. Stocks are nearly as bad. They're a mess of regulations and a dictionary's worth of jargon. Don't even get me started on options, puts, calls, or commodities. The markets are made of razzle-dazzle, a gambling arena bigger and more profitable than any casino owner's dream, and more complicated than a Byzantine mosaic.

Compared to credit and investing, insurance is simplicity embodied. It's still gambling, of course. Property insurance policyholders are betting bad things will happen, putting down money on a wager that they'll crash the car before it's paid off, or their home will burn down, or they'll get hit by some other policy-covered disaster.

Or not! Maybe nothing will happen, and that's a win too. That's the beauty of it. Everybody wants the same thing: long, happy, uneventful lives—policyholders for the obvious reasons, and insurers for the profits from regular, on-time premiums and no claims to pay out.

It's like tossing a coin to the universe for a little extra hope of safety, the modern equivalent of pouring out a bit of wine to keep the gods from getting angry at you for enjoying your meal—or putting out milk and bread for the Fae. It soothes a superstitious itch, or it pays the bills.

Either way, everybody's happy, and insurers rake in profits.

See, at the population level, misfortune is a numbers game. The chances of disease, disaster, accident, age, misadventure, mayhem and even death become shockingly predictable at scale. A whole school of mathematics grew up around that reality, because when it comes to numbers games, the people with the most math win. Actuarial math gives insurers the house a big edge on all their gambles they make with their customers.

Actuaries work the math of life like card counters at a casino blackjack table, only the house respects and rewards them instead of kicking them out to the curb. Actuaries are some of the highest-paid professionals in the insurance business, because a little knowledge is a profitable thing. Their employers need those statistics to hedge policy bets.

There's only one job in the industry that pays more, in fact. Mine.

I'm an actual-ary. I don't do math magic. I do *magic* magic.

I make futures happen the way my insurance company clients want them to happen.

See, math only takes you so far. On a personal, individual level, policy payouts can still get expensive, and insurance companies are in it for the bottom line.

If a case looks bad enough, an actualary gets hired to fix the outcome. We're the little magnets that aren't supposed to be under the craps table controlling how the dice fall. Hey, I said it was a numbers game. I didn't say anyone played fair.

You'll never find us on the organizational charts. We're freelancers, every one of us. Consultants. Sometimes we even do pro bono work, if the situation is interesting.

And sometimes our jobs get seriously weird—usually with life insurance.

There's *always* a payout with that, death being one of the two big Inevitables, and as soon as you bring that third player —the beneficiary—into the picture, the whole 'everybody wins' aspect breaks down.

Life insurance bets are all about timing. That's why older people have to pay higher premiums for a new policy, and most policies have wait periods before coverage kicks in. Life insurers want their clients to live forever. The longer a policy-holder lives, the more money the company keeps after settling with beneficiaries. The clients, on the other hand, want to pay in as little as possible before they die. That's how they maximize the winnings they'll pass to their heirs.

This difference makes life insurance more adversarial than property insurance, and insurers love to hedge those bets by making the idea of doling out benefits in small chunks very appealing. Because, you know, the beneficiaries will die too, and if they die before the benefit profit is all used up…then the insurance company wins twice.

Unless they make a bad bet.

Take the case of Granny Fannie. She was my last job for a certain client now on my banned-forever list.

Don't blame me for the woman's nickname. Her great-grandchildren gave it to her long before Fannie's kids and grandkids relocated her to a nice little apartment in a nice senior living community in a nice little seaside town.

Fannie never liked the nickname, and she hated the idea of moving away from the great-grands and all the neighborhood kids she babysat and granny-ed, but she was a practical woman, too. Her income from Social security and a life-benefit monthly check from her husband's life insurance policy would go a lot further if she moved.

So, on her seventy-ninth birthday, she threw a big block party at her old city walk-up and invited all her family, neighbors and friends. Everyone pitched in to get her essentials packed up and her other belongings parceled out while she was still living.

Quilts, old hats, knickknacks, baby books, and big-ticket furniture pieces all went into boxes or onto backseats. A few items went with her, but most were carried away by local families who could use them best. Three days after that, Fannie was all settled in her new independent-living apartment several states away.

"Resurrected like Christ," she said at the time, as she rocked in the wooden chair where she'd nursed four babies. She pronounced the food in the cafeteria edible, she charmed the staff, and she spent hours in the common room watching prehistoric-looking herons in the marshy wetlands next door.

She also took walks around the retention ponds—well away from the alligators—marveled at the pelicans flying overhead, and learned plant names from the landscapers. By the end of her first month, she thought she might even learn to love her new nest.

My job, unfortunately for both of us, was to make sure she never got to enjoy a second month there.

The number cruncher in charge of her account had gotten nervous about how much she was costing the company every month. Then he looked at how much *her* life policy payout would cost them, panicked at his bottom line, and called me in.

Most days an actualary's job is like being a guardian angel. I don't enjoy the cases where I have to shorten life lines, but I'm only human, and those jobs are by leaps and bounds the most lucrative ones. I was weak, I succumbed to temptation, and I signed on the dotted line.

It should've been easy. Fannie already lived a long, meaningful life. I checked the infinite possibilities and picked a not-uncommon end, one without pain or suffering: hit by a reckless driver at an unfamiliar intersection near her new home. That fit the bill.

I tugged the lines of the universe just so and sat back to watch Fate unfold.

Only Fannie didn't die. She looked both ways, she didn't trust that kid in his shiny, red sports car, and she dodged death by a hair.

That happens, when dealing in probabilities and adjusting infinite dimensional possibilities. No big deal. Lethal opportunities abound in the daily life of the elderly, and I still had three weeks.

I adjusted her lifeline accordingly and proceeded to plan B.

Fannie dodged death again a few days later, when she didn't slip in the shower and fall, because she listened to the lecture she got from the manager after the prescription incident, and she used her call button when she had trouble opening the stall door.

Plan C? Zero for three. She didn't die of smoke inhalation, although she did set the building on fire with her toaster. She was living the high life, and I was failing. I hunkered down and pulled out all the stops, to no avail.

She didn't break her neck in the puddle at poolside on her way to water aerobics. She didn't choke on a piece of biscuit.

She had her first physical and was proclaimed fit as a fiddle, as healthy as a woman ten years younger.

I'm not bragging when I say I'm good at my job, so at this point, I was getting mighty suspicious of Fannie's good luck.

I took a closer look at her life line. After a long, in-depth examination of all the lives her life touched, I called the office.

"This one is not happening," I told my liaison. "I'm out. My advice is, take the loss. Do not mess with her. Seriously. Do not."

He didn't listen. More fool him.

My replacement had no better luck than I did. Unlike me, he didn't have the sense to back off when all the reasonable, likely death probabilities were exhausted. The fool tied whole handfuls of actuality into existential knots.

More disasters and fluke accidents occurred the next month in those ten square miles of Florida than happened in the whole rest of the world.

Parts dropped off an airliner and crashed into the building. Cars smashed through the front windows. An overturned tanker full of poison gas derailed on a nearby railway. A dozen mice infected with hantavirus got loose from a research lab and went to ground in the neighborhood.

Granny Fannie skated through every incident without a scratch. So did all the innocent bystanders. All. Of. Them.

Don't even get me started on the property damage, though. Can you guess which insurer turned out to be responsible for the majority of those policies? Yup. When you poke reality too hard, reality bites back.

That company is going to be cleaning up their own mess for decades, I'm sure. Without my help, or the help of any other responsible actualary, either. We do have a network.

Florida stories were all over the news. Late night hosts made jokes. The internet overflowed with memes. My replacement actualary and his boneheaded liaison kept trying.

And Fannie kept surviving.

The doofus duo was contemplating an earthquake time-line when their corporate overlords finally contracted a case of common sense, pulled the number-cruncher off the case and fired him.

The actualary? He didn't get paid, and he got stripped of his powers too, once an anonymous tip to the disciplinary committee finally worked its way through the bureaucracy.

Fannie was the big winner. She loved every one of her fifteen minutes of fame on all the big media outlets, and she got a book deal out of it. Some enterprising young cousin of hers sold the rights to a Hollywood producer for a fortune.

"The Luckiest Woman in the World," they called the miniseries, and they were right.

Only it wasn't luck. It was Fate. Or more precisely, Fate's goddaughter.

See, one of the brats from Granny Fannie's old neighbor-hood grows up to become one of the world's greatest scientific minds.

A snot-nosed little kid who went home with a quilt from Fannie's moving party will eventually unlock the mysteries of trans-dimensional travel and change the future of humanity. Messing with probabilities to protect the people she loved? Child's play.

The moral of this story? Do not mess with the golden years of a super-genius's beloved babysitter.

Just don't.

THE THING IN THE PANTRY

This one would've been in a concept anthology about a haunted house. The plan was for each contributor to pick one room from a public-domain floor plan for a Gilded Age mansion and write a horror or horror-adjacent story centered on that location. The anthology never got off the ground, but by the time it collapsed, I'd written this little piece.

———

THE DOOR OPENED. Metal scraped, and light burst over the small room from the bare bulb screwed into a socket overhead. The Darkness shrank back in alarm.

The small, trapped shadow of the light's pull chain danced wild against the bounty displayed on the pantry's racks and bins. An unforgiving glare glinted off metal blades, pots, and pans, birthed reflections on rounded glass jars, and kissed the ranks of boxes and plastic containers with a faded rainbow of colors. Darkness lurked behind every full container and closed bin, waiting to see what shape the invasion would take.

Light could drive it back, but it never prevailed. Darkness knew how to drive away all the Things that brought in light. The Things came, they fussed, they re-organized, tidied, and they *took*, but in the end, they all retreated.

This space belonged to Darkness, and Darkness didn't share. It had been here first, it hated thieves, and it fought dirty.

The pantry was the heart of the kitchen, home of culinary dreams. When treated with respect, Darkness kept the shelves stocked with all the raw ingredients of comfort and happiness. It wanted nothing more than the quiet satisfaction of seeing its territory well-tended.

In its experience, too few Things understood the power of a good pantry.

Today, a New Thing stood framed in the pantry doorway, with sunshine and fluorescent glow at its back and bags in its hands. It studied the shelves, made disapproving noises, and began moving things. Darkness extended a tendril of curiosity and pushed itself like smoke against a jar of cherry preserves. The jar tipped, slid towards the edge—and the Thing picked it up to examine its label.

Light lanced deep into the shelf, obliterating the thread of power. Darkness retreated. The Thing put down the jar, picked and put down other items, inflicting painful assaults on Darkness each time.

The Thing called over its shoulder into the kitchen. "Hey, Jordan! Look at all this stuff the previous owners left behind. It's all good, too; I checked all the expiration dates."

Someone else in the light said, "Dates on what?"

Shade passed across the doorway, and a second Thing appeared, bigger and bulkier than the first. Darkness stirred as the second thing's shadow touched it, like sensing like.

Thing Two said, "Wash the pots and things before you use 'em, and throw out that food."

"What? Jordan, that's three hundred bucks of groceries, maybe more. You said we were were tapped out, between the down payment and the repairs. How can we afford—?"

"I said pitch it, Harley." Jordan retreated, leaving only its voice behind to dim the bright air around Thing One—

around *Harley*. "I'm not taking that bait. There could be laxative in the flour, salt in the sugar, rat poison in the cake mix—look there's a box of it right there on the floor, and that's the old-fashioned kind, too. No telling what else those crazy mofos might've done."

"Who would play horrible tricks like that on perfect strangers?" Harley sighed. "No, never mind. I don't want to know. I'll get started on supper."

"Work fast. It's getting late, and that upstairs bathroom needs cleaning too, so I can shower before I eat."

"Couldn't you—?"

"Don't even think about finishing that sentence. I'm the one paying for all this, remember? I'm the one with a real job."

"I know." Harley's voice went small and dark.

"And don't you forget it. I'll be setting up the entertainment console so I can catch up on the games I haven't been playing since you packed last week." Jordan's voice retreated. "Fix me something nice and then clean up. I can't believe how ungrateful you are."

"I'm sorry." Harley shook out a big trash bag and regarded the shelves again. "What a waste."

Every box, bag, can, and jar of food the Darkness had set up went into the garbage. Shadow after precious shadow dropped into stretchy white plastic and disappeared into the greater light. Afterwards the vegetable tubs and bins were scoured and left open, and new mouse poison was scattered on the clean floor under the shelves.

The bright light drove Darkness far behind the shelf uprights, deep into the corners, up by the ceiling. Its fortress was stripped bare, and it clung desperately to its last redoubts, feeding patience with spite and anger. Light never lasted. Not here. A chance to retaliate would come soon enough.

Harley finished cleaning and unpacked the meager contents of the grocery bags onto the new wide, bare spaces.

Darkness regarded the new things with jealous hatred, and once again, it extended a single dusky line of rage. Waited for the right moment.

Harley reached for the cord to the light fixture. Like a runner awaiting the gun, Darkness crouched ready. It moved at last under the rising shadow of Harley's arm.

The cord scraped again, cha-chink, and Darkness leaped off the shelves to reclaim the room, all but a slice of floor and wall lit by the open door where Harley stood gazing at the light like he didn't want to go into it either.

Darkness flexed, and a box of dry pasta slid, tipped over… fell rattling to the floor. Another box followed. A glass jar landed unbroken in the nest of cardboard, then shattered under the arrival of canned peaches falling from on high.

"Hey!" Harley leaped backwards into the brightness of the kitchen. "What was that?"

"Are you making a mess already?" Jordan called from another room. "God, you're clumsy. Make sure you clean up every bit. If we end up with ants, you'll regret it."

"We won't get ants. Or mice. I promise." Harley stood in the doorway looking down at the puddle of pasta sauce. The pool of red liquid, dotted with lumps of poison, flecked with basil and tiny bits of glass, spread far under the shelves.

Darkness nudged at the stockpot on its rack, just enough to make it swing.

Harley looked up. Looked down at the sauce. He smiled. "Be a shame to waste it," he murmured, almost as if he knew Darkness was listening.

Harley reached for the pot and the copper-bottomed saucepan beside it. The pasta was collected by the handful into the pot. The spilled sauce was scraped off the floor and went into the pan. Another handy trash bag swallowed the bigger pieces of broken glass. Harley carried it all away into the light.

"Hey, Jordan, I'm making spaghetti and meat sauce, nice

and spicy the way you like it. Then I'll do the cleaning upstairs. Eat whenever you like."

"Like I'd do anything else. You don't eat until you finish your work. Don't expect me to wait."

The door closed, and Darkness swelled out to embrace its full territory.

So many changes to undo. So much work to be done to repair the pantry's tidy, perfect system. Boxes of cereal here. Cans of beans there. Soy sauce, crackers, pickles, tea in tins, coffee in bags. More rat poison on the clean floor to keep the mice from breeding. Everything in its place, just the way Darkness liked it.

The screams started soon enough. They didn't last long.

Later, much later, Harley opened the pantry door to hang up the sparkling clean pot and saucepan.

He didn't turn on the light.

Darkness snickered.

THE CATCH

This science fiction story was inspired by a news clipping about towns trying to ban pets completely. I've mentioned that my short works tend to be either much more serious than my novels or more comedic, but this one somehow fell right in the middle. It's a weird little thing and flawed at its foundation, but I still love it.

———

TROUBLE WALKED into my life on a rainy Tuesday morning. I was avoiding morning paperwork by contemplating my office door, and trouble's arrival significantly improved the view.

The dress had practically been painted onto her body, and her glistening raincoat hung over it like folds of mist. She wore her dark hair was long and loose, and an expensive scent drifted into the office as my door swung open.

The rent-sucking lawyers upstairs saw a lot of clients who wore that kind of money, but they didn't often brighten up my day. I let my eyes wander in appreciation and regretfully prepared to inform the woman that she had gotten off the elevator one floor too soon.

She leaned elegantly against the door's edge, striking a

pose right off the cover of a pulp novel. *The Fragile Face Of Fear,* or *Beauty Beseiged.* Something like that.

"I'm in trouble," she whispered.

Perhaps she was in the right place after all. I had heard that tone of voice enough to know it well. I gave her another look, down and up again. She didn't flinch.

"Domestic problem?" I carefully suggested.

Her bright lipstick quivered enticingly as she waved both well-manicured hands in an eloquent, eye-catching gesture. "I have to get rid of him, and I heard you were—" She paused, searching my face.

"Discreet." I hurriedly offered a chair. "I am. Discretion is my bread and butter."

She sat on the edge and regarded me with confusion. The bafflement was as common a reaction as her initial fearfulness, so I ignored it.

My decor was at fault. The one window behind my desk was frosted, which kept the room dim even in sunny weather. The desk itself was gray, like the computer, the file cabinet, and the peeling paint on the walls.

For some reason people expected a cynic in a trench coat to inhabit the environment. I did own a trench coat, but I gave off absolutely no aura of forceful masculine authority. It invariably disappointed clients.

"Start at the beginning," I said.

"I have a dog," the woman announced. "And they're inspecting my building tomorrow. If they find him, I'm dead. What more do you need to know?"

She waved her arms again, treating me to a hefty dose of the perfume. It cost a fortune, and no copycat formula was available. Someone was trying to impress.

I was not impressed. She might be financially destroyed if caught with a dog inside city limits, but death was an exaggeration. Owning an unlicensed dog was a misdemeanor with monetary penalties, not a capital felony.

It isn't a dog's world, these days. Human overpopulation, municipal concern about public health, and the cost of waste removal have slowly but surely pushed cats and dogs out of the hearts of the country's urbanites.

Everyone said it would never happen, but it did, of course. City governments all over the country are licensing and taxing the remaining holdouts to death in hopes of encouraging them to change their ways. As maintenance costs rose higher and higher, most people have transferred their affections from furry friends to briny aquariums or dusty aviaries.

Others keep unlicensed pets under wraps and hope their homes don't get inspected. There are still thousands of dogs and cats in this city alone. With legal right to inspect and eyes glittering at the prospects of huge fines, municipal employees and land managers all love to crack down on violators.

The violators, panicking like this one, come to me for solutions. I poured the woman a cup of coffee while I refilled my own cooling mug.

"I'll need a name," I told her. "Personal use only. Make something up, if you like."

Most of the frightened little girl act disappeared, engulfed by sophisticated assurance. Her chin lifted and her blue eyes sparked.

"I'm Monique Bathwell," she said in a far loftier tone than the earlier one.

"Bathwell? Of *the* Bathwells? Oldest daughter of Augustus Bathwell?"

One arched eyebrow answered my question.

The Bathwells are our local royalty, as notorious for extravagance and shady political influence as they are envied for the immense profit of their overland transport firm. Everyone knows some of the family profit arrives from various illegal sources. No one talks about that.

"Why does a Bathwell need me?" I asked. It was a logical

protest. "Surely someone with your resources has lawyers on call who could make a deal, or—"

"Family resources, subject to family interference," Monique interrupted in a voice like ice water. "I'm currently persona non grata with my father, and I don't want him involved or informed. So I'm on my own."

She gave the perfumed shrug another try. I held my breath.

Augustus Bathwell was the president and CEO of Bathwell Trading Company. Rumors of cutthroat business tactics and personal brutality trailed after his reputation like smoke after a fire. No flame had ever been revealed, due to a lack of live or talkative witnesses.

I wanted to add myself to Augustus Bathwell's 'persona non grata' list the way I wanted to play Russian roulette with a fully loaded pistol.

"Um," I said.

"Please." The icy demeanor cracked: black despair ran fast beneath it. "I can pay you. I knew I couldn't keep him, but I didn't realize they'd inspect so soon. I can't find anyone to take him, and I heard you—"

She broke off and shrugged yet again. This one was the most expansive yet, and it did interesting things to the neckline of her dress.

I knew she was doing it on purpose, but I still enjoyed the effect.

"You heard I relocate animals for a price." I acknowledged. There was no danger in admitting that much. Pest control was my legal stock in trade; specifically humane pest control. "I live-trap raccoons, skunks, and release them in forested districts, I relocate bird nests and bat colonies before trees get culled, I transfer bee swarms to local hives instead of fumigating them, etcetera."

For the last few years, the etcetera part had included finding adoptive country homes for a variety of family pets.

That part was illegal as hell, but I did it anyway. It balanced out the guilt over my *other*-other job.

Now we'd come to the meaty part of the conversation. "I'm also the city dogcatcher," I informed her.

"I already knew that," Monique stated baldly. "Name your price."

I named an outrageous sum five times higher than I usually charged. "Take it or leave it."

Most of my prospective illegal clients panicked when they realized they'd asked the dogcatcher to save their beloved beasties from the dogcatcher. Not Monique. She just assumed I was dirty.

I couldn't decide if I should be flattered or insulted.

Monique nervously rolled her coffee cup between her fingers, but whatever doubts she had, she kept to herself. "I don't have time to haggle. You're my only hope."

I gathered the particulars of her case, arranged an evening meeting, and discussed payment. After she left, I let the fax machine chatter off the work requests it had been patiently holding. I also opened a desk drawer and placed my visitor's cup on the scanner inside it. It paid to be cautious.

Using her fingerprints, I ran a background check through a slightly illegal tap on the municipal computer network. Both the social registry and the police gave Monique a clean pass. I dealt with my deposit after reading the file. One fictitious but well-documented deceased relative and one call to a local broker, and I was temporarily rich.

I was also busy. One complaint about a huge wild parrot and five scheduled trap inspections came from private clients, while the city had me slated to check four possible pet ordinance violations.

I wanted to crawl back into my chair and sleep away the rainy hours. Instead, the phone rang. The snowy image of a beefy middle-aged man in a suit that screamed out plainclothes cop glared out of the screen at me.

I gave him my best professional smile. "Top o' the morning to you, Dutch."

"Don't you use that fake accent on me, Jeffrey Nguyen. I told you to *ask* before using the police computer."

"I'm fine, thanks. How's the wife?"

Dutch sighed. "She's fine. I'm fine. Enough friendly chat. Did you have to route your data to me after you were done snooping? You overwrote an hour of my work."

Oops, I thought. "Sorry. I just wanted to use my new toy. Guess who just walked out of my office; stiletto heels, Mackay dress and all."

Dutch glanced to one side, at another screen. "Monique Bathwell or a really good bathtub clone. That laser scanner I gave you does a nice job."

He hadn't given me the stupid scanner. I had paid for half of it myself. "It didn't have to work hard. She left prints all over my mug."

"Not very bright, but then she wasn't weaned on criminal procedures like her brothers. I hear her papa's a little miffed at her. The little lady got mice in the walls?"

"Just wants my pretty face," I said.

"You be careful, Jeff."

I hung up on him as the computer coughed up a late work order.

I grabbed my coat and hat along with my equipment belt, but I still got soaked on the way to my van. The drenching made a perfect start for the day. It was, as I had expected, monotonous, physically grueling, and emotionally draining.

Rescuing the housewife from her 'huge green parrot' was the only bright point. The parakeet had been far more damaged by the good lady's broom than she had been by the bird's 'raking talons,' and she kept the bird after I caught it for her.

Three of the four following investigations were obviously crank complaints: people harassing their neighbors. I still had to perform the inspections. The last inspection was the worst, because I did find a dog there.

The old woman cried when I unearthed her arthritic, incontinent Lhasa from its closet hideaway, and I felt like a monster. I had to impound a pet or provide a body for the city, and they preferred bodies: it was cheaper.

I wanted to offer a third alternative—take the dog out of the city and file a clean report—but the dog was too old and unhealthy for any of the foster families who had openings. I consoled myself with the thought that the animal was half-dead already, and the woman let me finish the job on the premises.

I skipped lunch.

My live-trap checks and releases came next on the schedule, but even the sight of a sassy raccoon bobbing into the dusky forest preserve did not help. I was still feeling guilty when I started my last assignment.

It had arrived late, and it looked bad. It was an 'animal removal required,' and I got confirmed removal orders only when no one else wanted the commission. That meant an uncooperative owner or a vicious animal, and the order said I was hunting a cat. Four of them, according to the complaint.

I was visualizing tigers trained to rip out throats as I walked into the apartment building. The address was a pricey one, and the concierge pointed to a first-floor corridor as soon as I entered the lobby. I admired his observational skills. The trench coat hid my uniform.

Maybe I just looked like a dogcatcher. Maybe I just looked like a killer.

When the occupant of the corner apartment cracked open his door, I smelled cat: plural in number and lacking in hygiene facilities, judging by the intensity of the stench.

The man staring coldly at me through the narrow opening was big, but he didn't look violent. I challenged his silence with politeness.

"Mr. Weaver? I'm here from the city. There've been complaints. Could we talk about them inside?"

Then I caught a glimpse of the room past the barrier of Weaver's body. The apartment was a labyrinth of dusty boxes, stacked furniture, and black trash bags, packed wall to wall, floor to ceiling. It was no fit place for a human to live, much less animals.

The human wasn't my business. I shoved my foot and shoulder into the doorway before Weaver could slam it shut.

"Kitty-kitty-kitty," I called. "Here, kitty."

Some people just have a way with animals. I'm one of them. Three white handfuls of fluff charged around a pile of plastic tubs and scampered into the hall. They had climbed up my legs and were climbing into my coat pockets when their equally fluffy mother trotted out to join them.

I stepped back. The mother cat jumped to my shoulder and mewed in my ear.

"They come with me," I said coldly.

Weaver looked as furious as I felt, but I really didn't care. I wrote the ticket, threw it at him, and walked away.

The cat's hiss was my only warning of trouble. I ducked, and the metal pipe that would've split open my skull caught me across the shoulders instead.

The next strike glanced off my ribs, and the third smashed into my ear despite my attempt to roll with the impact. The cat launched from my shoulders just before the floor hit me in the face.

In a total panic I rolled onto my back, grabbing at my pockets and belt. Squirming reassured me that I had not pulverized the kittens, and I had the comforting weight of a weapon in my hand by the time Weaver dislodged mama's four kilos of teeth and claws from his face.

I hit Weaver in the face with the flashlight from my equipment belt. The flashlight broke, but he fell down. I dragged him into the apartment.

It was worse than I'd imagined. The place was a literal garbage dump. There was no sign of anyone living there other than an overflowing cat box and a dish of cat food.

Recalling the too-perceptive concierge, I decided not to leave by the front door.

It took me ten minutes to clear the window enough to exit through it. My head was throbbing hard by the time I got to my van. I put the cats in a carrier and put a few safe blocks between me and the building before I felt it was safe to pull over.

I picked up my phone, started punching numbers and forgot what I was doing before I finished.

I rested my aching head on the window and tried in vain to think of a reason someone might want to lure me into an abandoned apartment and beat me senseless.

The car door unexpectedly opened. I spilled out of it and into someone's arms.

"I was going to call you," I told Dutch.

"That was twenty minutes ago," Dutch said, propping me upright. "I couldn't understand a word you said. Patrolmen spotted your vehicle for me. Sit down, will you?"

I sat. Dutch waved fingers in front of my nose and asked how many.

"Counting the thumb?"

"Wiseass. What happened?"

I told him. The straight facts sent away the dark uniforms which had been hovering in my peripheral vision. One returned in a few minutes and pulled Dutch off for a discussion. I heard only: "—other suspect in custody."

'Other suspect' sounded bad, considering how hard I had hit Weaver. "Am I in trouble, Dutch?"

"Good lord, no," Dutch said. "We lost the bogus security guard, that's all." Then he remarked, "You're looking green."

I was feeling worse with every second. "Could you drive me to my office?"

I didn't think I could manage the van now, but I had paperwork to finish and other work to do. While Dutch started the engine, I spent some time mentally sorting it into stacks of 'can't avoid' and 'easily procrastinated'.

The next thing I heard was: "Jeff, wake up. Doc said you shouldn't snooze for twelve hours or so."

I found myself in the van on the passenger's side, head against the window, and I felt utterly sick. I sat up. That felt worse.

Dutch was driving. He kept his eyes on the road. "Feeling better?"

"No," I said honestly. I felt after my ribs, which were aching and bandaged, and examined the concrete scenery. "Where are we?"

"On your way to the office from the hospital. Docs said you might do more fade-outs from the bang on the head. Guess you were in one at the time. Funny, huh?"

"Hilarious."

"Why do you think you got mugged, Jeff?"

I had been thinking about that. "Well, the work order came off the municipal network. Private customers have to call my direct line."

"So you were set up by somebody who has strings in city hall and friends in back alleys. Like our good friends the Bathwells, with whom you've taken up acquaintance of late. I guess Papa is unhappy with his daughter and any idiots who associate with her."

"Figured that out all by yourself, huh? You should be a detective when you grow up. What time is it? I'm supposed to meet a client at seven."

"Almost six, and you're almost to the office. I assume the client is Monique Bathwell. I'm staying unless you kick me out."

"I couldn't kick a flea right now. Stay. I need to think."

"About what?"

"I don't know."

I kicked my jellified brain into submission and wondered. I thought about Weaver. I thought about cats being left in a storeroom long enough to smell, and I wondered who owned that building. Then I thought about the cats again.

"I think there's more to this Monique Bathwell case than a family tiff," I told Dutch. "Whoever ordered that beating used a family of purebred Persians for bait."

"So?"

"Purebred animals from good bloodlines sell for big money, and licensing makes the prices astronomical. If someone—and there's always someone—wants a pureblood for prestige, they might pay real well to get one under the table."

"And distribution is Bathwell's specialty. If he's supplying pets, he might see you as a competitor." Dutch pondered something. "Was your latest client's problem supposed to be purebred?"

"Didn't ask."

Supposed to be, was the phrase Dutch used. I felt like a fool now for swallowing Monique's story. She must have been bait too. Augustus Bathwell was careful. He would check on rumors before taking irrevocable action.

He had checked, and I had snapped at the lure like a starving bass.

I mused fuzzily about my stupidity long after Dutch installed me and the cats in the apartment behind my office. The kittens adopted me as their new best friend, so I sat on my bed and let them burrow in my shirt. They gnawed at my bandages, I watched the clock. Dutch called his fretting wife and paced.

The studio was a remodeled stockroom with the office door on a long side and the one to the loading dock at one short end. It was my refuge for nights when I was too tired to drive home. Dutch could cross the room in three steps and did so several times. I hadn't turned on the lights, but my aquarium's glow lit his face.

"You're falling asleep," he said with annoying accuracy. "She's not coming, Jeff. It was set up from the start. Start thinking about your options."

"I won't be bullied." I wouldn't stop helping people just because Augustus Bathwell felt threatened. I would not be beaten.

"Seriously, Jeff. Would you be willing to bring this into a courtroom? Personal police protection, immunity from prosecution for the, um, indiscretions that tie you to Bathwell? It's small potatoes, but they got Capone on taxes. We want Bathwell, Jeff, and so do the Feds. He's involved personally. We could get him."

"I won't be bribed with safety, either." It was tempting, but even with immunity, I would lose my city job. A stray suspicion hit from nowhere. "What kind of meds am I on, Dutch? What did the doctor give me?"

He looked peeved. "I told them you were too doped up to remember the instructions. There's a bottle of painkillers in the bathroom."

"A high enough dose to affect my judgement, maybe? High enough you think you can pressure me into helping you make your case?"

Dutch stared at the wall and said stiffly, "I had to ask."

"Like hell you did." The betrayal stung, and I hurt enough already. "I won't agree to anything tonight, so you might as well get on home."

He left without another word. I sat in the dark and started to feel frightened.

I should call a friend for company. I should call another friend who had access to illegal weaponry. Hell, I decided, I should call a travel agent and book a flight to Mexico.

I didn't call anyone. I couldn't run while I had responsibilities, and even the responsibilities would have to wait until I felt capable of driving.

Mama cat climbed into my lap to nurse her babies, and I dozed despite my best paranoid efforts to remain awake. We all jumped when the office doorbell rang, and when the door from the office opened, I cursed Dutch for leaving it unlocked.

The intruder paused, dim light from the security system streaming past her.

Her. That silhouette was unmistakable. My heart settled into a normal rhythm again.

Monique was breathing hard. "Mr. Nguyen? Are you there?"

Well, I was there, and I was a fool. The light switch was within reach. I reached it. "Here. Shut the door behind you."

She hurried across the room, then stopped short when she caught sight of my unimpressive self. "I heard—I thought—I was afraid you might be—"

"Beaten to a pulp? Dead, maybe?" I wondered if she was hiding a weapon. "Sorry to disappoint you."

"Why would I be—? I don't understand. What—?"

Her lipstick was the same shade as earlier in the day. The shrugs and unfinished sentences were the same too. She was dressed far more casually than she had been that morning. More practically, too. The dark shirt, loose pants, and low boots were high quality but designed for action.

"So you're not here to finish the job for dear Papa?"

"You think I tried to hurt you? I didn't—I wouldn't—oh. I was afraid he'd scared you off!"

She sat down on the floor with a thump and burst into tears.

Tears were no surprise. I practically expected tears from any woman who wanted to pull my strings.

I knew I had to wait until the emotional storm passed, but I felt helpless. I called Mama back to my lap so I could give a little surrogate consolation.

The cat arched her back under my fingers and kneaded my sore chest with her paws. She was as fascinated by the bandages around my chest as the kittens had been.

In time she extricated a wire and a tiny button, which she contentedly began to lick. Someone's ears were no doubt being assaulted by loud slurping. I rescued the bug and closed my fist around it.

"Did you see a fortyish Hispanic-looking gentleman in a rumpled suit on your way up here?" I asked Monique,

She sniffed. "The man who brought you home? He's in the coffee shop on the first floor. I know I'm late. I'm sorry. I wanted to wait until you were alone, but he never left. I snuck past when he went to the restroom."

I checked my watch and found I had lost another two hours to my throbbing headache. And Dutch was still watching me. I thought about that.

Monique was watching me too, steady again if a little smeared in the cosmetic department.

"What now, Mr. Nguyen?" she asked, sounding sad.

She expected me to boot her out the door. Fool, I told myself. "Where's the dog?"

"In the car." Her relief was that of a reprieved prisoner; doubting and hopeful. "You'll take him after all?"

"How do you feel about moonlit drives in the country?"

Hesitation, then, "Why?"

"Your father's tried to kill me once today. I figure he's less likely to gun me down if you're right next to me."

Monique's face darkened like a cloud. "What if I don't feel like being a hostage?"

"Then I won't rescue your dog."

The threat made me feel like a monster for the second time in one day, but it was the only lever I had.

Monique's chin came up. "I love moonlit drives, actually."

"Great. Grab the cat carriers and help me herd kittens. We're taking your car. "

Her car was a low-slung black sports coupe with tinted windows. It looked fast and sleek under the dim fluorescent garage lights, and it was occupied by a dog previously described by Monique only as 'big.'

It was actually a pedigreed male Rhodesian Ridgeback who nearly filled the rear seat. I was grateful the smooth-coated giant canine made room for the kittens and their mother, because Mama would've lost any territorial disputes.

Candy, Monique called the beast, which figured.

Monique drove. I gave directions and watched for anyone tailing us, and we left the city far behind us.

We safely arrived at our destination. I was so tired I dropped the key to the front door twice on the way up the steps. The second time, Monique picked it up for me.

She jammed it into the lock with angry force. "This is the best you can do with all the money people pay you? A rundown little shack in the middle of cornfields?"

"Yup." My home was a classic little ranch house in a classic little ticky-tacky subdivision, only it sat on a full acre with solid six-foot fencing all the way around the yard. That privacy fence had cost me cost an arm and a leg, never mind the security system. And she called it a *shack*. "Sorry to disappoint."

Inside, Monique tossed the key onto the dining room table and the pile of mail I'd been ignoring. Then she draped herself on my couch, looking ready to embark on a full-tilt tantrum.

If she didn't want to say goodbye to her supposedly beloved dog, that was no skin off my back. I left her there to sulk and took Candy and the cats into the back rooms.

There was a lot of feeding, watering, and cleaning to be done back there. The house currently held three dogs, ten cats, two parrots and an aquarium of finicky saltwater fish. They all required daily care.

I wobbled my weary way through the work, apologizing

for the lateness of the hour. Then I released everyone from confinement—one by one, and obviously not including the fish—to meet the new arrival.

Introductions sometimes got tricky, but my current tenants were a tolerant, inclusive bunch. Also, it's one of the situations where being good with animals came in handy. A few minutes of growling and wary circling with fur at full puff, a few gentle reminders from me, and everyone settled down.

The cats resumed ignoring the dogs as beneath their notice, and the dogs commenced an energetic round of play-wrestling. Their furry hijinks restored my sense of humor, and we all returned to the front sitting room together in a noisy happy mob.

Monique was still there, sitting on the couch with her feet curled under her. Candy went straight to her, wagging his whiplike tail hard enough to move his whole rear end. The rest of my houseguests followed, excited to meet a new human.

They don't get out much, and I don't entertain, for obvious reasons. Monique commenced petting them all and cooing over them like she meant it.

I'd expected her to get out while the getting was good. Did she truly think she was a hostage? Didn't she understand that she could just leave? Or had she wanted to say good-by after all?

"Go home," I said. "We had a deal. I'll honor it."

She stood up. "The money goes towards feeding all these animals until you find them homes, isn't it?"

"That's part of it. Licenses, bribes, kickbacks, too. It adds up."

"How long does it take?" She stared at the three-legged old yellow Labrador retriever romping around the room with her much younger dog. "To find buyers, I mean."

I'd had Blondie for a year, and two of the cats had been

with me even longer. "For a dog as sweet and as valuable as Candy, maybe a week."

"Oh." It came out very quietly.

She hadn't really faced the loss until then, and her pain hit me almost like a fist.

"Take all the time you need to say goodbye," I told her. "Just remember: it won't be healthy to stick around here for long."

Candy stayed with her. My other critters joined me when I retreated to the den, and they kept me company while I sat in the dark room and made some fast plans.

Thanks to the miracles of computerized financial networks, I soon wheeled and dealed myself into fair and retroactively legal ownership of five more animals. As soon as those transactions cleared, I made arrangements with a friend to ensure the future safety of the animals.

Once those details were hammered into final form, I knew I could finally relax. The computer screen cast a gentle glow over the desk, the printer hummed as it spat out the documents I would need, and I sat back and picked up my coffee.

Several seconds after I swallowed the first mouthful of delicious hot liquid, I remembered that I hadn't made any. I promptly choked, caught between the impulse to spit it out and the need to protect the electronics.

"It isn't poisoned," Monique said from the shadows nearby.

She was right next to the desk, sprawled on a loveseat that was usually occupied by two or three cats. Candy, in Monique's lap, heaved a sigh of pure doggie happiness, and the three other dogs draped over her feet sent me apologetic glances.

They weren't watchdogs, they were saying, and they liked her.

It looked like she was smiling at me, but it was hard to tell in the dim light.

"Uh," I said after a second. "Why are you still here?"

"I thought I'd leave in the morning."

That was a lot to process. I took my time with it. All my bridges had been burned when I brought her out here. Either I was a dead man or a safe one. I wasn't a stupid one, though, so I made no assumptions.

"You can use my bed," I offered. "Let me grab some clean sheets. I won't be sleeping. The doctor says I'm supposed to stay awake."

When she leaned closer, I saw that she was definitely smiling.

"I saw your huge bed," she said. "There's plenty of room for two, and I bet I can keep you awake."

She did, too. I didn't fall asleep until the sun was coming up, and then she poked me in my sore ribs and woke me right up again. Four dogs grumbled and shifted around when she moved, making the mattress shift and nearly pushing me out.

That's why I have a huge bed.

I rolled to face Monique.

She smiled, all tousled and sleepy eyed, face blotchy with the remains of yesterday's makeup. "I want to help."

"No, thanks. You've helped me enough already. I've lost my job, been arrested, beaten up—"

"Please."

She had a way of saying that word. It tore my heart out every time.

"Fine, you can help. Stay here and watch the place until a guy in a rusty white van shows up. He'll be looking after all my critters for a while."

"You're running away? Now? You're that scared of my father?"

Before I could think of a face-saving answer, I was interrupted by the sound of the front door being kicked open.

"Mr. Nguyen," someone called in a smooth, slightly accented voice. "We have business. Please appear at once."

Monique gasped. "That's Papa!"

"Scared?" I asked with a grin I couldn't hide.

Her glare withered. "Yes. You should be, too. Get up!"

"No. I don't jump when he says jump. This is my house and I'm staying right here in my bed."

"Fine." She scrambled into yesterday's clothes, then disappeared into the bathroom. The bathroom had a window. Monique had a well-developed sense of self-preservation. I wondered for a moment if she was ditching me, but no.

She was back in a flash, hair combed and face cleaned of yesterday's makeup. Dutch's surveillance bug, which I had removed for obvious privacy reasons, dangled between two manicured fingertips. "This is why you aren't worried, isn't it?"

"I am worried, but yes. That's my secret weapon. Bring it here, please?"

I hadn't been idle while she was washing up. I'd moved to the side of the bed nearest the wall and evicted the dogs. They did their best to trip Monique as she returned to the bedside and sat down next to me.

In fact, Bathwell's physical presence on my property raised my odds of immediate survival. I had never expected him to move so soon or so personally. The emotional involvement must be clouding his judgement.

Also, he never would've come after me himself if he knew the police had enough evidence to charge him. Since he *was* here, it meant I might get a chance to do some damage to him. That felt good.

"I suppose those are your reinforcements," she said wryly as she handed over the wire. Candy draped himself over her feet in a show of loyalty. The other dogs watched the door with expectant faces and wagging tails.

"Can't hurt." I blew into the microphone. "Wake up, boys. Keep your ears peeled and your recorders running. A little door-bursting, heart-pounding action wouldn't be frowned on."

No allies immediately appeared, and our passive resistance apparently puzzled the opposition. Minutes passed without further action.

Finally, noise drifted down the hall. The dogs barked. I told them to be quiet and sit down, then prodded at my pillows and sat up.

The trio of men who appeared in the door attempted to approach as a unified front. I waited for them to wedge themselves in the frame like a comedy act, but no. At the last moment, the one in the middle paused so he entered a second after the dark-suited linebacker types.

The senior Bathwell was an impressive fellow. Gray hair, gray suit, steely gray eyes, and an air of energetic self-confidence crossed with lazy contempt.

He sat on the foot of the bed, centered to make us a conversational triangle. The bodyguards bracketed the door and eyed the line of silent dogs with professional wariness.

Bathwell cleared his throat. "I told you to leave my house if you could not stomach my ways. I did not give you permission to steal from me on your way out the door."

"He was mine, Papa. I had a right to take him."

So Monique had *stolen* Candy? I gave the woman marks for bravery. She might not have been exaggerating when she had said she would die if the dog were found.

Clearing my throat made no impression on either of them. Daddy and daughter were too busy glaring at each other.

"Is this a case of the pot calling the kettle hot?" I asked.

Papa Bathwell turned his attention to me, and I was forcefully reminded of a snake. He stared at my shirtless chest. "You're injured, so I forgive the insolence of greeting me from your bed, but I don't tolerate insults. You've had one lucky escape. You won't get a second one."

"I don't feel lucky." The bruised ribs were turning an interesting shade of blackish-green around the straps. My face looked spectacular too, far worse than I actually felt.

"You're still alive. For now. Be grateful."

That hit hard. Paranoia aside, I hadn't really believed I'd escaped a murder attempt. I managed to keep my voice steady enough to stall for time. "So the beating wasn't a message to back off?"

"You interfered in my business and in my family affairs. You cause problems. I dispose of problems."

That's when one of the linebacker-types by the door unbuttoned his blazer to reveal a holstered pistol. His face looked vaguely familiar. It took me a precious second to place him, but it came to me: he'd been a security guard yesterday.

"Moving down in the world?" I asked.

He grinned. Jerk.

I still played nice and issued a fair warning. "I wouldn't recommend trying to shoot me."

He tried anyway. He should've known better. They all should've known better than to walk into my house.

I didn't even have to move. The dogs knew what to do when someone showed them a gun, and they did all the work.

Neither bodyguard had noticed how close the animals were getting to them while Bathwell was talking. Dogs are good at that.

Before the faux security guard's pistol cleared the holster, his wrist had a three-legged, geriatric retriever dangling from it. Candy got into the spirit of things, knocking the man off-balance and then leaping onto him once he was down on the floor. Both dogs laid across the man's body and licked at his face and neck while he wailed and flailed like a colicky baby.

The second bodyguard was smarter than his colleague and didn't try to draw on me or the dogs. My other two canine boarders contented themselves with pinning him to the wall with their forelegs. Their tails were wagging, but their growls meant business.

He kept his arms raised, hands fisted but empty, and he held still. The only un-smart thing he was doing was looking to Bathwell for instructions.

I gave my unseen law enforcement listeners about a minute before they got impatient and barged into the situation. A minute could be an eternity when guns were involved. I was going to have to get creative.

"Think hard," I told Bathwell before he could speak. "The walls have ears. So far you're only looking at charges for attempted murder. I wouldn't make it worse, if I were you. Unless you'd like to bribe me to leave town?"

He would never be stupid enough to bribe me now that I'd warned him he was under surveillance. I just wanted to distract him with the suggestion. Or to insult him, since he clearly didn't think logically when he was angry.

To my shock, Bathwell laughed. "You have nerve, but you aren't very smart. There won't be any criminal charges against me, today or any day."

He must be very sure of his ties in the judiciary system to make that claim. Or else he was still that confident in his ability to dispose of me without implicating himself. I didn't like either option.

I had nothing to lose by making my case. "Look, I'm smart enough not to mess with you, and you're smart enough to know it's cheaper to buy me off than to clean up a body. If you're not worried about being recorded, give me enough cash to start up somewhere else."

Bathwell's eyes narrowed. He wasn't convinced.

"He's lying to you, Papa," Monique said. "He doesn't need your money. He could've left town any time he wanted."

She wasn't wrong. If I'd really wanted to run, I could've hopped any flight I wanted, and I could've done it flying first class. Hell, I could've paid for a charter, and Monique had to know that. She'd seen me playing with my finances.

That left me wondering why she'd decided to turn traitor now, of all times.

Bathwell turned that considering stare on his daughter. "So you think he has too much integrity to work for me, do you?"

Tears welled up in her eyes. "Not everybody's like you."

"You're a fool." Bathwell reached inside his suit jacket for something.

My heart sank.

"All right, nobody move!" The supremely trite order came from the hall, outside the room.

Naturally, everybody moved. The bodyguards shook off their furry opponents, Bathwell lifted something from his inner pocket and pulled it free, Monique ran for the bathroom, and I dove for the floor between the bed and the wall.

Diving anywhere was a horrible idea. Pain exploded along my injured ribs, my vision snowed over, and I lost track of events for a time, too busy gasping for breath to pay attention to the pandemonium elsewhere in the room.

Rights and regulations were being recited by the time I got myself together again. I peeked around the end of the bed, past furry paws and various pairs of booted feet.

Dutch's feet were among them, heading my way. He grinned down at me. "You look like crap, dogcatcher."

"Took you long enough to barge in here. I could've been killed."

He laughed and tossed something at me. I let it fall to the floor.

It was a hefty bundle of nice, untraceable cash bills.

"Frightening stuff," Dutch said. "You were about to be thoroughly bribed."

Monique was standing next to her father while he was

handcuffed. She looked like she was on the verge of tears. I could forgive her the torn loyalties, I decided, and told myself I was a fool.

She frowned when she saw me staring, then said brokenly, "He didn't believe you, but I knew if I said you were lying, he'd change his mind. I was trying to help."

I should've known.

I held out my arms, and it was enough of an apology. After the hug, I pulled the wire from Monique's shirt pocket and offered it to Dutch. "You'll want this back."

"I'm sorry about planting the bug, Jeff. It wasn't my idea. The Powers That Be approved the no-consent warrant. You walked into the end of a case that's been building for three years."

He *was* sorry, too. It showed. I shrugged. "I could've flushed it. I didn't."

"You'll get called as witnesses, both of you." Dutch watched the departing officers and their uncooperative burdens. "They'll all be free on bond after arraignment."

And I would be a sitting duck for every hit man in town. "How long before trial?"

"Months, at least. You know how it gets. The judge will tell you not to leave town, too."

"Unacceptable. We're willing to help, but we want something in return."

He eyed me, the wire and Monique with equal suspicion. "We, is it?"

"Yeah, and you owe *us*." I grinned at him until he smiled back. "Here's the deal. My pet sitter is already on his way here. We agree to show up and testify, you turn your back and let us disappear until that day."

Dutch turned his back and folded his arms. "I see nothing."

Four hours later—after a stop for passports and other falsified paperwork—Monique and I boarded a chartered flight heading to the Caribbean.

Yes, Candy came with us.

As Monique played with her dog and I watched the city fall away beneath the wing of the plane, I reflected that not all trouble was bad. Sometimes it added a little spice to life.

THE FINAL BATTLE

Once upon a time in the Nineties, a friend in charge of the printed program for a local comic convention needed filler copy. "Write me a short story," she said. "Something heroic and funny, if possible." I wrote this. She printed it. Here it is.

———

THE HERO WADED through hordes of faceless minions and danced through the booby-trapped halls of the arch-villain's stronghold without a single misstep. He passed like a ghost through a vast command center where flunkies monitored the global progress of their master's fiendish plans. Then, at last, he stood on the threshold of his archenemy's inner sanctum.

Hinges wailed as he pushed the door open.

"Finally!" a querulous voice snapped. "Don't stand there letting in the cold air. You're late with my reports."

The long narrow room had a muddy stone floor and a sweeping skylight. Tables full of seedlings in trays and pots crowded the walls. Two muscle-bound minions stood at either end of the farthest table, facing the door. They eyed the hero suspiciously. A thin old man wearing a black robe was using a pair of trimming shears to poke at a potted plant near the middle of the table.

"Spit it out," the old man shouted without looking up. "What are the quarterly figures on insurrectionism? Are they up or down?"

"Uh," one of his minion said.

"Sir," added the second, "that isn't your secretary."

"It isn't?" The villain looked up, squinted, and then he shrieked. "You fools! That's Spruce Tree, Master of Cone-jitsu! Why are you just standing there?"

"It's a tree," the second minion protested. "Sir."

"He's a hero! I pay you to kill heroes! Do I have to do everything myself?" The villain waved both hands in a commanding gesture of unspeakable evil. "Attack!"

The minions lumbered forth to do their master's bidding.

They were clearly no students of either gardening or martial arts, or they would have chosen more wisely.

Spruce Tree's exultant cry of "Bonsai!" shook dust from the rafters, and he felled the first minion with one sweep of his lowest bough. The second minion, clearly cut from a more intellectual cloth than his companion, paused in his forward charge.

"Bonsai?" he said. "Don't you mean 'banzai?'"

"You know nothing of bonsai!" cried Spruce, advancing on roots as strong as the earth itself. He and the minion met in a slow-motion clash of punches, kicks and spins.

It was a cinematic masterpiece of a fight, complete with an aggressive soundtrack of grunts and snarls. At last, in a breath-taking demonstration of botanical dexterity, Spruce sent the second minion's body flying after the first.

Meanwhile, the villain ducked behind his experimental plantings. From the safety of his cowardly retreat, he called out, "Flee while you can, you misbegotten cabbage!"

"I laugh at your feeble insults," said Spruce. "Come out and fight me."

"Me? Fight you? Oh, no."

The villain cackled as he leaped toward a large red button concealed behind a pot of geraniums. An alarm blared, and a hidden portal in the wall opened.

Black smoke swirled, and a figure emerged from the inky shadows within.

The smoke paled to gray wisps that drifted around the monster's dark form. Noxious tendrils crept along the floor before it, discoloring all that they touched. Plants on the nearby tables wilted and blackened.

Spruce's limbs rustled as he drew back from the hazy apparition. "You summoned *Agent Orange* to this plane of existence? You dared?"

"I have nothing to fear," the villain said with pride. "But you do."

"All that live should fear the Agent." Spruce's sap ran cold for the first time in his long life, and he hastened to retreat. "You fool!"

He could not move fast enough. Agent Orange oozed forward at the speed of thought, and his vaporous shroud enveloped them both.

Spruce's branches drooped. His needles pattered to the floor, brown and withered.

In mere moments, Spruce Tree —valiant Defender of Good, undefeated in fair combat in all the centuries of his life —toppled to the floor with a splintery crash. Soon, the destructive fog reduced the fallen hero's powerful trunk and powerful limbs to a steaming pile of compost.

Agent Orange returned to its master's side, leaving Spruce's corpse to molder where it lay.

"I have done as you commanded," the monster announced in a guttural monotone.

The villain waved a hand in dismissal. "Yes, yes, you did well. Now go away. I'm busy."

He returned his attention to his plants and plans, cackling

in maniacal glee, and he failed to notice that Agent Orange stood motionless.

The villain tried out a larger laugh, a hearty *muahahahaha* of Ultimate Evil. "The final step in my master plan, finally complete! Only the threat of Spruce Tree stood between me and global domination. Now I can become the greatest evil mastermind of all time! Now all shall bow before me! Now I... ack!"

Seeping abscesses erupted on his skin. He raised his hands, horrified, and before his eyes, the rot ate away his flesh. He shrieked in terror.

"Now you will die, fool," Agent Orange said with great satisfaction. "You should have read the fine print in your summoning manual."

He gave a booming laugh and disappeared in a puff of story logic.

"Nooooooooo!" The villain clawed at his decaying face and gave one last, bubbling shriek of despair before dissolving into a puddle.

His remains seeped into a crack between flagstones and disappeared.

Across the room, the pile of compost that marked Spruce Tree's corpse stirred.

A single tender shoot of green emerged. It wavered upright, and then, like a ray of hope, the first needle appeared.

FIVE STAGES OF GRIEF FOR A FUNERAL THAT WILL NEVER HAPPEN

A GUIDE FOR THE NEWLY IMMORTAL

The first paragraph of this story popped into my head while I was doing research on second-person stories, and it refused to be ignored until I wrote it down. The rest fell into place with remarkable speed. I polished it up, and now it's here.

———

You won't believe it. No one does. Not at first. You'll rationalize away the earliest signs that you aren't going to die. This is normal.

When you twist your ankle moving boxes down the uneven back steps at the old place, you'll ignore how fast the pain goes away. It won't seem important. Moving house is an all-consuming project that keeps you too busy to think about anything else.

You're good at keeping yourself too busy to feel pain. We all are. Life gives us plenty of opportunities to practice that skill.

You won't notice the ankle doesn't swell up the way it did when you tripped during your last 5k, when she brought you ice packs and kisses all evening as a consolation prize. That was back when you could run a 5k together, and you try not to remember those times because a broken heart hurts much worse than a sprained ankle.

When you smash your thumb hammering in a nail to hang a picture at the new apartment, you'll decide you didn't hit it as hard as you thought. The bruises turn a spectacular yellow and purple, the colors of her favorite little spring flowers, so you'll pretend you didn't hear the bone crunch when you hit it.

Of course the fingernail grows back. Fingernails do that. That's normal, you'll tell yourself.

You'll wonder, though.

The itch of doubt will get fierce after you cut yourself dicing up vegetables with the expensive new knife your dad bought you. He bought it because he knows what you're going through, he said, and practical gifts are the only way he knows how to say I love you.

And you use it to cut up vegetables for a stir fry even though you'd rather order greasy takeout, because that's how you say I love you, too, by using what you're given instead of doing what you want.

Knives are sharp, your reflexes are dull. Insomnia is a killer.

Well. It's a killer for most people. Not you. But you don't know that yet.

You won't be able to ignore the spurting blood, or the way the bone gleams white at the bottom of the cut when you flex your hand. It's obviously a bad cut, the kind she would've told you needed stitches. She would've wanted you to drive to the emergency room.

But she isn't there, and by the time you get a towel wrapped around your palm, the bleeding has stopped. The cut is scabbed neatly by the time you're pouring your second glass of wine. Gone by morning.

You'll wonder, but not for long, because it did hurt, and it bled, and it's easier to believe you overreacted than to believe your body can repair an injury that should have required surgery to fix.

Death is inevitable. Everyone knows that. No one gets out alive. From cradle to grave, four legs in the morning, two legs at noon, three legs in the evening, death and taxes. All that jazz.

You won't believe you're not going to die like everyone else you know, not even when the signs become obvious.

This is denial.

It's normal. The path from life to eternal life is a long one, with many twists and turns, but denial is the place everyone starts.

Everyone immortal, I mean. Obviously. That's you.

How long will you keep denying the truth? Hard to say. It's different for everyone who takes the journey from now to forever It's normal, though, and it's difficult, but you will move past it. Eventually.

The next stage is anger.

You probably won't recognize anger when you stop flailing around in the cold dark ocean of mortality and realize you'll never drown in denial or anything else. From denial's side, anger looks a lot like acceptance with a little annoyance mixed in.

Denial will cling to you like seaweed as you wade from the unexamined expectation of aging onto the firm sandy beach of knowing death is an experience you'll never have. Denial will feed the anger you don't even know you're feeling yet, even as you strip away its final vestiges like wiping ocean salt from your skin after a swim.

You'll test yourself. You'll start small, with little injuries, and move to more dangerous one. You'll try drugs, you'll defy gravity, you'll graduate to ever-bigger, ever-harder, ever more terrifying activities.

They will all fail to kill you.

Denial will lose its grip, but the annoyance will become an

impatient itch of emotion you can't find the right way to scratch, a ferocious unhappiness that will cling to your mind and show up in uncomfortable, pinching places. It will chafe.

What have you got to be angry about, after all?

You're healthier than you can ever remember feeling. It won't take long for you to realize you've regained the energy and endurance of a teenager without the tumult of hormonal upset, awkwardness, and anxiety. Your body is optimizing itself. You aren't taller, nor more attractive, nor preternaturally strong, but your senses are as sharp as can be, exhaustion is transient, and sleep feels more like an appetite than a need.

You'll feel guilty for feeling annoyed about this, the way you felt guilty about impatiently tossing sprinkles on top of the cupcake batter instead of frosting them the way she wanted, back when she still had enough of an appetite for cravings.

She wanted cake. Not store-bought. Only a fresh box cake would do, and you'd come home exhausted from the second job you only took to help pay for extra comforts her medical allowance didn't cover.

You were tired. You made the cake, but you didn't pretend you were happy, and you did a shabby job of it. The guilt came after the annoyance and fanned it into an incoherent rage you swallowed like hot coals rather than hurt her with it.

But you felt it, inside, guilt and resentment like magma seething in your core, shaking you to pieces because it had no safe way to escape.

That's how you'll feel about being immortal, right when you think you've accepted it. Burning up with anger you don't want to feel, won't be able to express, and can't begin to explain.

The body you grew in, the one whose limits you'd slowly come to accept—that body is no longer a biological entity with biological limits. Pain and shock remain in your physical awareness, along with ecstasy and exhilaration, but the rules of consequence no longer apply the way they once did.

Rage, rage against the dying of the light. That's what the poet said about facing death, but what of facing not-death? What of the knowledge that you won't die when people you love are already gone?

When you get around to thinking about that, you will feel rage like the all-consuming fire of a thousand flaming suns. Only the sun will someday go dark, some billions of years from now, while your light will never die.

Oh, yes. There will be plenty of time for you to sit in your anger and stew.

Eventually you will store up enough of that energy to channel it into bargaining with the universe.

This never works. You will do it anyway.

People love to call themselves rational, but really, we all want magic to be real. We discover as babies that we can affect our world by acting on it, and that lesson stays with us forever. We play with cause and effect in our cradles and never stop believing we can change reality by the power of our desires.

We can, of course, but never by merely wishing it so. The universe isn't so easily knocked off its course. The rules of cause and effect are obscure and complicated. The way they interact is only predictable if you observe them closely, analyze the results, impartially compare them to your expectations, and adjust your conclusions.

Humanity really sucks at that.

We also see patterns everywhere, and we seek meaning the way flowers seek the light of the sun. When we don't understand something, we look for patterns that explain it. And when we don't find a meaningful pattern we recognize, we make one.

You know what I mean. Step on a crack, break your mother's back. Toss a penny in the fountain, a wish will come true. Wear the blue socks, the home team will win. Stop buying coffee because her chemo seemed to work better that one time you were running late and skipped the usual stop.

Everything happens for a reason. You will desperately want there to be a reason for what is happening. So you'll go hunting for a purpose.

If you kill someone evil, you might think, or run into the burning building to save a child, if you make a fortune and devote your life to wholesome and selfless causes, maybe those acts will expunge your guilt and extinguish the rage.

This phase is the most dangerous for the newly immortal, because it's the one most likely to result in being noticed. That way lies investigation, incarceration, dissection…any number of horrific outcomes.

None of that will kill you, obviously, but pain and frustration won't end the anger and guilt either—and it will damage you. Trauma wounds the soul.

Wishing won't make water poured from a larger glass magically fit into the smaller one. Toddlers learn that lesson eventually. With luck, you'll re-learn it on life's larger scale without making a spectacular mess of your psyche, but most of us inflict deep scars on ourselves during this stage of existence.

I hope you'll heed my warning and avoid discovery. I hope so, because you will need all your strength to endure what comes next.

There's one bargain we all make, a deal as old as death, base on the human belief that as long as we remember those who have died, they're not entirely gone.

This idea will seem like a comfort at first. You will decide that living forever means everyone you love will be immortal too. All you have to do is remember them.

I could warn you against attempting it, but we all inevitably latch onto this idea. It's a floating chunk of wood drifting in the ocean of our grief, and you will cling to it. And for a time, it will keep you afloat.

Until it doesn't.

Details of your life will slip out of mind, cherished memories pushed aside by new experiences. There's only so much room inside your skull. Inside your consciousness.

You are still only human, and to be human is to forget. Memories are ephemeral creations of confabulation and sensation. Facts are facts, but living is all about feeling. We are the stories we tell ourselves, endlessly growing new narratives in the decayed remains of the old ones.

The little things will go first. What was your father's middle name? What was the name of your grade school? Not important, you'll assure yourself. You can keep reminders. You'll get obsessive about records. Images. Recordings. Documents. You will hoard the past like a dragon.

It won't help. Time is relentless. You will disappoint yourself over and over by negotiating with a universe that does not care.

Remember that awful summer you had six jobs and hated them all? Which came first? The pizza joint? The garden center? You'll forget even the humiliation that tainted those memories for decades.

You'll decide those weren't important memories either, because rationalizing is a thing people do very well. If you were mortal, you would die before that trick stopped working, but it won't end there. Not for you.

Where did you go on your first date? Not the one that led to marriage, but earlier. How many lovers did you have? What year were you born in?

Time will sand away all those facts, once so crucial to your identity, and they will disappear. You can keep all the records in the world, but facts on a page will cease to have the meaning they once did.

Nothing you do will stop friends and families from growing old and dying, over and over. Memorizing their names and life stories will begin to hurt too much to bear. Making new friends will feel pointless.

In due time, the future you once feared most will come to pass. One day, you will look at that one picture of her you loved, and she'll just be one more face among so many others. You'll look into her eyes and you won't care.

Welcome to despair.

What happens when nothing matters anymore, when life is too much of a burden to carry *and* one you can never put down? What happens when you've lost everything, and it doesn't hurt at all, and that in turn causes a pain you cannot bear?

What happens when you want to end your numb, wretched, meaningless existence, and you can't?

Nothing.

Maybe the universe laughs. Maybe God has tea with the Devil and they chuckle over the cosmic joke they've played on you. Who knows? That's theology. This is a guide to the practicalities.

The practical answer is that you keep going, or you don't. That's the choice.

The mortal risks of despair no longer apply. This is a curse not a blessing. Your actions now have eternal consequences. You are neither omniscient nor omnipotent, and some decisions can't be unmade.

If you walk into the ocean to lose yourself in its peaceful, unpeopled depths, you'll still be there when the sun goes nova and boils away the seas. Crawl into a cave and pull the entrance down behind you, and you'll be buried alive until the continent goes to pieces around you. Throw yourself into a volcano, and you'll float through its molten innards in obliterating agony until the planet's core cools.

Despair is the final resting place for many immortals. Too many.

Do not be one of them.

Come back to this guide and revisit this section whenever you are foundering in the numb monotony of despair and dreaming of oblivion. There are other options.

Sleep away a few centuries or a few millennia. Hide yourself in a wilderness or an urban wasteland, become a ghost in the night, a spooky story told to children. There are a million-million options that won't leave you with regrets until the heat death of the universe.

A long list of suggestions is appended to this text. They're all time-tested winners, wordplay intended. Try one of those options. Try all of them. Dream up a hundred more. Take all the time you need to just not be. Just don't do anything that can't be undone.

I promise you—I promise on my undying honor—it will get better.

Everything under the sun has its season, they say. As long as despair doesn't lure you into an irreversible act, you will eventually be ready to crawl out of whatever pit you've dug for yourself, literal or figurative, and slide back into the world.

You don't get a choice about having a future. You do get to choose what your present will look like, forever. When you finally accept that, you'll wake one day, wherever you've gone to wait out the storm, and the air will taste sweet again. You will feel alive again.

That is the priceless, precious reward of self-acceptance.

But wait! You aren't done yet!

Don't make the mistake of thinking that achieving acceptance means you've won a prize or crossed some invisible finish line. Life was never a relentless forward progress, cradle to grave. Neither is immortality.

Acceptance, despair, denial, bargaining, anger—they're more than stages in a process. They're states of mind. Feelings are forever. You can't check off boxes on a list and be done. Bargaining will whisper poison in your ear, telling you that you don't deserve joy. You'll dodge a heated patch of rage only to spin out of control into an icy slick of despair.

This is what it means to be alive.

So, remember this: every time you fight, bargain, and endure your way through the other stages, you will find the imperfect present waiting patiently for you to experience its joys. Acceptance may seem elusive and fragile, but it's the glue that holds the universe together. Nothing in eternity is more powerful.

What happens next? Only you know the answer to that question. Take all the time you need.

Welcome to the never-ending party. Rock to the music of the spheres.

DOGCATCHER

Sometimes, just sometimes, I write fiction that resists any attempt to add fantastical elements. This one dates all the way back to my pet store days, when I was working next door to the local animal shelter. One of my regular customers worked in pest control, and I enlisted their help in coming up with fictional situations to inflict on my fictional characters.

January 2

KEEPING a journal helps you sort out your feelings. That's what the book says, and I need a New Year's resolution, so here goes.

A woman spat on me today. I was visiting an apartment complex to check a complaint about a feral dog. She was coming home with groceries. We met in the parking lot. She saw the tool belt and stopped to take a closer look at my uniform. Then she crumpled up her pretty face and spat in mine.

Chin up, shoulders flung back, she stuck her nose in the air and marched past me to one of the buildings. It was one of those upscale country places, lots of windows and expensive furniture inside, lots of grass and trees and space outside. She slammed the door. I wiped my face.

I found the dog in a ditch near the edge of the lot. Big old guy, black fur going gray around the muzzle, no tags, no collar. From a safe distance I counted his ribs and his teeth—too many of the first, not enough of the second—and let him talk to me. His body told me about life in a running pack, of fights for rank and killing rabbits, cowering in rainstorms and stealing garbage in lean times, and of remaining behind when he could no longer keep up.

The scent of the animal shelter clings to my clothes, which meant that I told him about chains and metal fences, lifeless wet concrete and darkness. He understood the future I promised him: fear, helplessness and death without dignity when the waiting time was over. He let me know he would take off my arm with his rotting teeth, given a chance.

I shot him. He was feral and dangerous, no doubt about it, and I'm allowed to exercise discretion in the interests of safety, mostly because the city saves boarding fees.

I don't feel like a murderer, but I keep seeing that woman's eyes, with all the hate boiling up.

Sometimes I hate my job.

April 19

I'M NOT DOING great with my resolution. I hate paperwork. Tonight, though, tonight I sure as hell need sorting out, so here goes.

I'm still a little drunk. Maybe that's the real problem. Maybe not. What am I, anyway? An official exterminator with an official truck and an official badge and official paperwork up to my ass, all so I can kill animals for official reasons. All so people can spit on me and yell at me when I'm drunk and depressed.

Sort it out. Where do I start? When I worked for the park district, nobody spat on me. Just a lot of dirt and sweat and long hours and low pay. No one spat on me when I went into business for myself doing Humane Animal Control. I relocated wild animals. Except mice. And bugs. Those I cheerfully and efficiently exterminated.

The public liked the idea so much I had to hire help and learn to handle red tape, accounting hassles, and employees. It was great.

I got greedy. That's where I went wrong. See, when you live in a little city near a big growing one, compromises get made on services. By compromise, I mean they pay contractors. Last fall, I put in a low bid and got animal control badges for me and all my guys.

I thought it would be a good idea to give strays some consideration too, but maybe I was fooling myself. The stories the guys have been telling me, the stuff I've had to do…hell.

I hadn't seen this guy since I left the nature center. Never saw him in my bar before tonight. Now I know he hunted me out. He was always looking after some orphaned beastie, always asking advice and not following it. We got along okay just the same, talking about the shame of destroying wildlife habitat for ticky-tacky swampland developments.

"How can you be a party to mass murder?" he asked. I wouldn't remember the words except that he kept repeating them. "No one has the right to kill another living, thinking creature. How could you sell out and slaughter helpless animals for a living?"

I didn't have an answer. I walked out of the bar and walked home. Too drunk to drive. I have to work tomorrow. Shit.

I thought I'd be bringing the best possible attitude to a lousy job that someone had to do. Maybe it was a mistake. Maybe I'm wrong.

Then again, maybe not. You can't empty the ocean with a

teaspoon, and that's what his kind try to do, trying to save every single animal. I'm not stupid, dammit.

Sort it out. Like hell. I can't think right now.

April 20

THIS MORNING, Dale and Steve, and Jim tiptoed into the office like my basement stairs were made of eggshells. I guess my hangover looked as bad as it felt.

They got coffee and equipment and talked in whispers. I didn't bother to eavesdrop. It looked like the kind of argument you might hear from a flock of penguins when they're convincing the most gullible one to jump first and find out if there are sharks in the water.

Steve walked into a swarm of wasps without a bee suit last week. He's the one who asked me what was wrong.

I couldn't say I was feeling lonely and nauseous and defensive. I told them all to shut up and get the hell to work.

Sometimes I think I missed some class in school that everyone else took. I understand animals, but people never stop confusing me. I was sure they'd all be pissed off. I would've been. They just moved faster.

I handed out the work phones I don't let anyone take home, checked with the answering service to confirm overnight work orders, and handed out the day's work assignments. I used an answering machine and a blotter pad for scheduling until Dale put everything on a computer and calculated the return on investment for the overnight service. His method works better.

Steve and Jim took their assignment sheets and left.

Dale has a way with looks that makes you want to agree with him just so he'll stop. He looked at me and asked if I wanted some time off. He handles dispatch whenever I do payroll or filing anyway, and I knew he'd stand there and stare until I said yes.

So I said yes. I rescued my truck from the bar parking lot, went to the forest preserve, and watched ducks all day. It didn't help much, but it was better than trying to work with clients in that condition.

The headache and queasiness retreated, but the frustration and shame stuck around. When my appetite made a reappearance, around sundown, I gave up on meditation and came home.

All the food I'd bought over the weekend was gone. Hungry employees are worse than a plague of locusts. It's one of the hidden costs of running a home business that they didn't warn me about in night school.

The freezer door didn't slam loud enough to satisfy my temper. I swore a lot to make up the difference, and Steve came upstairs to investigate. His mouth and both hands were full of pizza. My pizza. My supper.

I threw a glass at him. It missed. He beat me in the cursing competition that happened afterwards. Some days I can't do anything right.

I went downstairs to sulk in the office. Jim was there, off the clock but not gone. None of the guys have anybody waiting at home, and I'm too spineless to throw them out. Another hazard my management courses didn't mention.

Anyway, Steve and Jim put a few pieces of (my) pizza and a few beers (also mine) into me, and somewhere along the line I told them about the bar scene.

Jim has enough energy for three people, a mind like a spring-loaded trap, and a mouth that won't quit. He started delivering his opinion of fanatics in general and my animal-rights buddy in particular, and about the plans he has in store for all the jerks we see day after day.

My ribs were starting to ache from laughing by the time

Dale came down the stairs. The shopping bag he launched at Jim hit Steve instead, and everything spilled out where I could see it. I saw the receipt first, and I got ready to yell. I changed my mind a second later.

Naming the business exhausted my creative powers. I'd never thought I needed marketing beyond a name and business listing. Maybe I was wrong.

Dale had drawn up a real company logo and bought us all company jackets and tee shirts to go with our official badges and the city-leased trucks. I sat there looking at mine until Dale said in a tight, worried voice that he'd filed an expense report but would pay out of his own pocket if I didn't like the design. I told him to shut up and put on his damned coat.

They look good. The outfits make the guys look more official, like a team or something. They said I looked good too. They're lying, but I don't care.

Maybe we're doing something right, or maybe not. I don't feel so lonely doing it now.

June 10

ALL IN ALL, today was pretty average. And that, all in all, is pretty depressing.

Start with two normally rational human beings, both firmly entrenched in their respective gingerbread houses with chemical-green postage-stamp suburban yards. I'm talking matching lawn furniture and privacy fences and everything.

Give one of these hypothetically sane people a dog — not an exotic breed, just a basic dog. A puppy, really, all floppy ears, big paws and tongue. The neighbor has a cat — a basic cat, gray striped fur, green eyes and a loud purr.

Add a spicing of unpleasant incidents. Kitty comes home with bald patches, claw-marked puppy cowers in the attached garage, holes get dug under the fence line, unsavory droppings are found on the wrong patio. Allow a few months for fermentation.

This is a recipe for complete chaos, and it stinks.

Me and the guys, we're animal control officers, right? What a joke. The animals didn't need controlling, their owners did. We inherited this mess from our predecessors. I'd like to think we would've handled the earlier scenes better, cooling both sides down before things got so far out of hand, but I don't know. It might have been a no-win situation from the start.

I do know this: Jim was called to the dog-owner's residence by a police patrol unit. When he arrived, the officer in charge of handling a 'domestic dispute' (it was a brawl, according to witnesses) told him to impound the puppy.

Jim reasonably asked for a reason.

The owner was being charged with keeping a vicious animal, the cop said. The dog had allegedly bitten the neighbor's cat and then bitten the neighbor.

This dog weighs less than twenty pounds soaking wet and doesn't even have half his real teeth yet. If he had teeth, he would trip over his feet long before he reached anything he wanted to bite.

I'm afraid Jim started laughing, which wasn't very diplomatic.

Cat-owner, on the scene, became irate again and started shouting about bureaucratic incompetence and obstruction of justice and his rights as a citizen. Jim stopped laughing and started applying verbal band-aids. He called me afterwards, and I had him drop by the office to give everyone time to cool down before papers got filed and everything became permanent. He arrived, dog in tow, just as Dog-owner called me.

Dog-owner was furious because he'd lost a major battle in the undeclared war with his neighbor. Put the dog down, he told me. It wasn't worth a legal fight.

I got a call from the police station later saying that Cat-owner had dropped charges due to lack of evidence. In other words, none of the alleged bites had broken skin.

This puppy has been sitting under my kitchen table all afternoon, staring at me with these incredibly big brown eyes whenever I check on him. I could send him home, except his owner doesn't want him back. I called twice to make sure.

I could send him off to the shelter, except that this time of the year, they're up to their eyeballs in puppies, and this one's a little too old. He wouldn't stand a chance against the younger furballs. He'd get put down in ten days, right on schedule.

I can't send this damned puppy off to be killed. He keeps looking at me.

July 9

ONE OF MY biggest commercial competitors has a great tactic for getting animal nests out of chimneys: light a fire to destroy the nest, and if any animals escape through the chimney, he shoots them.

Yes, I am being sarcastic about the "great" part. It's monstrous and cruel, and I got to clean up after the bastard today.

I was in the living room taking a break when the call came in, but the customer's voice carried all the way up the stairs. Dale gave me a real long look when I poked my head into the office where he was frowning at the speaker phone.

Dale's look said I shouldn't take field calls when I have paperwork to finish. I looked right back and snagged the assignment sheet. He was right, but I was tired, and it was almost quitting time. Either I took care of the call, or someone else got overtime. I'm not rich.

The address was a miniature estate in an expensive new

subdivision. I worked out the story before I reached the end of the driveway. Homeowner remodeled and tore out all the landscaping. Some jerk with a bulldozer destroyed a raccoon's home. The raccoon made the best of a bad situation and made a new home in a convenient location. Homeowner noticed unwanted guest, got bargain price, received a bargain job, and found out too late that the bargain didn't include removing leftovers.

See, this raccoon was a mama.

The client met me at the door: past middle-age, with that harried look divorced executives sometimes get when they've been alone awhile. His expensive suit was covered with grime, and the story I'd expected was spun on the way to the scene of the disaster.

His living room was as big as my whole house and ten times as filthy. The coon's nest had fallen into the fireplace at some point after the exterminator left. Charred branches and soot all over a parquet floor.

I smelled burnt hair halfway across the room. On the hearth was a laundry basket, with four things wriggling around on a flannel shirt inside. Only fused bone remained of their feet, and their blistered faces were speckled with seared fur, like bits of pepper.

The client had found the mess when he came home from the office. He'd called his veterinarian, who was kind enough to recommend my firm. We hadn't gotten the job first because our fees were too high. He was very sorry.

I wanted to spit on the old miser, but I didn't. I cleaned the fireplace and the room, put the babies into a cardboard box and took them away.

As soon as I got them inside the truck, I broke their necks, fast and painless. Maybe I don't have the right to take another creature's life, but mercy still means something to me. I saved four babies a few hours of futile agony. I can live with that responsibility. I cried doing it, but I won't lose an hour of sleep.

Afterwards, I made out an invoice for triple my normal hourly fee and took it inside. Consulting rates plus emergency services, I called it. The guy didn't even blink. He pulled out a checkbook and asked if I thought I could save the babies.

God help me, I told him the truth.

He called me a cold-hearted monster and threw the check on the floor after he finished writing it. I picked it up and walked out. I mean, I couldn't very well hit a paying customer, no matter what I wanted to do. I sat in the truck and tried to cool down before facing rush-hour traffic.

I don't know how long he stood there waiting. I just eventually noticed him. He was standing all tight and quiet and mad-looking, right next to the door. I unrolled the window and waited for him to rub a little more salt in the wounds.

He asked if he could bury the babies in his yard.

I think I babbled something about disposal of animals inside city limits; it violates at least three ordinances. He nodded and asked again.

Those poor raccoons are fertilizing a maple sapling that'll make a good home for squirrels someday. I don't know who needed the gesture more, the client or me. I know we shook hands before I left, and he took half a box of my ad flyers to distribute in the neighborhood. That's the one bright spot in the whole tragedy. Maybe I can keep it from happening again. I guess that's why I keep doing this.

August 7

I DON'T KNOW what to do about this damned dog. I have zero yard-space and negative time to spend on walking and petting. He whines if I leave him upstairs and piddles on the floor if I leave him in the office. And every time I even start to think about getting rid of him, he looks at me. Worse than Dale.

It was my own fault. I couldn't file him into a category. He isn't a public hazard. Not a feral stray. Not a sick animal or a vicious one. Not an unfortunate but everyday occurrence in my job. He's a living breathing—howling—dog, and my heart isn't hard enough to kill him for the sins of carpet-soiling and being a nuisance. Not when he's my dog, even if ownership fell on me by default.

I refuse to start brooding about all the other perfectly sweet pets abandoned on the highways or left tied to the front doors of vet clinics. I do what I can, but I'm not crazy.

I have to do what I can.

I know, I know. That means I have to name the stupid beast.

Stupid it is, then.

August 20

I spent a few hours in hell today.

I'd just dropped off the morning's Animal Control haul—two abandoned kittens and an evicted dog—at the nearest shelter with space, and the truck dropped its transmission all over the parking lot when I tried to leave.

Tim the receptionist came out to commiserate. Tim's a big, smiley old man with a shriveled-up face and a gentle touch with animals. He did dog-training for the military or something before he retired. Now he volunteers most of his waking hours to the shelter. Neat guy.

He looked over the guts of my truck with me, asked how old it was, and said that euthanasia would be the kindest solution. I think he was joking. Anyway, he recommended a tow firm. I called the city garage. It's their truck. I'd been leasing because my accountant said it was cheaper.

I also called Jim. He's been trying his hand at the switchboard since he fell off a ladder and broke his arm. He said Dale and Steve both had full schedules and couldn't pick me up right away.

None of my options were great. Hitch a ride with the tow truck and spend hours watching mechanics play with greasy pieces of metal. Call an expensive cab. Walk the full five miles home along the streets.

Or I could be sensible and wait for one of the guys to swing by the shelter whenever they got a chance. I stayed. My mistake, or my good luck. One or the other. I'm still not sure.

Tim told me to make myself useful in the office, ran down the check-in procedures as if I didn't know them by heart already, and started the afternoon cleaning.

I thought he was doing me a favor.

They're talking about building another shelter any day now. They've been talking five years. The corridors between cages are gut-sucking narrow, the windows are tiny and the lights few and far between. It's slick underfoot and the walls are grimy-greasy because the exhaust fan on the incinerator cuts out on heavy days. The noise is hideous. Five to forty dogs barking at once, plus a varying collection of miserable cats crying their hearts out.

Tim worked every day in that din and stink and wet, knowing many of the animals he was tending so conscientiously would be dead in a week. I got to sit at the front counter, where there was fresh air, decent lighting, and a waiting area with a vending machine and doors into two discreet little exam rooms.

I should've known there was a reason Tim chose scrubbing dog piss out of concrete over processing intakes.

First, I helped a Good Samaritan fill out paperwork for a stray mutt she'd found complete with collar, rabies tags, and half his tether. It wasn't too bad, but she was so happy about demonstrating her concerned citizenship that she made me ill.

She wasn't doing it for the dog's sake, she was doing it for the gossip value.

The next arrival donated a litter of kittens and swore up and down they were eight-week-old weanlings. I've seen my share of kittens from day one on up. These were four weeks old, maximum. The man acted like he was doing the shelter a favor, dumping his babies there. I smiled at him a lot to make him leave before I committed violence.

There were others, some good, some bad. The last sign-in was the worst, a poodle whose owner had been moved into an assisted living place that didn't allow pets. The owner's relatives, all five of them, kept explaining everything to me as if I wanted to know, wanting me to tell them they didn't have to feel guilty about getting rid of the old man's dog. Keeping quiet was the best I could do.

There's triage in most animal shelters, just like in a war zone: space, time and supplies are all limited. The poodle was twelve years old, arthritic and going blind. Better prospects already occupied all the available cages. Tim put the dog to sleep ten minutes after its real executioners left, about five minutes before Dale arrived to retrieve me.

The dog's eyes went all bright and glassy when the anesthetic took effect. When I mentioned how eerie it looked, Tim said in a weird soft voice that he doesn't watch any more. We talked afterwards, and he scheduled me for a four-hour shift on Saturday.

Dale called me a sentimental dumbshit and took me home.

Asshole. He's coming too.

I know Stupid doesn't understand why he got half of my hamburger at supper or why he gets to sleep on the bed with me tonight. I know, though. I know, and I am very glad I kept him.

August 30

I'VE NEVER DECIDED whether I hate winter or summer more. Winter is deadly cold, the ice makes driving a bitch, my hands never warm up, I have to deal with sappy Christmas music and holiday blahs…but in the summer, monsters come out of the woodwork. The heat makes them confrontational, I guess.

I get five times the number of problem calls in July than in February. This year, it's been non-stop wackiness through August. I'm not talking about evil people who walk into fast-food joints with rifles and take out their troubles on total strangers. The ones I deal with are relatively harmless. They don't have the same views as the majority of humanity, that's all.

Unfortunately, they also like to talk. Standing out in the hot sun with sweat pouring down my back and making nice with someone who wants to tell me about the Flat Earth or Raw Diets is enough to make me wish for a blizzard.

Two clients like that in one day was one more than I could handle without blowing off some steam in writing.

I was polite, I was understanding, I was a good listener, and by the time I left each of them, I was ready to press charges. That's what those people do to me.

I showed up at the first one's address with a fistful of police complaints from the neighbors about noise and odor and the appearance of the yard. As I approached the door, I began to sympathize with the neighbors. The yard was a minefield of dog droppings. Unspeakably stinky and, in the steaming heat wave we're having lately, unbelievably unhealthy too.

The homeowner refused to open her screen door even after I identified myself as a public employee and showed her my badge and explained about the complaints. She told me I'd stolen one of her dogs already and that she absolutely wouldn't let me take the others.

I had never been there in my life. Neither, to the best of my knowledge, had my official predecessors. Warning bells started going off in my head. I suggested that she was confusing me with someone else.

She admitted that the dogs might've simply disappeared. Ever since the aliens had taught one of them how to teleport, she'd had an awful time keeping track of them all. She told me about the aliens at length: antennae, flying saucers, blue skin and so forth.

Yeah, I thought I was being pranked too.

I looked around for a hidden video camera, but I couldn't find one. She kept right on talking, explaining how the dogs had started teaching each other the teleportation trick, and how she had to drive to various local pet stores to collect them from their wanderings. They called her on the telephone when they were finished with their shopping.

That's what she told me. Straight-faced.

She looked sane enough: dressed well, nice jewelry, styled white hair and lots of powdery makeup. She sounded like a refugee from the Twilight Zone. I was supposed to tell her that she had to cut down her dog population to legal limits or the city would fine her and impound the animals. I didn't think she would listen. We didn't speak the same language.

The dogs in question were milling around her ankles. Poodles, Lhasas, a Pekinese and an assortment of other small breeds — I counted twenty specimens. They barked constantly while their owner was talking. Twenty dogs, even small ones, can produce an incredible amount of noise. She ignored them. I got a headache.

I handed over the complaints, wheedled a signature for the 'agree to comply' paperwork by telling her it was a petition to the government for stricter radiation laws, and high-tailed it home.

I figured bold-faced lying would be easier than trying to explain impounding and eviction processes. I also figured no one would believe her if she ever claimed failure to receive legal notice.

And all that was easy, compared to handling the second case. I'll tell you about him some other time. I'm getting a new headache just from thinking about him tonight. I can't write yet. Maybe later. I have to feed Stupid.

September 20

I WENT BACK with Jim today for a followup with the first animal hoarder I met last month. It was tragic on one level, but it was almost funny, too.

Let me go back a step. After my visit and report, the police got more complaints and went to talk to her themselves. The poor bastards had no more success than I did. The woman insisted she only had four dogs, the rest were only visiting.

The police didn't pursue it further. The neighbors were furious, but not furious enough to get tangled in lawsuits, and the hoarder did hire a service to keep the yard clean, so that nixed the public health angle. Her lawyer knows she's got an odd worldview, but believing in little blue Martians isn't illegal —especially not when the client is rolling in money.

The angry neighbors started calling me. That got old real fast.

Dale gets credit for the bright idea of calling the hoarder's out-of-town daughter and explaining the situation. Daughter was sympathetic. We cooked up a plan. The police looked into the legal side, and somebody with approval power approved it.

Our scheme won't solve things permanently, but it bought everyone some time and peace of mind. Summary: Daughter invited mother for a visit. Mom took her favorite dogs with her. The surplus got impounded and farmed out to no-kill shelters all over the Tri-State area. That last bit was Tim's doing.

So, that brings us to today. Jim and I did a check-up visit and asked how she was doing, partly to find out if she was planning to file a complaint against us.

Nope. Her dogs aren't missing, see?

She told us all about a secret canine mission to colonize another solar system.

The neighbors are happy, she's happy, the city's happy. Everybody's happy except the dogs, who shouldn't have been stuck in the situation in the first place. Even the dogs might be happier now, to be fair. Tim reports two got adopted right away, and the rest are adjusting to their foster homes.

I guess that's what got me so ANGRY about the other hoarder I met the same day I met the alien dog lady. The animals are the ones who always lose when people start messing around in their lives.

I suppose I should get the story of the other August hoarder off my chest too. I think I can stay cool enough to write at this point.

At first, I thought it was the same situation as the first one. The yard looked similar: big holes, yellow bushes, piles everywhere, stink and flies and who knows what growing in the mess. The only difference was that this hoarder wasn't keeping all his pets indoors in the cool. Some of them were outside.

Plenty of water dishes—I looked—but the ten dogs I saw were too overheated to even bark at me. A scruffy little clump of cats had staked out the shade of a hand-painted lawn sign that said 'FurSavers.' I started wondering if the police could get the homeowner for running an unlicensed business on top of everything else.

They did. He was. Bastard.

That part came later. On the day I showed up, I noticed right away that the outdoor animals all looked skinny, and the whole yard smelled like Parvo.

That's when I started to really worry. Parvo is distinctive

and dangerous. It's highly contagious, hard to treat, often fatal, and wholly avoidable with proper hygiene and feeding.

I rang the doorbell and braced myself for anything.

The man who answered the door told me I could take my bloody hands elsewhere. He wouldn't cooperate if I got down on my knees and begged. He'd rescued his animals from being killed, and he would take care of them and find them all proper loving homes if the uncaring money-grubbing animal-haters like me would just leave him alone.

That, at least, was the gist of it. He took a lot longer, used more expletives, and repeated himself a lot. It's amazing how long some things stick in my memory.

My jaw got sore from gritting my teeth. I counted the indoor animal complement I could see from the doorstep—more dogs and lots more cats—and wondered how he fed them all. (He took donations from anyone he could convince to help. He passed out flyers with his address and everything. The operation did look impressive on paper. I have to admit that.)

When he ran down, I handed over the legal papers and recited my lines about complaints, warnings, and compliance-or-confiscation procedures. He lectured at me again. He was tired of being persecuted. I told him he was facing prosecution, not persecution. He slammed the door.

I filed the papers. Jim and Dale went back a week later and impounded the whole collection, despite the efforts of their owner and some friends who staged a sit-down strike in the yard.

Devoted friends, given the condition of that yard. Very devoted friends.

It got into the local newspaper. The reporter couldn't decide whose side she was on, so I'm not sure if the publicity helped or hurt. Dale says our business picked up. So, whatever.

I helped the shelter staff put down the infected dogs.

Fifteen of them, some so far gone they couldn't walk. We saved ten cats. Ten out of fifty.

Maybe the hoarder's head was so far in the clouds that he couldn't smell the stink. Maybe his intentions were good. I don't care. By saving so many more animals than he could handle, he was doing no more than killing them slowly and painfully.

Ignorance is not bliss. It's dangerous.

But when Stupid comes up and puts his head in my lap like he's doing right now, I know, deep down, exactly how that man felt. People like him scare me because I know they're irrational, but I still understand.

I'm not sure how to deal with that. I'm not sure I want to think about it too much. For now I'll just sit here, soak up Stupid's love, and be grateful.

October 3

Nobody will believe this one. I mean, I didn't believe it when I was looking at it. You'd think people would know better, that's all I can say. Who in his right mind would keep several hundred pounds of alligator in their backyard?

I stood and stared at that alligator for a good five minutes. It was sitting in a huge steel watering trough topped with metal hardware cloth. The trough was four feet long. The 'gator was too long to turn around inside it. A lot too long.

My first thought was to wonder how in hell anyone cleaned up after him.

The 'gator's owner (my client, God help us both) had two troughs. He said he tipped over one tub with a stick and lured the 'gator into the other one with chunks of meat. Then he levered the trough upright, again with the stick.

I was sorry I'd asked, but Gator-guy kept going, assuring me that he would've brought the 'little guy' indoors before frost, that he only kept the alligator outside during the warm months, and we'd been having an unseasonably warm fall.

I looked at the skinny wire handles on the galvanized tub and cringed. Gator-guy must have been reading my mind—or my expression—because he helpfully pointed out the ten-foot long metal chain attached to the currently unoccupied trough up by the house.

Totally safe, he insisted.

Ten feet was thirty feet short of the distance I wanted between me and an alligator. In my opinion the entire one-story *house* was too small to share with an alligator as big as that one.

This was not the simple "got him as a baby and he's outgrown the tank" problem I had been contracted to handle. Neither my muscles nor my gear were tough enough to wrestle seven feet of nasty, carnivorous brainless reptile.

This guy needed a licensed wildlife expert, not a pest control outfit.

I said as much. The comment slid off a very thick skull, the kind you might expect to find in the owner of a neighborhood safety hazard. Gator-guy pointed out that *he*, in fact, had no desire to get rid of his pet. He'd only called me because the neighbors had threatened to go to the police. Also, the tub was a lot heavier than he remembered, and he wasn't sure he could haul indoors alone.

Maybe he was trying to convince me to help him hide the evidence instead of surrendering the animal. I don't know. I didn't think of that at the time.

I could hear children squealing happily in the distance. They were enjoying the unseasonably warm weather too. I pictured the results if one of the miserable brats discovered this backyard monster and decided to tease it.

The picture made me queasy. Alligators move a lot faster than people think. Mind you, I don't like children. They're loud, they're messy, and they grow up into teenagers who burn cats alive and take potshots at birds. Still, I wouldn't wish impromptu amputation on anyone, even a kid.

I looked at the 'gator a little more, thought out an approach to the problem, and started doing calculations in my head. Then I went to make calls from the truck, where I could be private and honest.

Gator-guy tagged along and gave me this 'now what?' look, so I explained what I was planning. First, I had to call for help. Second, I had to talk to my insurance agent. Third, I had to call the zoo I'd already called once, to see if they had room for twice the alligator we'd discussed, and whether they could cover me, legally. Fourth, I had to write a new estimate. The quote Dale had given him had not included consulting costs, insurance outlay, use of additional personnel, or danger pay.

Gator-guy turned red and huffed a lot, especially about being charged for extra helpers when he handled the 'gator by himself all the time.

I told him his choice was to pay the fees now or wait until one of his neighbors filed public endangerment charges. Then I would return in my official role with the experts on subcontract and personally ensure that he paid twice as much in official fines. I also mentioned that I would share the nifty idea of filing endangerment charges with every homeowner on the block before I left.

I didn't tell him that I wouldn't trust him to help me with his pet even if we were the last two people on earth. I do have some sense. Gator-guy kept whining long after I was tired of countering objections, so I closed the truck window on him and made my calls.

Dale sounded intrigued, but he sent the other two guys to help. The insurance agent sounded unhappy, but admitted my policy covered alligator bites. The guy from the reptile house at the zoo drooled into the phone with excitement and said he needed to examine the animal on-site before allowing its redisposition to zoo proprietorship. His words, not mine.

He also offered to bring a zoo van for transporting the thing, so I was more than happy to wait. The thought of driving with the 'gator in my truck had been giving me shivers.

Steve and Jim showed up and made nice with the client, who was trying to talk to me while I redid his paperwork. The client went indoors to fume after he saw the new estimate, but he didn't tell us to leave. Fine with me. I had his credit card number. The zoo guy took his time. I shot the breeze with my guys, listened to tunes on the truck radio and enjoyed the sunshine for an hour, all on the client's payroll. Paradise on the half-shell.

When the zoo guy arrived and saw what he was adopting, he did exactly what I'd done: stood there with his mouth open for a good long time, then started swearing.

He was furious over the 'gator's living conditions, not staggered by the logistics of moving him, but his language was no better than mine. The client, who had emerged from the house thinking he would get more sympathy from a real expert, beat a hasty retreat.

As usual, dealing with the animal was easy compared to handling the humans involved. It wasn't easy, but it was straightforward physical labor, requiring no fake smiles or tactful silences required.

First, we dumped the 'gator out of his trough and tried luring him into the crate the zoo guy had brought. It didn't work. He crawled towards the bushes instead — the gator, I mean, not the zoo guy. The zoo guy used a lasso-stick and a muzzle. Once collared and muzzled, the 'gator was uncooperative about letting anyone touch his body and tail. Me and the guys did a lot of grabbing and shouting and getting the hell out of the way.

The zoo guy mentioned that if he had really believed my

estimate of the animal's size, he would've brought a tranq gun. By then, of course, the job was done. Jim swore at him. I would've laughed, but I didn't have the breath.

I'm going to get a kick out of visiting the zoo from now on. I'll point out my alligator to total strangers and tell them the whole story. Looking back, it was a hell of a lot of fun.

Some days I really don't hate my job after all.

TURNING BACK

This is another of my rare forays into non-fantasy storytelling. The inspiration for it sprang from a day hike I took with friends in the San Bernardino mountains.

A few weeks later, several "long-lost hiker's body found" stories hit the news, and, well, I couldn't stop thinking about all the ways we'd gotten lucky on that hike.

So I made up some fictional people and wrote them their own wilderness adventure. It first appeared on a now-defunct online essay platform called Readwave.

———

WE DON'T BELONG HERE. This rocky path high in the San Bernardino Mountains is no place for city slickers like us. We aren't dressed for the weather or the terrain, we have no maps, canteens, or first-aid kits, and no one else in the wide world knows where we are.

We don't belong, but we're here. The trail goes two directions: forward or back. The sun is glimmering behind a seductive green fringe of pine boughs, the cool breeze perfumed with the scent of pine is rustling sweet meadow grasses, and the trail is a dusty-brown invitation to continue into the shadowed forest again. Forward or back: decision time.

We decided once already. That's how we got this far.

A few hours earlier we were all lounging around a hotel pool in the blistering mid-summer heat of California's Central Valley. There are five of us: Dru, Gary, Alexis, Kyle and me, co-workers by necessity, friends by serendipitous chance. Our company pulls together its best people to set up new locations, and the job involves a month of six-day workweeks where the shifts routinely top twelve hours.

We were enjoying the twenty-four-hour break between week two and three, recreating as hard as we could at the hotel pool in floating chairs with umbrella drinks, when Dru found an idea in her third mai tai.

Dru is short for Prudence, but I've never met anyone with a less appropriate name. Moderation is for monks, she says, laughing, and she has a sunny persuasiveness that makes the most ridiculous ideas seem reasonable.

"Let's go for a drive," she says, and that is that. Alexis the designated driver chooses a route titled "Scenic Byway" from the rental van's GPS, and off we go.

Eight clogged lanes of highway become four, and then two. Brown, withered plains give way to scrubby hills, and the roads empty out. Twenty miles from millions of people, we are the only souls in the universe.

The road shrinks again to one lane with narrow shoulders, and the route twists and climbs uphill through tall trees as straight as telephone poles. Drifts of snow huddle at the tree bases, gray in the shade. Gary opens the windows, and we shiver in our tank tops and shorts.

"National Forest," declares a faded wood sign.

Conversation quiets to murmurs of "I've never seen so much green," and "I wonder what kind of bird that is."

Kyle, ever the curious one, checks online. "Stellar jay," he says.

Then his phone loses signal, so we christen the world for ourselves. Ship-mast pines, old-man bushes with clumps of leaves like shaking fists, and bat-squirrels who cling upside-down from branches. We laugh at every new discovery until we run out of road.

No tire tracks mar the smooth gravel of the turnaround. There is only a tempting trailhead, brown tongue in an arching mouth of trees, and a weathered sign that hasn't been painted in decades.

I trace the carved symbols by hand, and Dru says, "Let's see where it goes."

It's the kind of suggestion that gets people killed in wild places on the edge of civilization. People die every year because they mistake proximity for safety. Hypothermia, exposure, dehydration, and worse are only one injury, one slip, one wrong turn away. Nature doesn't forgive mistakes.

I'm the only one who knows how stupid this is. I'm the only one with any wilderness experience. Dru smiles. I say, "Great idea."

It's stupid, but risk is part of life too.

Dru skips along in her flip flops, Gary grumbles about blisters, Kyle and Alexis complain about sweat, but no one wants to be the first to give up. Then Drew stops at a narrow cross-trail and looks longingly down the side path.

"No turns," I say.

She walks straight past the intersection, but she asks, "Why not?" so I tell everyone a few gruesome stories about people dying lost in the woods.

Survival is about choosing risks. All decisions have consequences.

A snide remark from Alexis and a joke from Gary lead to an unforgettable discussion about survival and the human spirit. The conversation meanders like the trail. We walk, and we talk, and we soak up the joy that comes with baring your heart to friends while getting grit in your teeth, twigs in your socks, and sunburn on the tips of your ears.

One more curve, we agree every time we come around a corner and the trail goes on. One more, and another, and another, until we reach this overlook where the smoggy human grid of the valley spreads out below us.

We joke about zombies and escaping the apocalypse, we admire the way the trail dives back into the trees at the far end of the soft forest grass—so enticing—and we look at the sun, not setting yet but soon.

Do we turn back? Or do we toss the coins of our lives onto luck's table and gamble our futures for the thrill of *new* and *now*?

Life never lets us see the endings we don't make. That's what stories are for.

We stand in a meadow bathed by golden light and weigh a simple choice that will write the ending to all our ever-afters.

HOMECOMING

This Rollover Files short work offers a bit of Jack Coby's backstory, seen through the eyes of the woman who adopted him after his early-onset rollover. It started life as a reward for new subscribers to my official email newsletter, but it's been languishing in limbo since I switched newsletter services.

———

MARY ELLEN COBY was awake when the vandals parked in her driveway. The time was past midnight by then, but sleep never came easy or stayed long, not since Vincent had passed. She opened the front door in the dark and watched them clamber out of their pickup truck the way only a mob of young men could, all long legs and wide shoulders, swaggering and slouching at once.

They hushed each other's hooting laughter and shuffled across her front yard in a parade of pushing and shoving. Cans and bottles fell onto the grass in their wake, and the breeze of their passage carried the warm stink of cheap beer into the house.

She waited until they reached the new yard sign in front of the shrubs. They clustered around it and jostled each other like penguins at the edge of an ice floe, encouraging each other in voices slurred by liquid courage.

When one of them lifted a leg to kick, Mary Ellen racked the slide on the shotgun and spoke through the screen door.

"You boys lost?"

And if the words shook a little, if they sounded old, brittle, and small, well, that was fair because she was all those things. They weren't lost, of course not. No one stopped for directions at a darkened suburban house in the wee hours. Even an old lady with weak eyes could recognize a bunch of no-good vandals out to vent their frustrations on a poor, helpless lawn decoration.

All the same, she would give them a chance to take the easy out, give her a false address and skedaddle. These were her neighbors' children. They were near-adult and mostly ignorant, but they might yet grow up to choose better. Some of them would come to their senses in the morning, at home with only their consciences and hangovers for company. She would give them that lesson if she could.

"Well?" She came outside, felt the cool, spring air against her bare legs and the chill of the concrete step against her bare feet, and she wondered if she looked like a ghost in her cotton nightie and quilted housecoat.

The moblings bumped and elbowed one another. "We're doing community service, ma'am," said one, raising snickers from the others. "We're taking trash off folks' lawns and driving it to the dump. You don't want this filthy poz propaganda here, do you?"

Disgust dripped from his challenge, soaking the words with menace. He believed himself the hand of justice. So did his murmuring huddle of friends. Her heart quailed under the assault of their self-righteousness.

The street light at the end of the block made shadows of them, but in better light she would know their faces. These were the same boys who loped down the streets fall and spring in track jerseys, the ones who chased each other along home with hockey sticks or soccer balls.

These same boys had called her ma'am when they brought her casseroles and condolences after Vincent died, showing up at her door in dark suits while their parents waited in the car to let their teenagers practice proper manners.

"My lawn, my sign, my beliefs," she said. "Free speech, boys. I believe R-positive folks deserve fair treatment under the law. My late husband was poz himself, you'll recall, so I'll thank you to be more careful what you call filthy."

She spared a glance at the innocent target of the boys' hatred. The sign was painted on thin board, staked secure in the sod. Blue background with stars, a white cross bordered in red. The word *Unity* held its center, with the slogan *Love Is Positive* marching in a red circle around it. Each arm of the cross declared a principle: *Peace, Justice, Equality,* and *Freedom.*

She had known that sign would bring trouble when she'd hammered it into the ground that morning, but she'd never imagined trouble would take the form of direct action. This confrontation made her ache for the whole world.

Vitriol and violence had no place in the future she had worked hard all her life to build. This was the future she was stuck with, though, and she wasn't dead yet. She lifted the shotgun, aimed it in the group's general direction.

"Don't even think about going after my sign. You're trespassing, and I'm within my rights to fill you full of birdshot."

Behind her, Snazzy hooked claws into the screen door and mewed indignantly over this disturbance of their nightly routine. Mary Ellen shushed her. No one needed the distraction of a fluffy tortoiseshell cat right now.

Shuffling and mumbling ensued, a pause freighted with dangerous messages. They *really* wanted their prize, and they couldn't recognize a threat when it was shaped like a frail old woman any one of them could lift with one hand.

The cat's arrival probably hadn't helped matters.

The muzzle of the weapon wavered. It was heavier than Mary Ellen had remembered. "I'll count to three and waste one shell on a warning shot," she said. "Y'all should know I'm not wearing my glasses, and the police will call it self-defense if I put one of you in the morgue by accident. One."

Her adversaries scrambled into motion.

"Not so fast." She used the tone she had perfected on generations of irritating salesmen. It was a little raspy these days, but it still worked. The boys froze. She waved the shotgun. "I'll see to those other signs you stole, too. Unless you want me to report you to the police for vandalism?"

They shuffled, and one muttered, "No'm."

"Pick up your bottles too, or I'll report you for littering."

Soon enough the subdued combatants retreated from the field of battle. The truck headlights flashed on once it reached the street, and it rumbled slowly away.

She set the empty shotgun down in the corner by the door and jotted the license plate number on the pad by the telephone. Her vision was not *that* bad, thank you very much. And then she carried seventeen signs back to the garage one by one and loaded them onto a tarp laid over the back seat of Vincent's car.

Some were defaced past saving but not all, and the sullied ones could be re-painted. She would call the police come morning, not that they would do a thing about petty vandalism, but she wanted it on record. And then she would take the signs back to those who would treat them with respect. She brushed dirt off the top one to admire the handiwork.

Peace. Unity. Love. So painful, to hear such beautiful ideals labeled as filth. So frightening to see how hatred and fear could change people beyond all recognition. It chilled her to see how fast the poison spread when left unchecked.

Fire sparked to life inside her heart, a bright-burning desire for justice that drove out the cold fear. That flame had cooled to little more than embers over the years, but now it blazed up high and hot again.

A sign isn't enough, her conscience whispered. *You could do so much more.*

And if her body groaned in protest, if doubt roiled in her belly and cried, *Think of the risks, think of how much work it would be,* well, those little voices could shut themselves up.

Every day was a chance to make a difference, as she'd told Vincent more than once. She'd grown weary, and she'd been lonely in her grief, but the truth remained unchanged. She could do more.

So she would. Not out of guilt, but for herself. And for all the people a thousand signs couldn't save from hatred's bloody grasp.

———

THE IDEA of picking a cause based on emotional appeal alone offended Mary Ellen's sensibilities, so she took her time deciding what *more* would look like. There were lists to be made, of organizations and public services tied to the Unity movement and their needs. Matching their missions against her skills, time, and energy narrowed down her options.

She ended up with a list that went from a high labor/high reward strategy—sponsoring someone through their post-rollover transition—all the way down to the low work/low reward option of volunteering more actively with her current community groups.

Once everything was laid out logically, the decision was easy. Becoming an official Public Safety Sponsor was by far the most appealing choice. Once she got her certification, she would basically be doing what she'd done all her career, but part-time and from her own home.

She missed teaching. Sponsorship would bring that joy back into her life.

Most people didn't need much of an assist after rollover washed away their life's intended path. Adjusting to new powers wasn't easy, but the safety net did work, mostly.

Her Vincent had been a good example of the way the system should work. He only spent ten weeks in internment before being certified safe and sent home on medical leave. He'd needed months of additional practice to truly master his new minor talent for shaping organics, but Mary Ellen had been there for him.

Living off the meager rollover stipend hadn't been easy, but oh, they'd had such fun while Vincent was busy learning. They'd laughed together over absentminded alterations to furniture and clothing, and she still missed his ability to change the colors of cut flowers.

Not everyone was forgiving. He'd lost his job over a minor incident soon after his medical furlough ended. No one admitted it was a factor, of course, but everyone knew. Mary Ellen had helped him get through that crisis too. They'd gotten through all the troubles together.

If he'd been left on his own, he likely would have ended up bankrupt, in jail, or dead. That made Mary Ellen worry about the people who didn't have anyone.

Most people had family to help them get back on their feet and headed down a new road, or friends willing to take them in. Some belonged to tight communities that took pride in looking after their own. But a few always stood alone at the camp gates on release day.

Some people lost everything else when the universe bestowed powers on them. For them, the sponsorship program was a life saver, giving them new connections and a solid foundation on which to build a new life. The more Mary Ellen considered that, the more she felt inspired to help others navigate their difficult life changes.

All the same, it *would* be a lot of work. So much bureaucracy to navigate, classes to take, dossiers to review…putting a few more hours into her current volunteer work would be easiest. Easy had its appeal, especially after the nights when her aching joints wouldn't let her sleep, and on the days when she was just too tired to finish tasks she'd done easily for decades.

There was merit to the middle road, too. Making contact with new groups would only be socially exhausting, not physically taxing, and it would still get her out more, *doing* more. Maybe she simply needed a change of pace.

After weeks of dithering, she opened the news one morning to a lurid headline: FATHER AND SON SLAUGHTERED, MOTHER DISOWNS HER MURDEROUS OFFSPRING. The family name of an ex-student leaped out at her from the story beneath.

She'd taught Jesse Wakefield her last year before retirement. She'd *seen* Jesse a few weeks past, weaving drunk across her driveway, carrying signs he'd stolen from other people's lawns. He hadn't been perfect, but he'd been a good boy all the same. Now he was dead at his younger brother's hand.

Johnny Wakefield had just turned fourteen. Despite the dramatic headline, he would not face prosecution. First, he hadn't meant to hurt anyone. Witnesses were adamant on that point, and over a hundred people had seen the disaster unfold. Second, no court could deliver a steeper penalty than the death sentence he already faced.

He'd rolled early. That was a tragedy in its own right. The average age for a normal rollover rarely dipped below forty-five. When power came earlier than that, death followed soon after. Adolescent bodies simply weren't mature enough to handle the strain. Johnny's chances of dying before he saw his next birthday were one in four, and no early-onset rollover victims survived much past twenty.

The newspaper made a point of mentioning that Johnny had taken his first R-factor test a few months ago. Mary Ellen admired the subtle editorial touch. No one wanted to be accused of fearmongering. The authorities wanted people to remember that these cases were rare. There was a system. If this accident hadn't happened, Johnny would have started Positive Living summer classes next week, and he should have had years to build a career around the possibility of a mid-life shift.

There was no cause for worry. The system worked—except when it didn't, when a child had to grow up in an instant.

In an additional cruel twist of fate, early onset victims tended to roll into the most destructive powers. This case had been no exception. Johnny's lethal T-series power had manifested without warning while his family was attending a youth baseball game.

The witnesses said he'd looked like a human explosion, blood and flesh spraying everywhere as he transformed from an average teen boy into an eight-foot tall, clawed, fanged, armored behemoth. No one could have predicted it, and no one could hold Johnny responsible for what happened next.

He'd panicked, blinded by blood and the pain of a near-instantaneous changeover, disoriented by incomprehensible reports from new senses. He'd been staggering and flailing with uncoordinated limbs strong enough to smash concrete, crashing into things with armored skin harder than steel—and he'd killed four people without ever knowing they were there.

There was a standard procedure for handling hot rollovers in public spaces. *Give the subject experiencing rollover room to move, clear bystanders from the area, keep your distance, call the DPS hotline.* Every public school teacher knew that sequence. The school district mandated annual emergency drills.

The ones who had died during Johnny's rollover hadn't kept their distance.

Mary Ellen could read between the lines. Jesse, the dead brother, had always craved attention. He always had to be in the middle of the action. Like son, like father, she suspected, and like the other two dead men, they hadn't questioned whether intervention was the best option.

That combination of pride and altruism had cost them their lives, but a child would pay the price in guilt for the rest of his short life.

Mary Ellen couldn't blame Johnny's mother for turning her face away from her son. Well, she *could*, but she refused to allow herself the luxury of judging another woman's decision, one made in the throes of unbearable grief. The thought of what Johnny was going through all alone was what broke Mary Ellen's heart.

"Poor, poor, boy," she murmured, and Snazzycat meowed at her from across the room. "Silly cat, not you. You're a girl."

As Mary Ellen continued reading details, her vague yearnings about sponsorship solidified into confidence. *This*, her heart whispered. *This is what you're called to do.*

Early-onset rollovers would need an extra helping of gentle firmness during their transition phase. Her particular skills would be perfect for that.

Right now, Johnny should have been getting ready to attend his summer school classes, learning the practical aspects of various power types, and getting coached on the social and economic complications of R-factor diagnosis.

Instead, he was sitting in an internment camp surrounded by people three and four times his age, struggling to master a body nothing like the one he'd grown up in. Life wouldn't get any easier after that. Once he had basic physical control, he would be conscripted into the military long enough to be trained in ways to wield that powerful body safely in society—and he would have to stay enlisted long enough to pay back society for the cost of that training.

His path was set, but there were pitfalls aplenty along the way. What would he do during the interval between internment and military training? Who would teach him all the little life lessons most rollovers learned years before they came into power? Where would he go?

He would need someplace to call home. She had just the place.

Inspired now, she sorted through paperwork and found the sponsorship application she'd been ignoring. Time to turn it in and get the ball rolling on her licensing and training. When the time came, she wanted to be ready.

———

The local Public Safety office didn't know what to do with Mary Ellen. She could tell that much from the repeated rejection letters she received over the next two weeks, from the multiple forms stamped "DENIED," from the impatience in the voices of the switchboard operators who forwarded her daily calls to voicemail boxes of officials who never called back.

The rejections came without explanation, but she didn't need one. It was common knowledge the Department of Public Safety liked sponsors that fit a certain profile, and she didn't meet those unwritten standards. The Department liked couples, preferably young, white, heterosexual couples with school-age children, and most preferably pairs who both had positive R-factor tests.

Vincent had been gone these few years now, and Mary Ellen was as null as a zero. That was enough to unofficially bar her from helping others adjust to the unsettling changes she'd helped her husband learn to accept.

Never mind it was illegal to discriminate based on age, race, sex, or R-factor status. Sponsorship was an unpaid position, so the DPS could claim exemption from the employment laws. They gave the substantial room & board stipend to friends and families who knew the right people, and everybody knew their decisions were final.

Mary Ellen Coby was not everybody. She hadn't wasted the years spent navigating the administrative systems of the local school district. She knew exactly how to spike the wheels of a smooth-running bureaucracy.

It took only one a letter to her state representative—copied to the editor of the local paper, and typed on the letterhead of an ex-student who currently argued cases before the Federal Supreme Court—to get the ball rolling.

The Department's local Agent–In-Charge called to assure Mary Ellen that all volunteer applicants were given full and objective consideration, and that his staff had assigned her a case reviewer. A few minutes after that call ended, someone from the reviewer's staff called to schedule a convenient time to discuss options.

Mary Ellen dressed in her best business suit on the day of the interview and brought along a tray of fresh-baked lemon bars. Some people said baked goods made a woman look too motherly, made her easier to dismiss. Those people had never tasted Mary Ellen's lemon bars. The lucky recipients never forgot.

One of the receptionists working the front desk at the local Department offices had been another of Mary Ellen's students, maybe twenty years past. The woman exclaimed happily at the sight of the platter, and after the offering was whisked away to an employee break room, Mary Ellen was given a brisk hug of greeting and personally escorted to the administrative wing.

"Good luck, Ms. Coby," her student whispered. "I read about you in the paper. My money's on you."

The encounter warmed Mary Ellen's heart and gave her hope. Nothing else about the offices encouraged optimism. The walls were dingy white, and all the fittings had a worn, dirty look as well. Those signs of apathy and institutional neglect made her sad for the people who worked in such a sad environment.

The man waiting on the other side of the bullpen desk peered at her over the tops of sturdy reading glasses. He saw Mary Ellen seated and asked the usual visitor comfort questions—water, coffee, something else—like a perfect gentleman, but when she declined, he returned to his own side of the desk with obvious relief.

Once secure behind his defenses of paper and electronics, he tapped on a keyboard and consulted a screen.

Mary Ellen knew stalling when she saw it. "Where do we start?" she asked.

The man's mouth twisted up into a little moue of disapproval. "I am afraid I'm going to disappoint you, Mrs. Coby. You were only granted this interview to beg you to please stop applying. You simply do not meet the minimum standards. There is no way around the safety and privacy regulations. Your persistence is becoming an embarrassment."

"Why?"

"Excuse me?"

"Where do I fail? Lay it out for me. All legislated regulations are a matter of public record. I've read them all. Don't insult my intelligence. What *specifically* disqualifies me?"

She had seen people look less hurt when kicked in sensitive bits of their anatomy. His mouth worked again as he chewed over his answer. "It's a complicated issue, Ms. Coby—may I call you Mary Ellen?"

"You may not." He hadn't even introduced himself, and he wanted to use her first name? Not likely. She arranged her gloved hands atop the clasp purse in her lap and examined the sign on his desk. Glen Thacker could use a lesson or two in manners.

She had a different agenda today. "You may refer to me as Mrs. Coby, *Glen*, and you may now explain the rejections. I see advertisements and news stories about the sponsor shortage everywhere I look. I'm stepping up. Your refusal to make use of a willing resource makes no sense at all."

"But, um—" Glen pulled at his collar with one hand and petted some papers with the other. "I'm not sure how to say this, Mrs. Coby. Transition sponsorship is a complicated process and a major commitment of time, resources, and emotions. There are plenty of other ways you can help out R-factor citizens in need. The volunteer shortage is widespread. We have positions open in any number of suitable areas. We use a matrix of factors, not a checklist. I don't want to trouble you with a lot of boring statistics—"

"Trouble me," Mary Ellen said. "Please. In detail. I am a certified public accountant and hold a teaching license for grades six through twelve. Go right ahead and lay out the points one by one. That way I can address the shortcomings."

The polite ultimatum silenced him for a good thirty seconds of pointless paper shuffling. His desk was a mess. Vincent would not have approved of him at all. At least he hadn't said, *You're not poz, you wouldn't understand.* He might be timid and untidy, but he wasn't a fool. Mary Ellen wanted to give him a chance to succeed.

When Glen looked up, his jaw was set. "Ma'am, you leave me no choice but to be painfully blunt. You're poor, you're old, and you're alone. The Department cannot risk injuries or other damages to sponsors or their property. Please, *please* listen to me when I say sponsorship is a bad idea."

She reached over the desk to pat his hand. "There, now. Was that so hard? Isn't it refreshing to be honest? You're afraid of a lawsuit. I do understand that."

He pulled back, looking wary. Definitely not a fool.

"I'd prefer *you* to listen to *me,*" Mary Ellen informed him. "My income is fixed, but I am not destitute. I have very few expenses. I admit I'm over the *recommended* upper age limit, but we both know you can't legally raise that as an objection. And as to being alone, statistically speaking, a boarder would make me less vulnerable to being victimized or dying in a health crisis."

"Errm," said Glen.

"If you would like to see the research, I can provide it."

"No, I—no."

They went around and around the issue until Glen threw down his last trump card. "I don't have the authority to approve anything. I have to run this by my supervisor."

Mary Ellen gifted him with a smile. "You do that. While you're pretending to discuss me, you might want to know I have my eye on a specific probationer. I plan to put in a request as soon as I pass the licensing test and field trial."

"Who?" Glen's tense expression relaxed into relief when Mary Ellen told him. "Oh. Well. That changes everything."

She'd thought it might.

She was a problem for the DPS. A lethally dangerous boy-giant whose family didn't want any part of his transition back to society—well, he was a problem too. Mary Ellen was giving the system an easy way to solve one problem with the other. Bureaucrats could rarely resist efficiency.

Glen was practically bubbling with glee when he returned from his chat with the application approvals in hand. Before Mary Ellen left for home, she was scheduled for testing and home inspection and put on an expedited list for a trial sponsorship. She was also reminded to put in her other request as soon as her license came through, and to flag it to Glen's attention.

"If you want that one," he said, "I promise you, we will make sure you get him."

She thanked him kindly and took her leave. Glen obviously didn't think she was still close enough hear him when he muttered, "You deserve each other."

But she did hear it, and she smiled.

———

THE BUS from Camp Auburn arrived at the transfer depot at the crack of dawn. Mary Ellen took a taxi and made arrangements for Johnny's transportation to her place with the local transfer agent.

The small group of outbound travelers, two men and one woman, waited silently on seats in the passenger lobby. Outside, a gaggle of children played tag around the few cars in the parking lot while two men stood nearby, hands in pockets, looking casual while they waited for the arriving bus.

When the vehicle pulled in and discharged its riders, there was no mistaking which one was Johnny. He was half again as tall as the man who came down the steps before him and broad for his height. He moved awkwardly in his military-issue tan shirt and trousers. His feet were bare, but his head was covered by a peaked cap.

His jaw had a ferocious under-bite, leaving the tips of his lower fangs pressed against chapped lips, and he wore a pair of full-wrap sunglasses.

Most people looking at that massive body would never know he was only a fourteen-year-old boy. Mary Ellen found it impossible to see him as anything else, watching how he moved, the way he watched everyone else.

There was a certain way young adults carried themselves when they desperately wanted to be seen as *all grown up*. The message they shouted with their bodies— *don't mess with me, I know exactly what I'm doing*— was raw and brash, and Johnny was broadcasting it on all channels.

It always reminded Mary Ellen of the way Snazzycat looked right after she fell off the couch or smacked into a wall after chasing shadows: fear and embarrassment disguised as dignity.

Two women decamped from the bus after Johnny. The driver who opened the luggage compartment handed over suitcases to them, but he let Johnny retrieve his own bag, a duffle built to his massive scale.

One woman's homecoming began with hugs from three of the children and ended with an exuberant kiss from their father. The other woman was met with quiet, uncomfortable reserve from husband and son, followed by uncomfortably stilted conversation.

Mary Ellen's charge looked around the parking lot. His gaze passed over her, came back. Away, around, back to her. The mirrored lenses of his glasses reflected her tiny body, wrinkled skin, squinty eyes. His body language wasn't subtle. He was unimpressed.

She wasn't here to impress him. "You're Johnny Wakefield, yes? I'm Mary Ellen Coby. I'm your sponsor, so you're coming home with me."

He ducked his head. Mumbled. The sound vibrated through Mary Ellen's sternum and ribs, it was so far down the frequency scale, but the volume was too soft to be intelligible.

"What was that? Speak up, young man."

"That isn't my name anymore," he said, louder. The defiant, lisping words were slightly garbled. Mary Ellen made a mental note to contact a speech specialist for the boy. He went on, "I don't know if I have a real name. My intake forms just say JD413. Mom said I was dead to her and left the name space blank."

And then the internment staff had assigned him a *label?* That had to be one of the saddest things Mary Ellen had ever heard. "You are a person, not a number. I'll help you get that straightened out. What do you want to be called?"

He shrugged. "I don't care."

That was a whopper of a lie. Mary Ellen folded her arms across her chest. She could come up with nicknames all day long. "Pick something. Jay? Jaydee? Four-thirteen? Jade?"

The boy held out longer than most of her students would have lasted, but he caved when the list got to Lucky Jay. "Those are all horrible. Everybody in the dorm called me Jackass. That's fine by me."

He meant that, too. There was no accounting for a teenager's sense of humor. Maybe she wouldn't file a cruelty complaint against Camp Auburn after all. Just the same, she did have limits.

"I am not calling you that. Jack it is. You can pick a legal name when you're ready. I'll get you the paperwork."

Once again, he did that look-up-over-around-and-down-again maneuver, obviously hoping to see someone else, and just as obviously trying to hide his disappointment behind attitude. "So, I have to go with you? You're my guardian?"

"No, I'm your transition sponsor." Mary Ellen squelched annoyance at the camp staff who had clearly not prepared this boy for anything. "You're legally an adult. There's some complicated DPS regulation regarding internment and age limits, so you got emancipated whether you wanted it or not. I'll be giving you a place to live and offering you some guidance until next month when the Marine Corps takes you in."

"Maybe. If I live that long."

His nickname suited him. He was aiming to shock. Bad news for him, it took a lot more than the mention of mortality to shock Mary Ellen. "Yes, *if*," she said. "Do you want to spend the rest of your life standing at a bus station?"

The sunglasses were quite effective at hiding his emotions, but his head tipped to the side, and the confusion came out in his voice. "Um. No?"

"Glad to hear it." Mary Ellen took his thumb in her hand and tugged his arm. "Come on, then. Let's go. You won't get any younger standing here."

There was no moving him. She might as well be yanking on a tree branch.

He frowned, which made his teeth show more. "Maybe I don't want you for my sponsor."

Now, that was heartbreaking. It might sound like rejection, but it was rooted in trauma and pain. The boy desperately needed to feel like he was in control of something. Better to push away everyone than ever face the agony of being rejected again.

He needed the power of choice. Mary Ellen could work with that. Knowledge was power, after all.

She pointed to the waiting specialized taxi. "That's your ride. Either you come live with me, or the driver will take you straight to the nearest Marine barracks, where they'll throw you in a secure holding cell to wait until a new training cycle begins. Your choice."

Jack gazed thoughtfully at the truck for a full minute. When Mary Ellen tugged hard on his arm again, he allowed himself to be led over to it. The springs creaked as he climbed into the covered bed and settled on the single bench seat.

"You sit right there and make up your mind," Mary Ellen told him. "Take as long as you need. The ride's prepaid, and the driver has my address. I hope I'll see you at home."

Home. That was the lure she threw out, and she baited the hook with a smile. "I made cookies."

————

THE TAXI DROPPED Jack off at the end of the driveway. Mary Ellen stood at her front door and watched to see what he would do. He stood there, bag in hand, looking hopelessly lost or tremendously belligerent, depending on perspective.

She marched out to meet him, took hold of his thumb again, and led him down the drive to the back of the house. "This is where you'll be sleeping. I hope you like it. I worked hard to make it comfy."

His shoulders rose and hunched, and his eyebrows came down in a ferocious scowl. When his lip curled in disgust, fangs flashed, top and bottom. He took off the sunglasses and squinted at it. "That's a garage."

"Well, yes." She hit the little remote button to raise the

rolling door. "Where else? I can't have you in the house, can I?"

"I don't want to sleep in a filthy old garage."

"No?" Mary Ellen elected to ignore the insult to the perfectly clean building. "Where do you want to sleep?"

"In a bed, in a bedroom. Like a normal person."

She wanted to cry, hearing that, but she wasn't here to be nice, she was here to be kind. "Look at my house, Jack."

He looked at her instead, and his bloodshot, red-rimmed eyes boiled over with resentment and hurt. Mary Ellen gave back prime Teacher Glare and used her Pointing Hand, a gesture perfected during thirty years of teaching fractious, distractible little boys.

"Look at it. It isn't large, so it won't take you long."

He looked.

"That house was built on the cheap after the war. You're as big as my dead husband's old Buick, I expect you weigh more, and you have two feet, not four tires. If I drove a car into my living room, it would likely end up in the basement along with my couch, the dinette, and the sideboard, although that last one would be no loss. I despise that hunk of wood, but it was a tenth anniversary gift from Vince's mother, so he never would never hear of replacing it. He hated the ugly old thing too. The cupboard, I mean, not his mother, although she was a horrible old bat if I do say so. And I do. I'm only being honest."

She stopped there, recognizing the signs that she'd wandered far off-topic.

Jack's mouth was hanging open, and he had the same glazed expression Mary Ellen's daughter-in-law got when she visited and conversation went somewhere unexpected.

Mary Ellen waved away the point. "Never mind that. You want to wreck my little house, by all means, walk in the front door and put a foot through the seventy-year-old plywood. Or the kitchen door. They're both unlocked. Duck, please, so you don't bang your head on the lintel."

The look on Jack's face was nothing short of pitiable. "I forgot about the live weight thing. We had a class, but I forgot. I didn't think about breaking things."

"Oh, honey." Mary Ellen patted the back of his hand. "That's a luxury you'll never have again. You have to learn to think first and always."

"But I don't *want* to." The whine came out in a basso rumble so deep it made Mary Ellen's bones shiver, but it was still the fretful, plaintive complaint of a child.

Her heart ached for him hard, but this was not a time for comfort. "You don't have to stay. Public Safety would still be happy to drop you in a holding cell until the next class of USMC R-Basic opens up."

His eyes narrowed, and the fangs showed again. He didn't like that option, and no wonder, but he didn't have a choice until he earned full Public Safety certification. Which wouldn't happen until a full year's time in the Marine Special Battalion.

This was a hard lesson, but the sooner he learned it, the easier the road would be down the line. "If you'd rather have a place to call home before you go into training—and after, whenever you're on leave from the Corps—you'll take this garage and pretend a little gratitude. I don't insist you feel grateful, but manners matter."

His gaze swung from the house to the garage, to the perfectly adequate bed built to spec for an average T-series, the little bookcase, and the oversized steel frame chair with one of her crocheted quilts over the back—and then settled on her again.

"Okay, I guess."

She raised eyebrows at him and waited. Manners mattered.

He rubbed the corner of one eye with his knuckle and

sighed so hard the moving air ruffled Mary Ellen's dress. "Thank you, ma'am."

"Better. And you're very welcome."

He picked up his duffle bag and carried it into the garage.

Mary Ellen walked after him and showed him the button for the rolling door and also the hook for the remote. "After you've rested and unpacked, come to the kitchen door and I'll go over the house rules."

She was halfway back to the house when he called after her. "Missus Coby?"

When she turned, he was standing there in the shadow of the garage door, shoulders drooping, both arms cradling Snazzy against his chest. The cat fawned against his shirt, shedding orange, black and white hairs all over it.

"Oh, dear," Mary Ellen said. "That's Snazzycat. She must've snuck inside again. She's been curious about the new furniture since it arrived."

"What should I do?" The boy's voice rose to a panicky squeak. Snazzy rolled over, the shameless flirt, and waved a paw at his face.

"That depends. Do you like cats? If you don't want her in your room, shut the big door and set her down outside the small one. I'll get some treats from the house."

"No, please. I love cats, but you should take her away." He stepped forward hastily, offering up the cat in both hands, and the truth came out. "I picked her up before I thought. I didn't —I don't—I don't want to hurt her."

This, too, was a lesson. Jack could not be responsible for the whole world being breakable. Snazzy squalled, indignant about being dangled at arm's length.

Mary Ellen caught Jack's eyes, met his fear with all the confidence she could muster and then some. "Snazzy is a big girl and can take care of herself. Don't you worry about her."

As if to prove the point, Snazzy dug her back claws deep into Jack's tough skin and used the leverage to squirm loose.

Once she was standing free atop Jack's hands, she looked disdainfully at the long drop to the ground and walked right up Jack's arm to stand on the boy's shoulder.

There, she settled in. Her claws flexed, and she started purring. Jack went somewhat cross-eyed trying to look without turning his head.

"See?" Mary Ellen said. "She's fine. Unless you hate cats."

"No'm. She's soft. I'm—I—never mind."

I'm still afraid, he'd almost said. He didn't have to admit it. Mary Ellen knew.

"Sit yourself down," she said. "I'll close the door for you and be right back with cookies and milk. And cat treats, for later when you want some privacy and need to lure Snazzy to the door."

"I don't want to be any trouble," he said, and if his voice cracked and wavered, Mary Ellen would swear on her deathbed she hadn't noticed it. The confession was about so much more than sitting down and resting while someone brought him a snack.

"It's no bother at all," she assured him.

He slumped in the chair with Snazzy curled up against his chin, and he scratched the cat behind the ears like a pro, using just the veriest tip of one nail. "I just want to do good," he said in a near whisper.

"I know, dear." Mary Ellen patted the boy's knee. "And you will. Trust me."

She would see to it.

CAMPFIRE

An all-new Rollover Files story! This tale expands on the Public Safety protocols mentioned briefly at the end of the second story in the mosaic novel Rough Passages. It takes place during the years after the events of The Sharp Edge Of Yesterday.

———

```
INTERNAL USE ONLY
DPS Unit TO94 Permanent Closure Report
Appendix C: Selected surveillance audits
supporting reclassification, read into
evidence during the Board Review. SEE ALSO
Appendix F: Historical Incidents re: TO94

DPSOXXXXX4594
CA-TRANSCRIBER SURVEILLANCE DUMP BEGINS:
09MAY2010
1315HOURS LOCAL
```

HELLO, and welcome to Campfire Island! I'm Samantha, the official orientation guide, and you're Arrival Number 1192, which is a pretty important bit of trivia you'll learn about later. Move to that green painted circle, and Transit will teleport your personal kit to the accessory pad down here—and there it is!

Congratulations, your transfer to Terminal Outpost 94 is complete.

Sorry there isn't more of a welcoming committee, but they never give us much warning. They being the Department of Public Safety, obviously. There's a long triple blast from the warning siren five minutes before Transit, one final blast before the 'porter does their thing, and then boom. Newbie time.

Climb on down from the arrival scaffold, it's too hot to stand around in the full sun this time of day. We're right on the equator and—whoop, careful. Dignity is the first casualty of rollover, am I right? Good thing sand makes for a nice soft landing.

Do bits of you always flake off when you move? It's like you're covered in bark or lichen or something. The texture is pretty, like coral, what I can see of it under the ugly Extremis coverall the DPS issued you.

Sorry I didn't try to catch you, but it isn't safe. I'm not wearing this skimpy white outfit because my bony ass looks good in it. My skin's hot enough to fry eggs. Extremis cloth is the only material I can wear that doesn't go foof immediately, and it only comes in white. Or translucent, if it's thin enough. Even that doesn't last long, so I only cover the essentials. They're impossible to requisition, too. Once you get some clothes you like, or stop wearing clothes, I'll gladly barter you something for that coverall or the extra they packed into your Arrivals kit.

Anyway, I'm a pyrokinetic. Don't ask me to prove it. Lack of control was the sin that got me labeled Unsustainable and exiled here.

I can see how you earned the designation. Guess we won't be doing the "what's your name, where are you from" routine, you not having a mouth and all. Or a nose. Oh, dear. How long will you last if you can't eat or drink or…breathe? You must be breathing, right? How long have you been like this? Can you hear me?

You're acting like it, but I don't see ears, either, and that stuff all over your skin must be thick since there's bolts holding that thing on your arm. Is it a heart monitor? Careful, let me get closer for a better look—hey, is everything I say coming up on the screen? It is!

A transcriber, huh? That is sweet tech. Very science-fiction-y. So you can't hear or speak, but you can see. Oh! Words in a new color! That must be you?

Good thing I brought my reading glasses with me. Yes, magnifying glasses on a steel rod, otherwise I'd melt them. Hold up your arm, please.

<I can feel vibrations. If I pretend I'm talking, this thing makes the words, but it takes forever slow. My name is Eleanor Hemmings, and I feel sick. I rolled weeks ago, they reassigned me today and sent me here. I hate this. I hate everything. >

You poor thing. Of course you do. And of course you feel sick. The trip here hits everyone hard. Doesn't matter what kind of teleporter is in charge of the transit. It's the distance.

I can call for help if you need to be carried. No?

Come this way, then. There's a spot where you can sit and rest. Do you know sign language—er, you do still have fingers? It's hard to tell with all those lumps.

Whew, good. Not much dexterity, though. Pity. And that thumbs down is no, you don't know sign language? Okay, then. Orientation is mostly me talking, but here's a sign for *stop* if you've said something you want me to read, like questions, and I don't notice.

The green parts of your skin are paler than a few seconds ago, and the browns are going gray. Is that a reaction to the sun? Or nausea? You don't know? Not to worry. There's a bench with a nice view on the other side of this big, green blob of concrete.

This is the camp radio station. All the buildings here are blobs like this, built back in the Forties. We call the big ones huts and the little ones cabins. Not important. I'll explain more later.

Take it slow. It's okay to go at your own speed. Being angry is okay, too. I wish I could do more to help you walk, but I don't want to burn you.

That transcriber is handy, but you should still ask someone to teach you sign language. There are four other non-verbals on the current roster, so signing is considered polite. People like teaching other people things, too. It's a way to pass the time.

I think your skin is reacting to the sunlight. The colors are getting brighter again. The little lumps in the cracks shimmer like gems, too. Pretty.

I will keep mentioning your appearance, by the way, and I won't apologize for it. Poz-A and proud isn't just a slogan here. It's a way of life. Radical acceptance means talking openly about things that make nulls uncomfortable, like our bodies. The sooner you get used to it, the better for everyone.

Don't flap your arms at me, I'm serious. Unsustainable is a big umbrella term, but dramatic physical changes are typically part of it. I'm an outlier, looking null like I do. I'm an outlier in a lot of ways, to be fair.

A few more steps. Your mobility isn't great, but it could be worse. Number 1106—that's Esteban Coolidge—he showed up in a big canvas tank full of water and nearly boiled in the sun before we got him down to the beach. Not sure when you'll meet him. He prefers the deeper waters outside the reef and only comes in for supplies. And to help in emergencies.

Here you go. Shade is all these palm trees are good for, they don't give us bananas or coconuts or figs or anything useful, but they do look pretty and keep the bench cool.

Head down, between your knees. We keep a bucket under the bench in case of vomiting, although you won't need that. You rest. I'll grab your dossier and bags and be right back.

BREAK

Back in no time as promised, bag and DPS file both intact. Three cheers for Extremis lamination, am I right? I hope you don't mind, I've been looking through the paperwork. It's the easiest way to get to know you, especially since you can't tell me anything.

Once we're done with Orientation, I can burn the file for you, or you can burn it yourself with a little effort. Or bury it, frame it as a souvenir, whatever you want. No one will ever ask for it again.

That's the one perk of landing in this particular Department of Public Safety camp. We are officially exempt from all the baloney. No daily inspections or curfews, no restrictive diets or physical fitness tests, no so-called adaptation therapists laying on guilt trips, no disgusting cafeteria food.

Folks who transferred from camps on the mainland say it's paradise. I say it's still a prison, there's still 24/7 orbital surveillance, but it could be worse. Let's see here...

You're only nineteen? Ouch. You're the first early-onset ever assigned here, as far as I know, so you're younger than the rest of us by thirty, forty years.

Keep that to yourself, is my advice. No one will ask, and I won't tell. No one will ever guess, not with that skin texture. Unless you want that bunch of old fogies to treat you like a child. Up to you.

You might've set a new record for physical mods, too. Photosynthesis and osmotic filter-feeding? Huh. I wondered how long you would last without eating, but it looks like you'll be fine. We're all about the sunshine, and the freshwater cisterns refill every month on the sixth, same day Transit 'ports in the rest of our supply order. Esteban has a portable immersion tank around somewhere if you need to soak—hey! I said, 'No touching!"

Oops. Didn't see you sign, "Stop." I was reading your file. What did I miss? All the words I see on your arm screen are mine—no, here come yours. Oh, dear. The time lag on this thing is horrible from your side. No wonder you're frustrated and angry.

<I'm embarrassed. I do mind. This is humiliating. I want to die and get it over with.>

No, sweetie, no. Living well is the only revenge we get. Thrive to spite them all. Mind what, though? Me reading your file? Hm.

Look, I don't have to ask permission to read it, full clearance is part of my Orientation job, but I am sorry for hurting your feelings. I try not to make things worse, but sometimes I fail. Nothing about what happens to us after rollover is easy.

I'm going to get you a slate from inside the comms hut. Then I'll see you writing down messages right away, and you can hit me with the slate if I get distracted or I'm being too annoying. You sit and enjoy the view. This is the highest point on the island, and it's gorgeous at sunset.

BREAK

Feeling better? I hope so, because we also don't have a doctor, just a hut stocked with medical equipment, supplies, and pathetic instruction manuals from like, 1950. All your colors look better. Brighter. May I join you at the end of the bench? Thanks.

I like sitting here because you can see nearly all the buildings on the island between the palm trees. Like a live map. People are peaceful from a distance.

I see you're writing on the slate, I'll wait.

Yes, the colored bumps are buildings. Most everything is

down at beach level except this radio hut. That and the Transit scaffold were built on the highest point, for safety.

The trio of big white cylinders over here are freshwater cisterns. The water pressure is gravity-fed, so don't expect much. The big yellow bubble is the medical unit—without a doctor— and the blue hut next to the scorched-looking palms is the community center.

<The colored bumps are buildings?>

I already answered that…oh, no, do any words you think come out on the transcriber? That might be more confusing than not having one at all. And awkward, if you're only thinking something private. Oh. Oh!

That's what got you exiled, isn't it? They made you into a walking audio recorder, bolted that thing on, and someone felt threatened by a thought they saw on your screen?

They set you up to fail. That makes me so angry for you. The DPS motto might as well be, "We make things worse pretending to make them easier."

Let me think.

Okay, look. Here's how we go on. I'll stop talking when you start writing or do something to get my attention—but hold off on showing me your slate until it shows up on your transcriber. Okay?

<OK>

That's better. We can make this work. Get someone to make you a cover for your screen so you can choose whether to show it or not. Your thoughts should be no one's business but your own.

Knowing the DPS, chances are good they're somehow still collecting your data, so make sure people know first thing. We all know we're under constant observation, but the more obvious reminders make some folks twitchy.

Sorry, I get worked up about privacy. Where was I? Telling you about the island, right.

Before you ask about the building colors, the Army engineers added dyes to the original concrete pours. They say they did it to prevent people from getting lost, but that excuse doesn't fly. No one gets lost on an island three kilometers long and two wide. I think they were using up bits of leftover dye batches. It's garish, but you get used to it.

This hill is artificial, too, lava raised up from the seafloor by some Army earthmover. That's why it's all rough and black under the top layer of coral and sand. They did good work. The path is a perfect spiral on a sweet grade. You wouldn't break a sweat even if you could sweat.

The four rainbow clumps of smaller bubbles are the residential neighborhoods. Four cabins in each color per grouping, the white bubbles at each end are laundry facilities—yes, yes, I'm stopping.

<I am so lost. Stupid. I can't remember all that. It's too much.>

You are not stupid. You don't need to memorize anything. There's no test. It's my fault you're feeling overwhelmed. I'm doing a bad job. It's been months since our last arrival. Over a year since the one before that. And like I said earlier, I never get enough warning.

I promise it's me, not you. You can do this. Wait one sec. There's an Orientation instructions binder inside. I should use it.

BREAK

Take this, I can't hold it long. On page one of Instructions For Orientation Guide—all in capital letters, pretentious as all get-out—is a recommended welcome speech. I was supposed to say all that right after you arrived. It's horrible and pompous. Skip it.

Page two, get-to-know-you topics. Bullet points for name, ID matrix and address preference, power series and rank, rollover story, all categories optional, etcetera and so on. We're past all that, it isn't import—OW.

I said you could hit me, I didn't say hit me hard. Let's see your question.

<You know all about me already. I don't know you. Not fair.>

That's valid. My dossier would've told you I'm Samantha Martindale, series and rating P1-W. You can see the parts about me being white, 165 cems tall, pushing 66 kilos, brown eyes, gray hair. 63 years old, birthday May 12, female, cis-het-demi, background hopelessly Midwestern, prior employment record long and boring. Financial middle management.

I was Arrival number 17. Back home in Cincy, I rolled hot —yes, literally, I never get tired of that joke, ha, ha. One thing led to another, and I woke up on the Transit pad here with six people standing over me arguing whether it was safe to touch me. It isn't, by the way.

Eleven years ago, that was. There were a lot more residents back then and a full complement of DPS support staff. Things changed.

Anyway, it's nice to meet you, Eleanor Hemmings. Sorry you're stuck here, but I hope you find some new friends and have some good times.

Elm? No? Old eyes, bad with handwriting. You prefer Ellie. Excellent. We're onto page four, Ellie. Of forty-three, but the last half is mostly charts and things.

<What's the trivia? About me being 1192?>

Save that question for the next person you meet. It makes a great conversation starter.

Speaking of meeting people, we're up to the fifteen-page personality assessment. They say it's there so you can be assigned quarters with compatible roommates. Hah. No tests for you. We have loads of empty housing. Outpost 94 was built for a population of four hundred souls. Your arrival puts us at one-forty-nine.

Pick a neighborhood, pick a cabin, it's that simple. They're all marked with a two-sided door sign, blue for vacant, white for occupied, showing names and phone code if the occupant's socially at-home. Some folks build their own shacks instead, some pair or group up, others—Esteban, Gina, a few more—live off-shore.

I live in a nice shady spot behind the radio tower. The breeze is nice, and the night sky is stunning. When I missing walls and a ceiling, I'll sit in the comms hut for a while, but all the buildings turn into ovens if I stay inside too long. I melted one. You'll know it when you see it.

Moving on. Rules, regs and curfews. Skip, skip, skip, we ignore all that. Requisitions process, setting up a Personal Allotment account, and recommending a budget? Yeah, no. Forget DPS play money, exchange rates, lists of disallowed materials and restrictions on consumption in general.

The PX—that big orange bubble—is communal. Honor system. Browse all you like, take what you need. It restocks itself monthly except fresh produce, that's weekly. I mentioned barter. The crafty folks exchange goods and services. There's a weekly fish bake—see the ash pit—and other events. There's a bulletin board by the PX. People make up excuses to party and post times and locations there.

The comms hut is shared access, too. There's a reservations clipboard. If you're craving something not on the official lists or available locally, there's a good chance someone here knows someone back home who can get it 'ported out. Come up the hill, make a call.

Page twenty-seven! Nearly done. I'm to escort you to the assigned housing, which means I'll guide you around until you find a cabin you like and make sure you can find your way to the PX and other common spaces from it.

Ready? Take the white shell path down the hill. No, you go first.

BREAK

That's it then. Cabin assignment, contents inventory, PX visit, and return to quarters, check, check, and check. I'd ask why you chose a cabin in a cluster with no other residents right now, but it's none of my business.

Any questions? No? Here's your official Orientation gift. Yes, crayons, sixty-four colors, all yours. Write your name on the doorplate when—if—you're ready to be social. A blank white sign means, "Leave me alone." That's local tradition.

It's also tradition that any time you want privacy, you wipe your name off. If you pick a different name, it'll be honored. If you move cabins, wipe the door *and* flip the sign back to the blue side.

Congratulations. You're oriented and ready to start this new chapter in the book of your life. I'll leave you to—what's wrong?

<You're leaving me alone here? You aren't going to introduce me to anyone?>

I could, but honestly, it's a bad idea. You'll find out why. There are much nicer people to socialize with. Put your name up and wait for folks to drop by. Or take a walk and introduce yourself to anyone you're comfortable approaching. Or keep to yourself. No one will judge.

Remember, they've all been where you are now, lonely, angry, and hopeless. No one ever forgets how that feels. There's no official psychologist, but if—when— you want to talk, it won't be hard to find people who'll listen. People who aren't me, I mean.

Unpack and settle in. I didn't see anything on the social board for tonight, so plenty of people will wander past to check your door. You're the biggest thing to happen around here in a long while. Ask for help unpacking or moving furniture, and you'll make someone's week.

If you want, I can check on you once I transmit the proper

Orientation Completed codes back to the mainland. No? That's smart. I knew you were smart. You're better off avoiding me now this official part is done.

I'm glad I got to meet you, Ellie Hemings. I hope the rest of your life is full of kindness and light. Make the most of every minute.

DPSXXXXX4594
CA-TRANSCRIBER SURVEILLANCE DUMP BEGINS
21MAY2010
1006HOURS LOCAL

Hi, Ellie. You want to use the radio? I'll get out of your way. Sorry it's so warm in here. People usually give a holler or walk extra loud so I can clear out before they arrive. I'll put in a bell for you or something. Directions are by the board, it's easy—sweetie, I can't leave if you stand in the doorway.

You want to talk? Fine. I'm waiting. Nice lanyard you've got for your slate. Cowrie shells? I guess you've met Esteban, then.

<You're a liar. Liar liar LIAR.>

I have not lied to you. Dishonesty is not among my many crimes. Calling me names isn't exactly encouraging me to stick around. Let me out. Don't make me go through you.

Stop waving the paper in my face before I ignite it by accident. Did someone talk you into delivering the hate mail? If they bullied you into it, I'll have to have a little chat with them.

<DON'T YOU DARE LEAVE LIAR. I WROTE BECAUSE YOU LEFT OUT ALL THE IMPORTANT THINGS IN ORIENTATION. YOU HAVE TO EXPLAIN BETTER>

I don't have to do anything, missie. Don't shout at me in all caps.

Fine, fine, I'll look at your paper. No, put it on the desk. Do you want to start a fire in here with all the electronics? I'd tell you to calm down, but that's generally the worst thing to tell anyone when they're upset.

Oof. You couldn't write bigger here? Paper is cheap. Where did I leave my readers?

Your skin looks amazing now, by the way, especially those new cobalt blue lines. The caftan complements them beautifully. Gerry must like you. He doesn't barter his fancy patterns to just anyone.

All the little shiny lumps are getting bigger, aren't they? I wonder if you're going to flower. Or drop seeds.

Stop flapping your arms, I can talk and look for my readers at the same time. Ah, they're on the table by the clipboard. Behind you. The long metal stick, remember?

Oh, look, it's in list form. That's handy. Number one, we're stuck here until we die. Yes, obviously. Where's the lie? I told you we're a Terminal Outpost.

<HOW WAS I SUPPOSED TO KNOW WHAT THAT MEANT?>

Camp identification has been part of the Primary Prep curriculum since the Seventies at least. Did you sleep through your public safety classes in middle school? Not my fault.

Who taught you that sign? Rude. I'll take that as a yes.

Look, it wasn't part of Orientation, but I'll run through the basics if it'll make you feel better. Pull down the red Admin binder on that shelf. The table of contents for the appendices is in the back. Look for "DPS unit types."

They're all defined, see? Camps for long-term residence, stations for temporary accommodation. Offices, administrative-only, blah, blah blah. Any unit based outside US territory is an outpost. International waters, mostly. Conveniently outside US legal jurisdiction.

Flip to the org chart. It looks like a big web of boxes connected by numbered lines. Those are page numbers for transfer instructions. Military, Retraining, Secure, Special,

Transitional, Terminal, and Vocational. Terminal is a dead end. One line in from every other box, none out.

I don't know how many Terminals there are. Unit numbering isn't sequential, so there probably aren't 94. I hope not.

Anyway, it wasn't a deliberate omission. I am sorry the news came as a shock. If you're done pouting, I'll move on.

Two, why do they call you the Executioner? I didn't know anyone did. Huh. That's a good nickname. Much better than the one Esteban came up with. As to why, I'd only be guessing —oops. That's the temperature alarm. The electronics are overheating.

Can we please go outside now? I promise I won't run away.

Don't forget your list.

BREAK

This little glassy spot between the tall palms is where I sleep. Home sweet hollow. Fine, stand in the sun if you want. I prefer the shade. Put a rock on that paper so it doesn't blow away in the breeze. Where was I? Three, wasn't it?

Three, the siren goes off all the time, but you don't always bring someone downhill. What happens?

It isn't all the time. It's once a month or every few months, and it hasn't happened since you got here, so I know someone put you up to asking that one. Jerks.

You're upset, so I'll tell you. Three different things happen.

One, not everyone makes it through the teleport. Most Unsustainables got shipped here directly after rolling hot and hard. That can make people fragile. The second group are the true Unsustainables. They survive Transit but have too many physical anomalies to last long. They self-destruct from internal physical conflicts within minutes or hours. I was afraid you'd be one of those, remember? It's usually easy to tell, and I don't make them walk down the hill. Third…

What did I say about the arm-flapping? Don't rush me, I'm trying to find words that won't upset you worse.

Did you sleep through Civics too? Remember the imprisonment exceptions for poz citizens who can't be effectively locked up, like high-level Tees, Strongmen, and prime touchie-feelies? A quick recap for context: the exception means they're executed if they're convicted of particular crimes.

The anti-death penalty groups lost all momentum when telepathic verification became admissible and false conviction rates plummeted. I'm mentioning it because lots of those death sentences are quietly commuted to Outpost assignments.

By quietly, I mean secretly. You won't find that information in any official binder. I had to make friends in the mainland underground community to confirm it. They say the average sentence is five to ten years, followed by relocation with a new Social Service ID built from birth up, which means they disappear, so there's no proof it ever happens.

I know it's true because a few of those convicts don't get regular Outpost assignments. Their crimes were bad enough to get them re-designated as Unsustainables, and they end up at Terminal Outposts.

Yeah, like this one.

I am not telling you which of your new neighbors were violent criminals before they came here, just like I won't ever share info from your file with them. Your stories aren't mine to tell.

None of them are monsters, if that's what you need to hear. None of the monsters make it down the hill. I sleep fine at night knowing that. I'll sleep even better knowing I have a wicked nickname.

No, don't hug me! Why do you keep trying that? I don't want you going up in smoke before I cross off the rest of your complaints. There are a bunch more things on your list to go over. Young people are so emotional.

Four, the DPS abandoned the island a year after you got here. It's your fault.

It's hardly abandoned, and that isn't a question, but it is true. I am the reason the island doesn't have any staff in residence.

Five, you murdered all the DPS employees.

Okay, no. I did kill some, but murder requires intent. I'm quite sure I told you my pyrokinesis is mostly uncontrollable. The day I arrived, which was the day I rolled, by the way, I warned the camp administrator what I felt during my onset event. I told everyone what would happen. They said I was overreacting and ridiculous. The psychologist said I was hysterical, attention-seeking, and exaggerating.

Enough about them. I won't speak ill of the dead.

The second administrator listened better. After that crew evacuated, the DPS left the rest of us to self-govern. We didn't expect them to keep sending new residents, but they do. Moving on.

Six, everyone says they don't know why our arrival numbers matter and to ask you.

Now *that's* a big fat lie. Most of them know. Estaban especially. Maribel, and Leelee. For pity's sake, Leelee's been here longer than me. They usually jump right in with the explanation—oh. Oh, no.

You told them how old you are, didn't you? Ugh. Now they're babying you. It's good you're making friends, but don't let people disrespect you. Keep asking. Someone will eventually 'fess up and tell you the story.

No, not me. I was very clear about that point back when you arrived. It's a bad joke, and explaining a bad joke only makes it worse.

No more pushy questions. I'm done being nice. Look at that paper burn. All gone, up in smoke.

I am not your friend. Remember that. Go away.

Wait. One last thing. Do me a favor. When you do hear the siren go off, whenever that happens, run to the beach, swim out as far and fast as you can. Esteban will tow you, if you reach him in time.

———

DPSXXXXX4594
CA-TRANSCRIBER SURVEILLANCE DUMP BEGINS
10JUN2010
14:55HOURS LOCAL

WHAT ARE YOU DOING HERE? Do I invade your cabin? I do not. I don't have walls or a roof, but it's the same principle. Let an old woman enjoy her lunchtime nap in peace.

Try again. All those shiny lumps covering your outsides make your signs hard to read. They aren't popping, huh? Some of them are the size of softballs.

Don't apologize for startling me. I'm not surprised. I heard the bell on the trail and got out of your way. That's why I'm cranky. It's a simple system. I stay out of sight, and no one violates my privacy. No one except you.

Next time I hear you crunching along like a glacier, I'll take a hike. You'll never catch up.

Don't stomp away, that was a joke. You're here, the damage is done. What's on your mind? Write big, I left my readers in the comms hut.

<Bernice explained the bad joke about my arrival number.>

Goodie for you. Knowledge is power. Are you waiting for an apology? You won't get one.

Looks like I won't have to worry about avoiding you much longer, either. You're already filing off gnarly bits to keep the transcriber screen clear. Pretty soon you'll be so overgrown you won't be able to walk. Or see. You're filing the edges of your eye sockets too, aren't you?

I'm sorry. I wanted better for you. I hope it doesn't hurt.

<I don't want an apology. Nobody hates you. You're wrong about that. I am okay. Nothing hurts.>

That's a relief.

My goodness, look at those buds shimmer in the sunlight! They're huge now. And so many colors. It won't make up for being entombed alive, but for what it's worth, you'll be a really pretty statue.

Are you scouting places to plant yourself? You could set up near the water tanks with a trickle tube, a nice view, and plenty of sun. You'll have to convince someone else to scrape your eye sockets clear, though. Thinking about it gives me heebie jeebies.

No? Then what do you want? Don't make me guess all day.

Oh, for pity's sake, another list of grievances? That looks like Maria's handwriting. She played secretary for you so she could add her own complaints, didn't she?

I don't know why I humored you last time. I'm not in a helpful mood today. Go bother someone who cares.

<You care. It's a letter from everyone. We all signed it. Even Maria. She kinda does hate you. Read it.>

Even if I wanted to, which I do not, I don't have my—you brought out my reading glasses. You are annoying, do you know that?

< READ IT>

Have you read it? No? Fine, then I'll do it, but only because you should suffer though it too. Listen to this drivel.

An Open Invitation To Our Volcano Goddess Ugh. How many times do I have to tell people I hate that nickname? It's culturally insensitive and wrong. I don't do lava, I do fire.

Where was I?

Samantha dearest, first guide and vigilant guardian, fire on our moun-

taintop, alpha and omega of our island lives, we do not presume to under-stand you. Death walks before you and behind you. Death sleeps in your skin. You are apocalypse made flesh, and you carry in your heart the ashes of a hundred-hundred souls.

We who are condemned to your care cannot comprehend that existence, cannot condemn your retreat to empty solitude between warm welcomes. We can only beg your indulgence and keep space for you in our lives.

We entreat you to look upon us with favor, o living inferno. Walk with us, not around us. Come down from your aerie. Bring your fire to our firesides, accept our acceptance, let us share our lives with you for however much time we have left.

Remember us when we are ashes on the wind.

Good grief. Whatshisname wrote that, didn't he? The S1-W from New Jersey with the ponytail? Used to be a screenwriter. I remember his name now—Hammond. Arrival 465?

Ha. I knew it. He thinks he's a poet, but really he's a chauvinist dinosaur, worse than Esteban, and I'm not talking about their age. Goddess. Hmph.

For the record, if people insist on nicknames, I much prefer Executioner.

Look, they send me one of these "Please stop being a weird lurker, come to the parties" things every few arrivals. Bonus points for fancy language this time.

Here's my usual RSVP: Thanks, but no thanks.

What, did you think I'd be grateful? Sweetie, no. I don't need saving. I don't lurk because they hate me. I lurk because I hate getting attached to people.

Please don't look so sad. How do you manage to droop when your skin is so rigid? Look, I'll make you a deal. I'll come to one Friday night bonfire if you—wait, did you hear that?

Of course you didn't.

I'm so sorry, Ellie. You need to run. Now.

This is no time to be signing questions at me. The Transit

siren is warming up. It's only ten feet away, on the roof up there, and it clicks a few seconds before—

OVERLOAD

OVERLOAD

OVERLOAD

SYSTEM SHUTDOWN

SYSTEM RESTART

```
DPSXXXXX4594
CA-TRANSCRIBER ERROR REPORT 10JUN2010
15:02 HOURS LOCAL
OVERLOAD SYSTEM RESTART
CA-TRANSCRIBER SURVEILLANCE DUMP RESUMES:
10JUN2010
15:03 HOURS LOCAL
```

— op wasting precious time on that stupid thing, the siren probably broke it—there. It's working again. Get out of here. Run. See my words? See me signing? *Run*. Why? Because if this new arrival is the one that triggers me, you'll die. You can't stay here.

It is not too late already. You have three, maybe four minutes. There's a chance you could make it to the beach in time. Esteban likes you, he'll wait until the last second before swimming out beyond the reef.

No, not much of a chance, but you have to try.

You know why. You want the gory details? There'll be a glow, then there'll be a pillar of fire, and then the only thing left moving on this island will be me and the plants, dead fish bobbing in the lagoon, and steam rising off piles of ash.

I don't want to be watching you when that happens.

And you don't care what I want. Great time to be selfish, Ellie. You don't want me to be alone? What a load of crap.

Whatever. Let's go sit on the bench. We can both look at the ocean, and you'll die with a nice view.

Tell you more about my power? No.

I am not ashamed. Don't throw my words back at me like that. I'm comfortable talking about it, I don't *want* to.

<I'll tell you a thing you don't know. The DPS told me they were sending me here for *therapy.* This stuff on my outsides didn't get thick until the doctors cut off the first crop of bumps. It felt like they were stuck, and I thought it would help, but everything grew back worse, and they dumped me here.>

That's—I want to say horrible, but that's the Department for you.

It is not my turn. I didn't agree to barter secrets.

Fine. Stop flapping. Anything to keep you from sulking for your last few minutes.

I'm mainly a typical P1 contact pyrokinetic. Blast-furnace hot to the touch, otherwise nothing special unless there are too many people around me. Then I go up like a…a bomb that only targets animals. It took two cycles to learn that, and a third to find out my threshold is dropping every time. Four hundred ten. Three hundred. Two twenty-five. One-eighty.

Yes, that's how many died each time. Not counting my office back in Cincy where I rolled. I've never asked how many died then.

There might be a math pattern, but I'm no scientist. Don't try to make it logical. There's no explaining why my power works that way, like there's no explaining why you're a living terrarium or why I don't burn up myself. That's how most pyros go, eventually.

Every time, I hope I'll die in the firestorm too, but no such luck.

Anyway. With the island population at one forty-nine, every arrival might be the one that triggers me. Sometimes ships ignore the warning buoys and get too close, and I feel pressure building up. This is probably going to be it.

I'm sorry. I wanted more time for all of you.

What are you doing? No—how many times have I told you, don't touch—I don't want—oh. Oh. Look at that. You're hugging me, and you aren't burned.

This feels so good it makes me want to cry. I haven't been touched in so long, and you're so big and solid. Can you feel me patting you through all that armor?

What did I say? Stop shoving at me. Why are you pushing me down? You want me to do what? Sign slower.

You're big and solid, I could fit underneath, between you and the sand—oh. You think you can contain the firestorm? What if you aren't fireproof enough—ow, what did I say about hitting? Fine, it's your funeral. Help me scoop a hole, I'll kneel in it.

There. That's as small as I can make myself. Go ahead and hug me tight, again, sweetie, as tight as you can. Nothing exposed. Blech. Sand in my face.

That's the siren click. I hope you're right. If you're wrong, at least I won't have to see you—-

OVERLOAD

OVERLOAD

OVERLOAD

SYSTEM SHUTDOWN

SYSTEM RESTART

SYSTEM RESTART

SYSTEM RESTART

DPSXXXXX4594 CA-TRANSCRIBER ERROR REPORT

10JUN2010

15:09 HOURS LOCAL

OVERLOAD RESTART FAIL

CONTACT LOST

REMOTE SYSTEM RESTART
ENGAGING EXTERNAL MICROPHONE
DPSXXXXX4594 CA-TRANSCRIBER SECONDARY
SURVEILLANCE BEGINS:
10JUN2010
15:18 HOURS LOCAL

No, I will not hold it. Maybe it's my fault it fell off, but are you seriously complaining about your bark being smooth and thin again? It's your assistance device. Balance it on top of the binder. Once you get a new note board, you can bolt it to that. Or wait until you thicken up and sprout seeds again.

Don't worry about it. If it gets bad, we'll ask Esteban to paddle us both within range of a shipping lane and wait until someone gets too close and sets me off. Problem solved.

Now hush. The newbie is here. We need to go meet them and get to work. Where are my reading glasses?

BREAK

Hi, welcome to Campfire Island! Sorry I'm late, it's been a weird day, and thanks for staying on the Arrivals circle until we got here. Transit gets cranky if you move before I press the acknowledgement button down here.

Anyway. I'm Samantha, the official orientation guide, and you're Arrival Number 1193, which is a pretty important bit of trivia I'll explain in a second. This is Ellie Hemmings. I'm training her as my Orientation assistant. She doesn't talk much, on account of not having a mouth, but you'll learn to sign. Everybody does.

Move to that green painted circle now, and Transit will teleport your personal kit to the accessory pad down here—and there it is!

Congratulations, your transfer to Terminal Outpost 94 is complete.

Excuse me, but I need to raid your kit for the backup Extremis coverall Transit always shoves in there. I would apologize for my appearance—by which I mean being naked—but I wasn't expecting to meet anyone today.

Sorry there isn't more of a welcoming committee, either, but there's a reason for that. It's a long story. I'm sure someone will explain. Someone not me.

Please open the binder for me, Ellie. Are these little flowery blobs going to follow you everywhere? They're adorable, but I'm afraid of what will happen if they get underfoot. I don't think they're fireproof anymore, or not yet, and—

You're right, I'm distracted. First things first.

Climb on down from the arrival scaffold, Arrival 1193. Or, yeah, fall down. That works.

You're fine, sit there in the sand until you feel steady again. Dignity is the first casualty of rollover. We've all been there.

Yes, Ellie, I do give the same speech every time. We can talk about making changes later. Let's all get through Orientation first. Hand me his file, will you? I hope this doesn't get awkward.

Good news, Gareth Simmons! You don't get to learn either of my nicknames today. Lucky you.

Lucky all of us.

Here's to new beginnings, right, Ellie?

Turn the page.

STONE AND SALT

This story is the most unsettled piece I've ever written. Like its protagonist, it isn't comfortable with labels or expectations. It's dark—there's pet death in the first paragraph—but it isn't horror, it's fantastical but doesn't follow a typical fantasy story arc. It went through five titles and a dozen markets before I gave it a home here. It's the capstone to this story collection because I love it to pieces, whatever it is.

———

THERE'S A LOOK THEY GET, right at the end, after the anesthetic takes hold, before the final needle goes in. Their gaze shifts beyond mortality as they slide into the final sleep before death, offering a glimpse of eternity to the careful observer.

It gives me chills each and every time.

End-of-life care is the hardest of all my duties as a veterinarian, but someone has to do it, and I'm better suited to the task than most. That's what I tell myself anyhow, on the nights when I can't sleep for the memories of those glimpses.

I might be lying to myself about that part, but I know one thing for certain: if I ever stop feeling a cold shiver of awe at life's passing, I will close up shop forever and let someone else absorb the heartbreak. There's such a thing as a calling, and I have one, but I didn't ask for it. I can think of a dozen other jobs I could be equally happy doing.

So can my parents. Giving up my practice would make both of them ecstatic, albeit for different reasons. My mother wants me to embrace the conventional life she rejected.

"Frankie, *baby*," she says, "you need to settle down and find someone to take care of you." Not that she's offering to do it. She's never taken care of anyone, not even herself.

My father thinks all employment is demeaning. Or as he puts it during my rare visits to him, (never him to me, oh, no) "Dearest child, you cannot reject me forever. You have magic in your blood."

That's true, but mortality is in my blood too. So I live in my mother's world, where death is a regular visitor, and I take care of everyone who lets me help.

I kneel beside the dog I'm treating tonight, and I stroke his head. His name is Donny. He licks my hand and wags his stubby tail.

Do not cry, I tell myself, but I know I will.

Donny is a terrier mix, seventeen years old, twisted with arthritis and half-blind from cataracts. Cancer has ravaged his body, and the ridge of his skull is a sharp line beneath my fingers. His ribs stand out beneath his wiry pelt. I watch until they fall and no longer rise, listen through my stethoscope until the unsteady heartbeat slows and stops.

Death creeps through the shadows in the room and takes him away.

"Farewell, fierce heart," I whisper. "Run free and swiftly. Green fields and wide skies await you on the far side of forever."

And yes, I'm crying. Donny's owner hands me his box of tissues, in a decorative cover ringed with little terrier silhouettes. He says one last goodbye, whispering through tears and scratching Donny under his chin. I help him undo the buckle on Donny's collar. The ID tags jingle as John crumples the band into his fist.

When I first met Donny, he was a puppy small enough to fit in one of John's big hands. John's last call to my emergency service reached me at two AM Sunday: Donny hadn't eaten in two days, he was crying and couldn't stand. Could I do anything for him?

Well, yes, I could. Now John and I stand together in the living room, with night pressing against the windows and Death lingering expectantly in the shadows.

We went over the mundane arrangements beforehand, so I know what John wants next. Yes, cremation, yes, please return the ashes—so he can bury Donny in the yard without worrying about scavengers—yes, he can pick up the ashes from the clinic, no, he doesn't want to call anyone to stay with him right now.

That last choice worries me. This close to the new emptiness in his life, John is vulnerable to countless destructive influences he doesn't even know are real.

A warning prickle runs over my skin. I meet John's eyes, and there's a cold glow growing in their depths, like the eerie light of an arctic midwinter sky. The room chills, air thickening with power.

Death wants to stick around.

Folding Donny's blanket around him takes but a moment. I stand with the weight of him as light in my arms as a newborn child, as heavy as the world.

"John." Names have power. I invoke his in my calmest voice. "I'm sorry. It's always too soon."

He waves off my words, but the bleak, lethal power in his eyes dims to helpless, mortal sadness. I exhale slowly, and the magical pressure in the room eases.

Litanies like the rote call-and-response of condolence boost life's power and solidify the barriers between the seen and the unseen. Rituals sketch boundaries around the infinite and help humanity fill the rifts it carves in their lives.

"We had a good run," John says. He runs his thumb over Donny's collar and sighs. "Thanks for coming here in the middle of the night. Are you sure I don't owe you anything?"

Power blazes through me like lightning. My feet root themselves to the earth.

This is the reason I build costs for euthanasia and related services into the fees I charge for other procedures. "No charge," I say through magic-numbed lips, and the paralysis lifts.

———

THE SUN IS RISING by the time I get home after dropping off Donny at the clinic. My little patch of suburban heaven boasts two bedrooms, a tiny lawn, and a detached garage. Three cats and an aging canary await my return and their breakfast indoors, but I sit and rest in my truck after parking in the driveway.

Light creeps into the sky in shades of gold and rose. The warm truck engine ticks quietly. A few sleepy crickets are still chirping, and birds are greeting one another. Summer heat seeps into the cab, smelling of damp grass, mold, and metal.

I scrape up the energy to face my responsibilities with thoughts of a shower, tea, and clean clothes and get moving. Two steps away from the safety of my kitchen door, magic like a touch of moth wings flutters against the back of my neck.

"You are needed," a rasping voice announces. "You will come."

The herald's declaration comes wrapped in suggestive power, urging me to ask *where?* or *how soon?* and trap myself into acceptance of the answer.

I bite back the impulse to speak. The effort brings sweat prickling to my skin.

This is my father's sense of humor at work.

Delays are meaningless to those living on the far side of reality where time runs differently, but he finds binding others to his will entertaining. In service to his wishes, the court herald routinely resorts to shock tactics and petty compulsions like these.

And I routinely indulge in petty defiance. "I'm needed a lot of places. Get in line."

"You do not command us." The herald emerges from in-between, stands ankle-deep in the nodding marigolds that border my kitchen garden. "We must stay until we deliver the summons."

Heralds aren't the weirdest living beings I've ever encountered, but they are in the top ten. They're collectives who share space and move as one, as unified as a school of fish. But as always when they come where mortal eyes might glimpse them, they've attempted to look human.

Their advance is jerky, as if each limb wants to go in a different direction. Eyes like hot embers glow beneath bushy brows, sizing me up. I return the favor.

Gray skin ripples beneath an illusion of satiny white livery, and their face isn't quite symmetrical. Worse, the number of eyes fluctuates from moment to moment. The mouth twitches into two mouths, then three, before settling back to singularity.

They won't fool anyone who gives them more than a passing glance, but it's the best they can do.

My father's herald is on the small side, no larger than me, and glamour takes energy to maintain in daylight. Already the sun is burning through their illusions and gnawing deep into their body.

Pops sends them in daylight because he knows I hate to see any living being suffer.

I concede the fight. "Deliver your summons and be released."

"Details are provided within." They offer a scroll dotted

with wax seals. Misty tendrils of magic drip from their long fingers and the embroidered hems of their skirt. The scroll sparkles gem-bright in the glowing dawn. "Give me your reply at once. The Squire requires it."

"You don't command me, and neither does the Squire." Not diplomatic, and not strictly truthful, but right now, after Donny, I am in a mood.

No, that isn't right. I am *angry*. Angry at life, angry at myself, angry I share any heritage with people who treat family, friends, followers, and possessions so much the same.

My father isn't the only one who treats others that way, but he's the only one I can safely defy.

I walk past the herald and up the three steps to the house, grabbing the scroll on my way. My house keys rattle in my shaking fingers. I find the one for the kitchen door. The dead bolt slides back, the steel door opens, and a step takes me across the threshold into relative safety.

The phrase *don't kill the messenger* whispers through my mind on an ashy breeze of guilt. I turn back.

The herald awaits my reply: stiff-bodied and fire-eyed, shedding magic like smoke in the sunshine. Magic can be cruel. They literally cannot leave until I give them an answer.

The marigolds sprout dark new leaves as I watch, already grown knee-high in the last few moments, and the green tomatoes on the vines behind them ripen to red globes. Garden magic at work.

Foliage rustles and shakes. The herald's fingers dissolve. They can't truly die on this side of the veils, but they can feel pain, and the world is eating them alive where they stand.

I can't bear to watch it, no matter how deep my rage goes.

"Give Pops this message," I say. "Don't wait up. I'll visit when I'm good and ready."

They depart sideways through one of the holes in the world. I grab my phone and call my mother.

———

"I want to come with you," Mom says over tea on Sunday afternoon. "What can it hurt? I haven't been over cloud and under hill in forever."

"No, Mom." This is not an argument I want to have, but I can't avoid it any more than the herald could've left without my reply. I swore to tell Mom whenever my father called me long before I knew oaths would bind me. To this day I'm not sure if she knew the consequences when she asked me to make that promise.

I suspect she did. Parents keep secrets from their children. Both of mine specialize in half-truths and manipulation.

"Please, Frankie." Mom smiles across the little table in her elegant living room. She leans forward to pour tea. "Think it over."

The pot wobbles in her frail hands. A drop of grass-green liquid falls onto the spotless white lace doily.

Steam lifts from my cup, a delicate porcelain thing so thin the sunlight makes it glow. It's new, evidence that Pops has been visiting. Creations from his workshops have a particular expensive-but-useless look.

The tea has a bright floral scent and tastes like lawn clippings. Mom flutters her fingers over a waiting plate of home-made macaroons and macarons arranged in a colorful display. "Have a cookie, dear."

The macarons look delicate and crisp, while ruby-bright cherries nest within the centers of the golden-edged coconut macaroons.

Macarons are my favorite cookie in both worlds. I choose a pink one, crunch the meringue between my teeth, and swallow. It sits like a hot lump of coal in my stomach.

Wild pigs will tear me limb from limb before I ask Mom if she offers me hospitality gifts to ensure my good behavior. I want to believe she serves me tea and cookies because nurturing me brings her joy, not because I'm my father's child and she thinks to trap me into a bargain.

I will never ask if she's trying to trick me. I am my mother's child too, and I want to believe the best of people. I do not let her control me, but if it's in my power, I avoid bringing her pain.

Every conversation between us treads a thin line between solace and suffering.

When I finish eating, I lean back against floral upholstery decades out of fashion. Mom could afford new things, but the one time I suggested it, she said she loves what she loves, and it's none of my concern. The rebuke stung worse than a slap. I will never bring it up again.

All of Mom's furniture is old but tended with love, every worn surface gleaming clean, every threadbare cushion plumped and tidy. Mom has the same well-preserved look. Her white, brittle hair is braided back in tidy lines, and fresh cosmetics protect skin as thin and wrinkled as crepe paper.

I move my tea cup to one side. "You can feed me all the cookies in the world, the answer will be *no*. I will not carry you over."

She can't go alone, which pleases me as much as it frustrates her. Those of mortal blood can only cross between worlds at certain places, and the thresholds are bounded by rules.

Returning to the world of one's birth takes only an act of will—each land welcomes back its own—but mortals cannot usually cross into magic without help. The spells require power as well as the full and conscious consent of both participants. That's not to say everyone plays fair. Many powerful beings who enjoy mortal company excel at spells of persuasion, seduction, and entrapment.

And then there's me. Among my collection of meager magics is one small but unique talent: the ability to carry others with me between worlds, consenting or not. I don't do it as a rule, but I can. Never say the universe has no sense of humor.

For the main part, though, only the willing cross, and only the willing remain. The problem is, Mom never *stays*.

Time runs differently here and there, and mortals gamble on every passage. Some come home young to find a span of lifetimes has passed, others accrue a debt of time that comes due on their return. Those risks should be a deterrent, but they aren't.

Don't eat or drink, the old stories warn, but some are cursed to endless yearning with their first breath of the magic-soaked air. Mom is one of them. She's also cursed with an unsettled nature. The changelessness she craves also drives her away.

I turn the handle of my teacup, controlling one aspect of life in place of things I cannot. Like my mother. "Mom, you know what would happen. You'll get bored or homesick and leave, and how many years would you lose this time?"

How many years do you have left? I don't ask it aloud. We both know the answer is, *Not enough*.

Strangers assume Mom is my grandmother, in her eighties at least. In my baby pictures, she looked like a woman in late middle-age. She was nineteen and headstrong when she ignored her grandmother's warnings and let an elegant, eldritch stranger lead her by the hand across worlds.

A single night's adventure cost her decades, and I'm all she got in exchange.

My great-grandmother came away from a similar trip with the same result. That's how the family came to have this land and our riches. It's why Mom knew to return to the threshold and call to her lover once her child quickened, and then again when she held a living babe in arms.

Returning to Pops' world was all she wanted. She was willing to give me to Pops if only he would take her too.

It should've been the easiest bargain ever. Children are rare and precious among my father's people. They do not steal babies, but they aren't above begetting them on mortals in hopes of breeding true.

Pops was ecstatic over the achievement of my conception. He wasn't as enthusiastic about the result.

I've never met my—cousin, I guess she would be. My great-grandmother's fairy babe was born rich in power, and her father took her far away and deep into the territories of greater power long before I came along. I hear she's happy and nothing like me.

Me, I am a child of the thresholds. My magic is as diluted as fresh water at the edge of the sea.

The way Pops tells the story, he refused Mom's bargain because I was too weak to survive childhood in his world. Growing up in the presence of greater magics would've washed the life out of me long before I matured into my own power. The way Mom tells it, she loved me too much to leave me to the care of others.

The stories aren't mutually exclusive. In either case, Mom has been over and back again twice since my birth.

Once, I let her take my hand and cross over with me. *Once.* I was eight and ignorant. Mom kept me that way on purpose. She fooled me once. Never again.

My father welcomed us both and begged Mom to stay. His kind rarely beg, but love has made fools of wiser men than him. I know Mom returned for my sake that time, because I was there.

I was homesick for my room and my school friends. No one warned me about the cost.

Love is strange. Mom loved me enough to sacrifice years of her life to raise me herself. Pops loved her so much he would have sacrificed me without a second thought to keep Mom there.

Only a night and a day passed here when we returned, but Mom lost a decade more.

Years after that, she persuaded one of Pops' courtiers to

bring her over. She came back crook-backed and white-haired that time, spilling tales of years spent with Pops and how he wept when she returned here because she missed me.

Every time I cross over to see my father, Mom begs to come along. She can't help herself. The place has seeped into her blood and bones. Now she plucks a macaroon from the plate and takes a bite of chewy coconut.

"Please, Frankie? If you take me, I'm sure I'll stay this time." She licks the lie off her lips along with the crumbs.

Has she forgotten I can see truth and falsehood? Probably. She loses more than years every time she goes over and back. Baking both macaroons and macarons is her attempt to hide a sad truth: she knows I like one of them but can't remember which.

It's worse for the mortals who stay behind. Their bodies remain immortal, but as time stretches far past their normal span, they become thin memories of themselves. They're the closest thing to ghosts I've ever seen.

"No, Mom," I say the way I always do. "I can't protect you from yourself."

"That isn't your job, dear. I'm a grown woman."

The rest of the macaroon disappears into Mom's mouth, and she smiles again. I have her eyes, people tell me. Brown and warm, and twinkly when we smile. Lately I haven't been smiling much.

"No. N.O. Don't try to follow me, either."

Mom brushes the crumbs from her fingers. "All right, fine. But you will call me as soon as you get back, won't you?"

"I always will." She'd made me promise that, too. The oath tugs at my center, knotting my stomach. "You'll hardly notice I was gone."

We finish our tea and cookies talking about other, easier things. After she hugs me goodbye, she plants a papery-dry kiss on my forehead. "I love you, baby."

"I know, Mom. I love you, too." The words feel like a curse, thick and sour in my mouth.

There is nothing more to say. I grab my backpack and leave from the back yard, down the old path into the woods.

———

Mom's house has been in the family three generations. My father is right about one thing: I don't need my job to make a living. There's a trust and annuities that far exceed my income. The fortune was founded on fraud, yes, but the leaves and stones in someone's bank safe were written off the books long ago, replaced by real profits from real investments.

There may be a moral in that story. I don't know. I don't hate being rich.

The groomed trail takes me through a carefully maintained parkland. Birdsong and the rustle of green leaves welcome me. Pale spring sunlight glows on new grass, and deep blue skies promise of hot summer days around the corner of time.

I breathe in the heavy sweetness of peonies and lilac, and when I lick my lips, I taste early roses. My favorite threshold sits beneath the wide, white trunk of a half-fallen beech tree whose crown is held aloft by a supportive neighbor. Before I reach it, I collect an armload of flowers.

One step and another through the doorway of living wood, and I go from here to there. Simple as that.

My first step lands with a splash, and muddy water flows over the top of my shoes. On this side of reality, clouds and chilly silence rule the day. Drifting mist swallows the upper branches of gray-barked maples and rough oaks. The quiet is a soft, soggy thing, the air empty of sound and thick with water.

No one will ever call my father subtle. Powerful, yes. Subtle, no. The weather far beyond his territory responds to his mood. Being forced to travel through storm and wrack is a common punishment for my little rebellions. He nearly froze me to death in a blizzard once.

Since then, I've been packing the latest in expedition gear when I cross over. Weather is weather no matter its source, and modern mortal textiles are damned close to magical. Dreary and dank is no challenge for waterproof boots. I break out a featherweight rain jacket and rain pants and continue my journey in total comfort.

Not far along the muddy path I find my way blocked by a masterpiece of a spider web. The spiraling lines of it stretch across six feet of open air, centered over the path and anchored high and low with sturdy threads to the nearest trees.

It is a tollgate as solid as any ever built on a mortal road. If I turn aside, I will find a host of obstacles—hillocks, windfalls, briars, and worse—steering me back to the trail, or into a bog, or over a hidden cliff, depending on the mood of the web's builders.

This bit of land answers to a swarm of pixies who love a good prank more than they love flowers—and they are total suckers for nectar.

Centuries ago, these pixies claimed the patch of forest near the gate so they could zip across to our side and nibble on wild rose petals and sip from honeysuckle blooms. My great-grandmother planted flowerbeds for them, gardens which were expanded by my grandmother and mother in turn.

They love our flowers, but they still charge for the privilege of crossing their land. Blood or bargain, either will do, but a price must be paid. That's the way things are, here. Every scrap belongs to someone. Everything comes with a cost.

Pops would clear a path for me through his patchwork properties if I asked. His word is law, and his goodwill governs all who answer to him, including even the pixies.

I never have asked, and I never will, because I enjoy disappointing him. Since I have neither the wit nor the muscle to fight my way across his territories, he assumes I degrade myself by bartering with lesser powers.

We are forced by our natures to deal only in truths, so secrets have a particular appeal. He has his, I have mine. This my oldest one: I haven't paid a single toll since my first trip here, the crossing I made by accident.

Back then, no one had told me I was different. I mean, I *knew*, but no one explained, or trained me, or told me about the rules of this world. Mom was and is a big believer in the protective power of denial.

I was well into the woods before I realized I had wandered into a whole new world. I know now that I was never in serious physical danger. No one outside Pop's court would dare harm the blood-kin of their ruler. Not permanently, anyhow.

But when the first creatures I met demanded payment for my passage, I was seven years old, terrified, confused, and utterly lost.

The pixies had expected a drop or two of blood, a taste of my father's power by proxy. Instead, I'd offered up every childish treasure in my school bag and pockets. Textbooks, comics, shiny stones, blue jay feathers, pencils, foil-wrapped chocolates—I doled them out one by one to my astonished audience, and when I saw how much delight every new item brought them, I dumped out the bag and told them to keep everything.

I was raised to share, and I liked making people happy. I still do.

By chance, my meager gifts gained me more credit than I could ever spend. Offering all I had with no expectation of a proper return—there is major power in that kind of gift.

I learned that later. Then? Pure luck. There is a magic to luck too, I suppose.

The legacy of that first exchange sways before me now, the letters of my name and a recognizable smiley face crafted in an arc of sticky, water-sparkled silk strands. Impossible not to smile at the sight of it.

"Good work," I say, and I tip my head back to look for the web spinners.

A drop of water falls directly into my right eye. Three more drops splash my forehead—one-two-three—targeted dead center. That makes my welcoming committee four pixies, with one of them new to their wings.

I grin at the gem-bright flickers hiding behind leaves. "A first flight, is it?"

An affirmation of dewdrops spatters down on me. I sweep a bow to the trees. "I offer my felicitations."

First flights are careful, private affairs. Being allowed so close to a vulnerable new pixie, wobbly and fragile, is a precious sign of the swarm's esteem.

Pixies are immortal, but they're ephemeral too, eternally cycling through life stages and recalling little of each previous incarnation. No one in this group would've been alive for my last visit, not in their current forms. Individuals come and go, but swarm never forgets.

Many people in my father's lands—especially the courtiers who thrive on schemes and plots—disdain pixies as frivolous. Pixie disinterest in the past or future makes them politically useless, and their fertility wins them no friends among the more powerful sorts who conceive rarely and wrangle ferociously over dwindling inheritances.

Pests, they call pixies, but the dismissal is tempered with wariness. They are flighty, yes, but they are also fierce and numerous, and each swarm can hold a grudge forever. They guard well those they love. I feel honored to be included in that category.

Every time I visit, the pixies escort me past the shifting territories of far more predatory beings, straight to my father's personal estate. By the laws of power, they must do that much. My first gift paid all. Because I am determined that there be more to my life than balance and bargains, I continue bring small offerings of whatever I think they'll enjoy.

They're especially fond of violas. Tastier than pansies, they insist. I can't tell the difference.

"Shall we greet one another face-to-face today?" I ask as I lay flowers beside the path. "Or am I too terrifying to approach?"

The leafy canopy rustles, and crystal-chime laughter breaks the quiet, brightening my mood and freshening the air. One glittering pixie flits to a lower branch and showers me with kisses that scatter in a fall of icy green sparks.

Pixies are made as much of beetle wings and butterfly legs as they are of human parts. All their colorful bits and pieces are held together by delicate threads of magic.

This one responds to my teasing with a shake of her fist. "I am the Charlotte, and I fear nothing," she declares in a bumblebee drone. "We ask no toll, but we would welcome a compliment for our web."

I make a show of examining their work. They love this part so much. "It's some pig. Terrific, and radiant. Humble, even."

My literary references are answered with a chorus of peeping laughter and a shower of dew from the leaves above. I duck under the web to view it from the other side before rummaging in my bag. "Here are new words, freely given, to add to your glory. A book full of brave rabbits, clever badgers, and courageous mice."

Charlotte swoops in for the prize, which will be memorized and recited aloud long after the pages fade and crumble into the loam. "We will cherish it," she says with utmost solemnity.

I'll meet a Martin on some future visit, I'm sure. Moments like this make these trips bearable. "Are you the only brave one, dear Charlotte, or will others introduce themselves today?"

Three more glittery fliers drop into view, two green, one fiery orange and unsteady in the air. Charlotte joins hands with the wavering flier. "This one came to new wings at dawn. She has not yet chosen a name. We are joined by the Templeton and the Wilbur, who will lead the rest of our swarm in attendance. Be welcome, and travel freely under our aegis."

"Lead on, and I will gladly follow."

She ducks low to tickle my cheek with her toes, then departs behind a last, wet sprinkle of magic. A hum of wings announces arrival of the rest of the swarm. They swirl ahead through the trees, trailing laughter and light behind them. I wipe my cheeks clean and suck the wet flavor of starlight off my fingertips.

———

My father's house is a bright and shining palace on a hill, with roots sunk deep in magic. Its carved stones defy gravity, with airy exterior walkways and stairways connecting floors in impossible ways, and the windows on the outside don't match the rooms within. Turrets jut from every corner—a number which varies depending on your viewing location—and three spindly towers rise from the center, impossibly tall enough to be visible from the edge of Pops' estate.

The pixies leave me in a meadow where the turrets appear between the treetops. I take another step through ferns and brush, across the invisible boundary. Pop's magic hits my skin with a cool, bracing slap of recognition. A pale, smooth roadway appears where my foot touches the earth, curving through gloomy evergreens and undergrowth.

I've tried to arrive unnoticed, to creep through the estate

woods unseen, but I can't. Wherever I cross this border, the road appears.

The herald arrives from a gap in reality a moment later, sitting tall behind the wheel of his pride and joy. I can't escape them, either. They always arrive when I do, and they always insist on driving me the rest of the way.

While those of less political temperament care for most of Pop's territories, his personal property is all about rigid order groomed into a careful imitation of chaos. The cultivated forest is given over to wild pigs, pygmy deer, and albino peacocks, plus one roly-poly bear who used to be a gamekeeper.

The herald's ride is no more a real automobile than the forest is wilderness. It's a creature whose exterior is a perfect replica of a Model A station wagon. It even sounds like a Model A when it moves, although at rest it makes noises more like a snoring dog than a working engine.

I've never asked why it chooses that form. Some mysteries are not worth the price of an answer.

The herald uses the time spent on the drive to brief me on recent events and the backgrounds of everyone currently visiting my father. They say they must prepare me for court.

I ignore the briefing, like I always do. There's no point in listening. My father's people will never accept me. His courtiers made their disdain clear before I'd spent my first week in his court as a child. These days I rarely cross paths with them. When I visit, they hide themselves from me with magic I cannot match and snicker from the shadows.

That's fine. Their games are deadly, and I don't need trouble following me home. Besides, Pops only ever calls me here for one task, and the job is hard enough without getting to know the people involved.

Sometimes it's so hard I ask myself why I bother coming at all. There's nothing Pops can do to force me to cross between worlds, after all.

There are good reasons. First, it appears immortality is the main thing I did inherit from him, and forever is a long time to collect regrets and grudges. Second, Pops wouldn't be the one to suffer if I refused to use my talents in his service. Others would bear the cost.

Third, it's the right thing to do.

The trip takes as long as it takes. We pass without challenge under the trees, through meadows, over bogs. When the herald runs out of intrigues and gossip, we arrive at the castle. That's how it works here. Time is a pretzel, knotted and salty.

Pops meets me at the gate in the white marble wall. He's bundled in layers of ceremonial robes, and he smells of hard sugar candies and citrus fruit.

That's how he appears to me, anyway.

Long ago, the blind architect who designed my father's palace told me, "Trust nothing you see here," and he confessed he did not miss the lies his eyes once told him.

I keep his advice close to my heart every time I return here, reminding myself that my father built this place from a madman's dreams and delusions, and that all the people who call this castle home are masters at bending reality to their whims.

Some tales describe the inhabitants of this land as ethereal beauties whose perfection drives mortals to madness. Other stories speak of eternal youth and unearthly grace and go on and on about lithe bodies, silken hair, and pointed ears.

To me, Pops always looks like a middle-aged monarch from a children's book—bearded, portly, and jovial, all smiles and hugs and ho-ho-hos. Mom says he's stunning, dark-haired, and slim.

My whole life is rooted in illusions and lies. Is it any wonder I prefer the honest company of animals?

"Be welcome in my home," Pops says, and the words settle on my shoulders, a mantle of protection.

I give him a nod. "Squire."

He never lets me call him Father, or Pops, or Dad. Not here where words have real power. The open acknowledgement could be deadly to me or be used against him. I'm pretty sure which possibility worries him more, but the worry protects me either way.

When he embraces me, his magic smothers me in welcome. The pulse of his greater power beats in time with my lesser one, a harmony binding us together far closer than the pressure of our arms.

"I've missed you," he says, and it's true, of course. I have to remind myself that his love is a ridiculous, conditional one, like a tiger bonding with a chicken.

Disappointment binds us too, the ache of wounds that cannot heal. He wants an heir with strengths I will never have. I want the kind of father he can never be.

"What do you require of me?" I say, because it's best to remain formal, to keep the volatile mix of my resentments and obligations safely tamped down by manners.

He puts me at arm's length, and sorrow wells up in his eyes. "Come and see. My court awaits you at the fountain."

He's brought his whole household outside into the palace gardens because I haven't crossed its inner threshold since I met the architect. The winding paths are confusing, and the planting beds are full of strange and lethal flowers, but the garden is still safer than the halls.

Don't ask about the topiaries. Great power does not confer good taste. Lately I've been gifting Pops with concrete geese to classy up the place.

A pearly fog of magic hides the waiting courtiers from my sight. Few of them ever reveal themselves to me. Knowledge is power, and they refuse me their identities because they can.

The herald would be happy to undermine them by announcing them to me, but I don't ask. Pops likes them afraid, and they hide because they fear me.

I am a living reminder that immortal does not mean indestructible. A touch of humanity can harm them. Can destroy them. I don't have much mortality in me, but only a drop is needed. One touch from me at the right place, under the right conditions, and I could end any one of them. I might as well be a plague carrier.

Still, I do have my uses. "Who asks my aid today?"

Two people step forward, resolving into focus out of the misty crowd. One is tall and graceful. He sports waist-length purple hair and a flourishing mustache the same color. It's the vivid shade of nightshade blooms. Threads of yellow gleam in it when he bows low, nose to knees, and the mass of it cascades forward over his shoulders.

His companion is human and female, with black, curly hair, delicate features, and a body forever frozen in the gangly awkwardness of late adolescence. Her bow is a startled, clumsy mimicry of the man's limber extravagance.

When she stumbles, off balance, her companion catches her upright and slips his arm around her shoulders to steady her. His eyes, lilac shaded with lavender, lift to mine. The desolation in his gaze brings a lump to my throat.

No. I am not going to cry. Not this time.

"I give you my name—I am Rio," says the purple-haired man. "I place my trust in you, and put my heart in your care. This is Nevah, who chose to share my life. She no longer knows herself . Please, help us."

The *please* chokes me with its power, and my heart squeezes tight as the weighty responsibility of their names settles on my heart. I don't want to know Rio. I don't want to be bound to someone who sees mortals as creatures to be indulged and pampered until they are used up.

And yet here I am.

Nevah smiles when she hears her name. It guts me. They always look so young.

Magic gifts of beauty and health cannot erase the marks left by early malnutrition, illness, and ill-treatment. Wherever and whenever she was born, her life had been cruel. No surprise she stayed here in luxury to live happily ever after with her fairy-tale lover.

Even happily-ever-afters can come to an end.

Those who find true love here get a good bargain, but it isn't the full immortality of their mates. Their bodies cease to age, but time does not give up its grip on their minds. Their personalities slowly, quietly wither away until they dissolve to nothingness inside eternal shells.

Nevah can barely stand with her lover's support, and her eyes have a familiar, fixed quality. Motion and color attract her, but she glances from face to face without focus, seeking something so lost she's forgotten what it is. Long-held behaviors and self-preservation instincts are the last to go, but the spark of identity is lost, unable to form intent even to ask for release.

Her body will never completely cease functioning, but the fire of her spirit has gone to cold ash. Left here, like this, she will end up a breathing, blinking statue sustained by magic.

Those who bring over their lovers to share full, rich lives often condemn them to living death. They convince the objects of their affections to stay past the point of no return because they can't let go gracefully.

Maybe I'm being unfair. It's easy to judge.

One thing I do know is that are far fewer statues in my father's garden now than there were a few years ago. I cannot bear to let someone suffer when I can ease their way.

"Hello, Nevah," I say, and I hold out my hand. "I've come to help you home."

She reaches out, mirroring my gesture without thought, the way she copied her lover's bow. Her hand is chill and small, and she gasps when I kiss her palm.

"Will you come?" I ask.

She blinks. In her eyes I see the tiniest flicker of forever. I pull her close and scoop her up, tucked close against my chest.

My father nods, and a path opens before me through the lurking crowd.

Nevah is a slight burden, no heavier than a box of kittens, and I let my power flow and fill me, salty and weak, but strong enough for this one, awful purpose.

Three steps, because small magics work best in threes.

One step takes me from the courtyard to the edge of the estate, a second brings me to the gate in the wild woods. Pixies welcome us there at the threshold, showering glitter and pine needles onto our heads and serenading us with scraps of children's tales. Nevah giggles when they tickle her face with their wings.

They love the sound of laughter, and so they bring happiness to those I bring here. I couldn't bear to do this without their generosity and joy.

Rio steps out of thin air, proud and silent, and pixies array themselves in a sparkling wall of challenge. Rio sweeps them a deep bow, hands spreading wide in supplication.

"My heart is here," he says. "Name your price for passage."

They retreat with a rattle of wings. "Travel freely this once."

No one has ever followed me this far, not that it's a hard journey for any of Pops' courtiers. Mercy is a bitter meal, and my father's people prefer the sparkling, sweet intoxication of denial.

I wait one moment and then another to see what Rio does next.

He takes his lover's hand. She squeezes it.

Well, then.

Sunlight slants golden under the arch of living wood before us, marking the line between worlds. Bright-flowered rose bushes nod in the sunshine on the far side. The air of two worlds carries the richness of their scent.

One last step under tree and over cloud, and my arms are

empty. Dust and dewdrops blow across the rose petals, remnants of a prodigal life long overdue for its return to the earth.

Rio lifts a hand to touch a dark speck caught in his perfect, purple hair, brings it to his lips, and turns his lavender gaze on me. His tears fall in drops of amethyst and diamond to glitter against the green grass.

Mine spill down my cheeks, humble and sticky, tasting of salt.

We stand in my great-grandmother's garden, and we cry together, salt and stone.

Grief makes us weep, but we come into the world crying, too. Maybe these tears will someday bring change.

I hope so.

THE END

ABOUT THE AUTHOR

K. M. Herkes writes and publishes science fiction and fantasy books that focus on people with damaged souls and complicated lives. The resilience of hope and the power of community are prevailing themes.

Professional development started with a Bachelor of Science degree in Biology and now includes experience in classroom teaching, animal training, aquaculture, horticulture, bookselling, and retail operations. Personal development is ongoing. Cats are involved.

When she isn't writing, she works at the Mount Prospect Public Library, digs holes in her backyard, entertains the household feline, and dabbles in experimental baking.

———

The author is online as @kemherkes@wandering.shop in the Fediverse, but mainly posts updates on her website blog at kmherkes.com or via Patreon at patreon.com/kmherkes

POSTSCRIPT: COPYRIGHTS BY TITLE

COPYRIGHTS BY STORY

Herkes. First published in *Ludlow Charlington's Doghouse*, edited by Tina Jens (Crawdance Productions, 2022).

"What's In a Name?" copyright © 2022 by K. M. Herkes. First published in *Ludlow Charlington's Doghouse*, edited by Tina Jens (Crawdance Productions, 2022).

"Heavy Lies The Head" copyright © 2022 by K. M. Herkes. First published in *Ludlow Charlington's Doghouse*, edited by Tina Jens (Crawdance Productions, 2022).

"I'm No Empty-Headed Fribble" copyright © 2022 by K. M. Herkes. First published in *Ludlow Charlington's Doghouse*, edited by Tina Jens (Crawdance Productions, 2022).

"Ruler Of All She Surveys" copyright © 2022 by K. M. Herkes. First published in *Ludlow Charlington's Doghouse*, edited by Tina Jens (Crawdance Productions, 2022).

"The Thing In the Pantry" copyright © 2016 by K. M. Herkes. First appearance.

"Mirrors" copyright © 1987 by K. M. Herkes. First appearance.

"For Want Of a Nail" copyright © 1988 by K. M. Herkes. First appearance.

"Numbers Game"Copyright ©2015 by K. M. Herkes. First appeared in *Far Horizons*, edited by Pete Sutton, May 2015.

"The Catch" copyright © 1990 by K. M. Herkes. First appearance.

"The Final Battle" copyright © 1995 by K. M. Herkes. First appeared in the Chicago Comic Con program book, July 1995.

"Five Stages Of Grief For a Funeral That Will Never Happen" copyright © 2023 by K. M. Herkes. First appearance.

"Story Without A Title" copyright © 2018 by K. M. Herkes. First appearance.

"Dogcatcher" copyright © 1989 by K. M. Herkes. First appeared on Wattpad.com, 2016.

"Turning Back" copyright © 2014 by K. M. Herkes. First appeared on Readwave.com, 2014.

"Homecoming" copyright © 2018 by K. M. Herkes. First published in the *Brain Bubbles* newsletter, 2018.

"Campfire, or Waves And Ashes" copyright © 2023 by K. M. Herkes. First appearance.